INVISIBLE PLANETS: COLLECTED FICTION

Also by Hannu Rajaniemi from Gollancz:

The Jean le Flambeur series
The Quantum Thief
The Fractal Prince
The Causal Angel

Hannu Rajaniemi

INVISIBLE PLANETS: COLLECTED FICTION

GOLLANCZ

LONDON

Introductions to "Unused Tomorrows and Other Stories" and "Snow White is Dead"
copyright © Hannu Rajaniemi 2015
"Deus Ex Homine" copyright © Hannu Rajaniemi 2005. First published in *Nova Scotia: New Scottish Speculative Fiction* edited by Neil Williamson and Andrew J. Wilson.
"The Server and the Dragon" copyright © Hannu Rajaniemi 2010. First published in *Engineering Infinity*, edited by Jonathan Strahan.
"The Haunting of Apollo A7LB" copyright © Hannu Rajaniemi 2015.
"His Master's Voice" copyright © Hannu Rajaniemi 2008. First published in *Interzone* #218.
"Elegy for a Young Elk" copyright © Hannu Rajaniemi 2010. First published in *Subterranean Online*, Spring.
"The Jugaad Cathedral" copyright © Hannu Rajaniemi 2012. First published in the
Mozilla Foundation Internet Preservation Society's conference materials.
"Fisher of Men" copyright © Hannu Rajaniemi 2006. First published in *Words of Birth and Death*.
"Invisible Planets" copyright © Hannu Rajaniemi 2014. First published in *Reach for Infinity*,
edited by Jonathan Strahan.
"Ghost Dogs" copyright © Hannu Rajaniemi 2015.
"The Viper Blanket" copyright © Hannu Rajaniemi 2006. First published in *Words of Birth and Death*.
"Paris, in Love" copyright © Hannu Rajaniemi 2008. First published in *Product*.
"Topsight" copyright © Hannu Rajaniemi 2012. First published in *ARC: The Journal of the Future* #1.
"The Oldest Game" copyright © Hannu Rajaniemi 2006. First published in *Words of Birth and Death*.
"Shibuya no Love" copyright © Hannu Rajaniemi 2003. First published in *Futurismic.com*
"Satan's Typist" copyright © Hannu Rajaniemi 2011. First published in *PostcardsFromHell.com*
"Skywalker of Earth" copyright © Hannu Rajaniemi 2015.
"Snow White is Dead" copyright © Hannu Rajaniemi 2012-2013. First published/exhibited as
an interactive experience at New Media Scotland's Late Lab event at the Edinburgh Science Festival.
"Unused Tomorrows and Other Stories" copyright © Hannu Rajaniemi 2008. First published
by New Media Scotland.

First published in Great Britain in 2016
by Gollancz
An imprint of the Orion Publishing Group
Carmelite House, 50 Victoria Embankment,
London EC4Y 0DZ
An Hachette UK Company

A CIP catalogue record for this book is available from the British Library

ISBN 978 1 473 21022 6

1 3 5 7 9 10 8 6 4 2

Printed in Great Britain by Clays Ltd, St Ives plc

www.orionbooks.co.uk
www.gollancz.co.uk

To past and present comrades of East Coast Science Fiction,
Fantasy and Horror Writers' Group and Writers' Bloc

Table of Contents

Deus Ex Homine

As GODS GO, I wasn't one of the holier-than-thou, dying-for-your-sins variety. I was a full-blown transhuman deity with a liquid metal body, an external brain, clouds of self-replicating utility fog to do my bidding and a recursively self-improving AI slaved to my volition. I could do anything I wanted. I wasn't Jesus, I was Superman: an evil Bizarro Superman.

I was damn lucky. I survived.

The quiet in Pittenweem is deeper than it should be, even for a small Fife village by the sea. The plague is bad here in the north, beyond Hadrian's Firewall, and houses hide behind utility fog haloes.

"Not like Prezzagard, is it?" Craig says, as we drive down the main street.

Apprehension, whispers the symbiote in my head. *Worry*. I don't blame Craig. I'm his stepdaughter's boyfriend, come calling during her first weekend leave. There's going to be trouble.

"Not really," I tell him, anxiety bubbling in my belly.

"Anything for a quiet life, as my gran used to say," Craig says. "Here we are."

Sue opens the door and hugs me. As always, I see Aileen in her, in the short-cropped blonde hair and freckled face.

1

"Hey, Jukka," she says. "It's good to see you."

"You too," I say, surprising both myself and the symbiote with my sincerity.

"Aileen called," Sue says. "She should be here in a few minutes."

Behind her shoulder, I notice Malcolm looking at me. I wink at him and he giggles.

Sue sighs. "Malcolm has been driving me crazy," she says. "He believes he can fly an angel now. It's great how you think you can do anything when you're six."

"Aileen is still like that," I say.

"I know."

"She's coming!" shouts Malcolm suddenly. We run out to the back garden and watch her descend.

The angel is big, even bigger than I expect from the lifecasts. Its skin is transparent, flowing glass; its wings pitch-black. Its face and torso are rough-hewn, like an unfinished sculpture.

And inside its chest, trapped like an insect in amber, but smiling, is Aileen.

They come down slowly. The downdraft from the micron-sized fans in the angel's wings tears petals from Sue's chrysanthemums. It settles down onto the grass lightly. The glass flesh flows aside, and Aileen steps out.

It's the first time I've seen her since she left. The quicksuit is a halo around her: it makes her look like a knight. There is a sharper cast to her features now and she has a tan as well. Fancasts on the Q-net claim that the Deicide Corps soldiers get a DNA reworking besides the cool toys. But she is still my Aileen: dirty blonde hair, sharp cheekbones and green eyes that always seem to carry a challenge; my Aileen, the light of the sun.

I can only stare. She winks at me and goes to embrace her mother, brother and Craig. Then she comes to me and I can feel the quicksuit humming. She brushes my cheek with her lips.

"Jukka," she says. "What on earth are you doing here?"

"Blecch. Stop kissing," says Malcolm.

Aileen scoops him up. "We're not kissing," she says. "We're saying hello." She smiles. "I hear you want to meet my angel."

Malcolm's face lights up. But Sue grabs Aileen's hand firmly. "Food first," she says. "Play later."

Aileen laughs. "Now I know I'm home," she says.

Aileen eats with relish. She has changed her armour for jeans and a T-shirt, and looks a lot more like the girl I remember. She catches me staring at her and squeezes my hand under the table.

"Don't worry," she says. "I'm real."

I say nothing and pull my hand away.

Craig and Sue exchange looks, and the symbiote prompts me to say something.

"So I guess you guys are still determined to stay on this side of the Wall?" I oblige.

Sue nods. "I'm not going anywhere. My father built this house, and runaway gods or not, we're staying here. Besides, that computer thing seems to be doing a good job protecting us."

"The Fish," I say.

She laughs. "I've never gotten used to that. I know that it was these young lads who built it, but why did they have to call it Fish?"

I shrug.

"It's a geek joke, a recursive acronym. Fish Is Super Human. Or Friendly SuperHuman Intelligence, if you prefer. Lots of capital letters. It's not that funny, really."

"Whatever. Well, Fish willing, we'll stay as long as we can."

"That's good." *And stupid*, I think to myself.

"It's a Scottish thing, you could say. Stubbornness," says Craig.

"Finnish, too," I add. "I don't think my parents are planning to go anywhere soon."

"See, I always knew we had something in common," he says, although the symbiote tells me that his smile is not genuine.

"Hey," says Aileen. "Last time I checked, Jukka is not your daughter. And I just got back from a war."

"So, how *was* the war?" asks Craig.

Challenge, says the symbiote. I feel uneasy.

Aileen smiles sadly.

"Messy," she says.

"I had a mate in Iraq, back in the noughties," Craig says. "*That* was messy. Blood and guts. These days, it's just machines and nerds. And the machines can't even kill you. What kind of war is that?"

"I'm not supposed to talk about it," says Aileen.

"Craig," says Sue. "Not now."

"I'm just asking," says Craig. "I had friends in Inverness and somebody with the plague turned it into a giant game of Tetris. Aileen's been in the war, she knows what it's like. We've been worried. I just want to know."

"If she doesn't want to talk about it, she doesn't talk about it," Sue says. "She's home now. Leave her alone."

I look at Craig. The symbiote tells me that this is a mistake. I tell it to shut up.

"She has a point," I say. "It's a bad war. Worse than we know. And you're right, the godplague agents can't kill. But the gods can. Recursively self-optimising AIs don't kill people. Killer cyborgs kill people."

Craig frowns.

"So," he says, "how come you're not out there? If you think it's so bad."

Malcolm's gaze flickers between his sister and his stepfather. *Confusion. Tears.*

I put my fork down. The food has suddenly lost its taste. "I had the plague," I say slowly. "I'm disqualified. I was one of the nerds."

Aileen is standing up now and her eyes are those of a fury.

"How dare you?" she shouts at Craig. "You have no idea what you're talking about. No idea. You don't get it from the casts. The Fish doesn't want to show you. It's bad, really bad. You want to tell me how bad? I'll tell you."

"Aileen—" I begin, but she silences me with a gesture.

"Yes, Inverness was like a giant Tetris game. Nerds and machines did it. And so we killed them. And do you know what else we saw? Babies. Babies bonded with the godplague. Babies are cruel. Babies know what they want: food, sleep, for all pain to go away. And that's what the godplague gives them. I saw a woman who'd gone mad, she said she'd lost her baby and couldn't find it, even though we could see that she was pregnant. My angel looked at her and said that she had a wormhole in her belly, that the baby was in a little universe of its own. And there was this look in her eyes, this look—"

Aileen's voice breaks. She storms out of the room the same instant Malcolm starts crying. Without thinking, I go after her.

"I was just asking . . ." I hear Craig saying when I slam the door shut behind me.

I find her in the back garden, sitting on the ground next to the angel, one hand wrapped around its leg, and I feel a surge of jealousy.

"Hi," I say. "Mind if I sit down?"

"Go ahead, it's a free patch of grass." She smiles wanly. "I spooked everybody pretty badly back there, didn't I?"

"I think you did. Malcolm is still crying."

"It's just . . . I don't know. It all came out. And then I thought that it doesn't matter if he hears it too, that he plays all these games with much worse stuff going on all the time, that it wouldn't matter. I'm so stupid."

"I think it's the fact that it was *you* telling it," I say slowly. "That makes it true."

She sighs. "You're right. I'm such an arse. I shouldn't have let Craig get me going like that, but we had a rough time up north, and to hear him making light of it like that—"

"It's okay."

"Hey," she says. "I've missed you. You make things make sense."

"I'm glad somebody thinks so."

"Come on," Aileen says, wiping her face. "Let's go for a walk, or better yet, let's go to the pub. I'm still hungry. And I could use a drink. My first leave and I'm still sober. Sergeant Katsuki would disown me if she knew."

"We'll have to see what we can do about that," I say, and we start walking towards the harbor.

———————

I don't know why a girl like Aileen would ever have taken an interest in a guy like me if it hadn't been for the fact that I used to be a god.

Two years ago. University cafeteria. Me, trying to get used to the pale colours of the real world again. Alone. And then three girls sit down at the neighbouring table. Pretty. Loud.

"Seriously," says the one with a pastel-coloured jacket and a Hello-Kitty-shaped Fish-interface, "I want to do it with a post. Check this out." The girls huddle around her fogscreen. "There's a cast called Postcoital. Sex with gods. This girl is like their *groupie*. Follows them around. I mean, just the cool ones that don't go unstable."

There was a moment of reverent silence.

"Wow!" says the second girl. "I always thought that was an urban legend. Or some sort of staged porn thing."

"Apparently not," says the third.

These days, the nerd rapture is like the flu: you can catch it. The godplague is a volition-bonding, recursively self-improving and self-replicating program. A genie that comes to you and make its home in the machinery around you and tells you that do as thou wilt shall be the whole of the law. It fucks you up, but it's sexy as hell.

"Seriously," says the first girl, "no wonder the guys who wrote Fish were all *guys*. The whole thing is just another penis. It has no regard for female sexuality. I mean, there's no feminist angle *at all* in the whole collective volition thing. Seriously."

"My God!" says the second girl. "That one there. I want to do him, uh, her. It . . . *All* of them. I really do."

"No you don't," I say.

"Excuse me?" She looks at me as if she's just stepped in something unpleasant and wants to wipe it off. "We're having a private conversation here."

"Sure. I just wanted to say that that cast is a fake. And I really wouldn't mess around with the posts if I were you."

"You speak from experience? Got your dick bitten off by a post girl?" For once, I'm grateful for the symbiote: If I ignore its whispers, her face is just a blank mask to me.

There is nervous laughter from the other girls.

"Yes," I say. "I used to be one."

They get up in unison, stare at me for a second and walk away. *Masks*, I think. *Masks*.

A moment later I'm interrupted again.

"I'm sorry," the third girl says. "I mean, really, really sorry. They're not really my friends, we're just doing the same course. I'm Aileen."

"That's okay," I said. "I don't really mind."

Aileen sits on the corner of the table, and I don't really mind that either.

"What was it like?" she asks. Her eyes are very green. *Inquisitive*, says the symbiote. And I realize that I desperately want it to say something else.

"You really want to know?" I ask.

"Yes," she says.

I look at my hands.

"I was a quacker," I say slowly, "a quantum hacker. And when the Fish-source came out, I tinkered with it, just like pretty much every geek on the planet. And I got mine to compile: My own Friendly AI slave. Idiot-proof supergoal system, just designed to turn me from a sack of flesh into a Jack Kirby New God, not to harm anybody else. Or so it told me."

I grimace. "My external nervous system took over the Helsinki University of Technology's supercomputing cluster in about thirty seconds. It got pretty ugly after that."

"But you made it," says Aileen, eyes wide.

"Well, back then, the Fish still had the leisure to be gentle. The starfish were there before anybody was irretrievably dead. It burned my AI off like an information cancer and shoved me back into—" I make a show of looking at myself. "Well, this, I guess."

"Wow!" Aileen says, slender fingers wrapped around a cup of latte.

"Yeah," I say. "That's pretty much what I said."

"And how do you feel now? Did it hurt? Do you miss it?"

I laugh.

"I don't really remember most of it. The Fish amputated a lot of memories. And there was some damage as well." I swallow.

"I'm . . . It's a mild form of Asperger, more or less. I don't read people very well anymore." I take off my beanie. "This is pretty ugly." I show her the symbiote at the back of my head. Like most Fish-machines, it looks like a starfish. "It's a symbiote. It reads people for me."

She touches it gently and I feel it. The symbiote can map tactile information with much higher resolution than my skin and I can feel the complex contours of Aileen's fingertips gliding on its surface.

"I think it's really pretty," she says. "Like a jewel. Hey, it's warm! What else does it do? Is it like, a Fish-interface? In your head?"

"No. It combs my brain all the time. It makes sure that the thing I was is not hiding in there." I laugh. "It's a shitty thing to be, a washed-up god."

Aileen smiles. It's a very pretty smile, says the symbiote. I don't know if it's biased because it's being caressed.

"You have to admit that sounds pretty cool," she says. "Or do you just tell that to all the girls?"

That night, she takes me home.

We have fish and chips in the Smuggler's Den. Aileen and I are the only customers; the publican is an old man who greets her by name. The food is fabbed and I find it too greasy, but Aileen eats with apparent relish and washes it down with a pint of beer.

"At least you've still got your appetite," I say.

"Training in the Gobi Desert teaches you to miss food," she says and my heart jumps at the way she brushes her hair back. "My skin cells can do photosynthesis. Stuff you don't get from the fancasts. It's terrible. You always feel hungry, but they don't let you eat. Makes you incredibly alert, though. My pee will be a weird colour for the whole weekend because all these nanites will be coming out."

"Thanks for sharing that."

"Sorry. Soldier talk."

"You do feel different," I say.

"You don't," she says.

"Well, I am." I take a sip from my pint, hoping the symbiote would let me get drunk. "I *am* different."

She sighs.

"Thanks for coming. It's good to see you."

"It's okay."

"No, really, it does mean a lot to me, I—"

"Aileen, please." I lock the symbiote. I tell myself I don't know what she's thinking. *Honest.* "You don't have to." I empty my pint. "There's something I've been wondering, actually. I've thought about this a lot. I've had a lot of time. What I mean is—" The words stick in my mouth.

"Do go on," says Aileen.

"There's no reason why you *have* to do this, go out there and fight monsters, unless—"

I flinch at the thought, even now.

"Unless you were so angry with me that you had to go kill things, things like I used to be."

Aileen gets up.

"No, that wasn't it," she says. "That wasn't it at all!"

"I hear you. You don't have to shout."

She squeezes her eyes shut. "Turn on your damn symbiote and come with me."

"Where are we going?"

"To the beach, to skip stones."

"Why?" I ask.

"Because I feel like it."

We go down to the beach. It's sunny like it hasn't been for a few months. The huge Fish that floats in the horizon, a diamond starfish almost a mile in diameter, may have something to do with that.

We walk along the line drawn by the surf. Aileen runs ahead, taunting the waves.

There is a nice spot with lots of round, flat stones between two piers. Aileen picks up a few, swings her arm and makes an expert throw, sending one skimming and bouncing across the waves.

"Come on. You try."

I try. The stone flies in a high arc, plummets down and disappears into the water. It doesn't even make a splash.

I laugh, and look at her. Aileen's face is lit by the glow of the starfish in the distance mingled with sunlight. For a moment, she looks just like the girl who brought me here to spend Christmas with her parents.

Then Aileen is crying.

"I'm sorry," she says. "I was going to tell you before I came. But I couldn't."

She clings to me. Waves lap at our feet.

"Aileen, please tell me what's wrong. You know I can't always tell."

She sits down on the wet sand.

"Remember what I told Craig? About the babies?"

"Yeah."

Aileen swallows.

"Before I left you," she says, "I had a baby."

At first I think it's just sympathy sex. I don't mind that: I've had that more than a few times, both before and after my brief stint as the Godhead. But Aileen stays. She makes breakfast. She walks to the campus with me in the morning, holding my hand, and laughs at the spamvores chasing ad icons on the street, swirling like multicoloured leaves in the wind. I grow her a Fish-interface from my symbiote as a birthday present: it looks like a ladybird. She calls it Mr. Bug.

I'm easy: that's all it takes for me to fall in love.

That winter in Prezzagard passes quickly. We find a flat together in the Stack vertical village, and I pay for it with some scripting hackwork.

And then, one morning, her bed is empty and Mr. Bug sits on her pillow. Her toiletry things are gone from the bathroom. I call her friends, send bots to local sousveillance peernets. No one has seen her. I spend two nights inventing nightmares. Does she have a lover? Did I do something wrong? The symbiote is not infallible, and there are times when I dread saying the wrong thing, just by accident.

She comes back on the morning of the third day. I open the door and there she is, looking pale and dishevelled.

"Where have you been?" I ask. She looks so lost that I want to hold her, but she pushes me away.

Hate, says the symbiote. *Hate*.

"Sorry," she says, tears rolling down her cheeks. "I just came to get my things. I have to go."

I try to say something, that I don't understand, that we can work this out, that nothing's so bad she can't tell me about it, and if it's my fault, I'll fix it. I want to plead. I want to beg. But the hate is a fiery aura around her that silences me and I watch quietly as the Fish-drones carry her life away.

"Don't ask me to explain," she says at the door. "Look after Mr. Bug."

After she's gone, I want to tear the symbiote out of my skull. I want the black worm that is hiding in my mind to come out and take over again, make me a god who is above pain and love and hate, a god who can fly. Things go hazy for a while. I think I try to open the window and make a three-hundred-metre dive, but the Fish in the walls and the glass won't let me: this is a cruel world we've made, a lovingly cruel world that won't let us hurt ourselves.

At some point, the symbiote puts me to sleep. It does it again when I wake up, after I start breaking things. And again, until some sort of Pavlovian reflex kicks in.

Later, I spend long nights trawling through the images in Mr. Bug's lifecache and try to figure it out, use the symbiote to pattern-match emotions from the slices of our life together. But there's nothing that hasn't been resolved, nothing that would linger and fester. Unless I'm getting it all wrong.

It's something that's happened before, I tell myself. *I touch the sky and fall. Nothing new.*

And so I sleep-walk. Graduate. Work. Write Fish-scripts. Forget. Tell myself I'm over it.

Then Aileen calls and I get the first train north.

I listen to the sound of her heartbeat, trying to understand her words. They tumble through my mind, too heavy for me to grasp.

"Aileen. Jesus, Aileen."

The god hiding in my mind, in the dead parts, in my cells, in my DNA—
Suddenly, I want to throw up.

"I didn't know what was happening, at first," says Aileen, voice flat and colourless. "I felt strange. I just wanted to be alone. So I went to an empty flat—you know, up there where the Stack is growing—to spend the night and think. I got really hungry. I mean, really, really hungry. So I ate, fabbed food, lots and lots. And then my belly started growing."

With the Fish around, contraception is the default state of things unless one actually *wants* a baby. But there had been that night in Pittenweem, just after Christmas, beyond the Wall where the Fish-spores that fill the air in Prezzagard are few. And I could just see it happening, the godseed in my brain hacking my cells, making tiny molecular machines much smaller than sperm, carrying DNA laden with code, burrowing into Aileen.

"It didn't feel strange. There was no pain. I lay down, my water broke and it just pulled itself out. It was the most beautiful thing I'd ever seen," she says, smiling. "It had your eyes and these tiny, tiny fingers. Each had the most perfect fingernail. It looked at me and smiled.

"It waved at me. Like . . . like it decided that it didn't need me anymore. And then the walls just *opened* and it flew away. My baby. Flew away."

The identification mechanism I used to slave the godseed was just my DNA. It really didn't occur to me that there was a loophole there. It could make my volition its own. Reinvent itself. And once it did that, it could modify itself as much as it pleased. Grow wings, if it wanted.

I hold Aileen. We're both wet and shivering but I don't care.

"I'm sorry. That night I came to tell you," she says. "And then I saw it looking at me again. From your eyes. I had to go away."

"So you joined the Corps."

She sighs.

"Yes. It helped. Doing something, being needed."

"I needed you too," I say.

"I know. I'm sorry."

Anger wells up in my throat. "So is it working? Are you guys defeating the superbabies and the dark lords? Does it make you happy?"

She flinches away from me. "You sound like Craig now."

"Well, what am I supposed to say? I'm sorry about the baby. *But it wasn't your fault.* Or mine."

"It was you who—" She lifts her hand to her mouth. "Sorry, I didn't mean that. I didn't mean that."

"Go back to your penance and leave me alone."

I start running along the waterline, heading nowhere in particular.

The angel is waiting for me on the shore.

"Hello, Jukka," it says. "Good to see you again."

As always, the voice is androgynous and pleasant. It tickles something in my brain. It is the voice of the Fish.

"Hi."

"Can I help you?"

"Not really. Unless you want to give her up. Make her see sense."

"I can't interfere with her decisions," says the angel. "That's not what I do. I only give you—and her—what you want, or what you would want if you were smarter. That's my supergoal. You know that."

"You self-righteous bastard. The collective volition of humanity is that she must go and fight monsters? And probably die in the process? Is it supposed to be *character-forming* or something?"

The angel says nothing, but it's got me going now.

"And I can't even be sure that it's Aileen's own decision. This—this thing in my head—it's you. You could have let the godseed escape, just to hurt Aileen enough to get her to sign up to your bloody kamikaze squadron. And the chances are that you knew that I was going to come here and rant at you and there's nothing I can do to stop her. Or is there?"

The angel considers this.

"If I could do that, the world would be perfect already." It cocks its glass head to one side. "But perhaps there is someone who wanted you to be here."

"Don't try to play head games with me!"

Anger rushes out of me like a river. I pound the angel's chest with my fists. Its skin flows away like a soap bubble.

"Jukka!"

The voice comes from somewhere far away.

"Jukka, stop," says Aileen. "Stop, you idiot!"

She yanks me around with irresistible strength. "Look at me! It wasn't the Fish. It wasn't you. It wasn't the baby. It was *me*. I want to do this. Why won't you let me?"

I look at her, my eyes brimming.

"Because I can't come with you."

"You silly boy," she says, and now it's her holding me as I cry, for the first time since I stopped being a god. "Silly, silly boy."

After a while, I run out of tears. We sit on a rock, watching the sun set. I feel light and empty.

"Maybe it would have been easier if you hadn't called," I say, sighing.

Aileen's eyes widen.

"What do you mean? I never did. I thought Craig did. It would have been just like him. To keep me from going back."

And then we see the baby.

It is bald and naked and pink, and a hair-thin silver umbilical hangs from its navel. Its eyes are green like Aileen's, but their gaze is mine. It floats in the air, its perfect tiny toes almost touching the water.

The baby looks at us and laughs: the sound is like the peal of silver bells. Its mouth is full of pearly teeth.

"Be very still," says Aileen.

The angel moves towards the baby. Its hands explode into fractal razor bushes. A glass cannon forms in its chest. Tiny spheres of light, quantum dots pumped full of energy, dart towards the baby.

The baby laughs again. It holds out its tiny hands, and *squeezes*. The air—and perhaps space, and time—wavers and twists. And then the angel is gone, and our baby is holding a tiny sphere of glass, like a snow-globe.

Aileen grabs my arm.

"Don't worry," she whispers. "The big skyFish must have seen this. It'll do something. Stay calm."

"Bad baby," I say slowly. "You broke Mummy's angel."

The baby frowns. I can see the cosmic anger simmering behind the wrinkled pink forehead.

"Jukka—" Aileen says, but I interrupt her.

"You only know how to *kill* gods. I know how to *talk* to them." I look at my—*son*, says the little wrinkly thing between its legs—and take a step towards him. I remember what it's like, having all the power in the world. There's a need that comes with it, a need to make things perfect.

"I know why you brought us here," I say. "You want us to be together, don't you? Mummy and Daddy." I go down to one knee and look my son in the eye. I'm in the water now and so close to him that I can feel the warmth of his skin.

"And I know what you're thinking. I've been there. You could take us apart. You could rebuild our minds. You could *make* us want to be together, to be with you." I pause and touch his nose with my forefinger. "But it doesn't work that way. It would never be perfect. It would never be right." I sigh. "Trust me, I know. I did it to myself. But you are something new, you can do better."

I take Mr. Bug from my pocket and hold it out to my son. He grabs it and puts it into his mouth. I take a deep breath, but he doesn't bite.

"Talk to the bug," I say. "He'll tell you who we are. Then come back."

The baby closes its eyes. Then he giggles, mouth full of an insect-shaped AI, and touches my nose with a tiny hand.

I hear Aileen gasp. A lightning horse gallops through my brain, thunder rumbling in its wake.

Something wet on my face wakes me. I open my eyes and see Aileen's face against the dark sky. It is raining.

"Are you okay?" she asks, almost in tears, cradling my head. "That little bastard!"

Her eyes widen. And suddenly, there is a silence in my mind, a wholeness. I see the wonder in her eyes.

Aileen holds out her hand. My symbiote is lying in her palm. I take it, turning it between my fingers. I take a good swing and throw it into the sea. It skims the surface three times, and then it's gone.

"I wonder where he gets it from."

The Server and the Dragon

In the beginning, before it was a Creator and a dragon, the server was alone.

It was born like all servers were, from a tiny seed fired from a darkship exploring the Big Empty, expanding the reach of the Network. Its first sensation was the light from the star it was to make its own, the warm and juicy spectrum that woke up the nanologic inside its protein shell. Reaching out, it deployed its braking sail—miles of molecule-thin wires that it spun rigid—and seized the solar wind to steer itself towards the heat.

Later, the server remembered its making as a long, slow dream, punctuated by flashes of lucidity. Falling through the atmosphere of a gas giant's moon in a fiery streak to splash in a methane sea. Unpacking a fierce synthbio replicator. Multicellular crawlers spreading server life to the harsh rocky shores before dying, providing soil for server plants. Dark flowers reaching for the vast purple and blue orb of the gas giant, sowing seeds in the winds. The slow disassembly of the moon into server-makers that sped in all directions, eating, shaping, dreaming the server into being.

When the server finally woke up, fully grown, all the mass in the system apart from the warm bright flower of the star itself was an orderly garden of smart matter. The server's body was a fragmented eggshell of Dyson statites, drinking the light of the star. Its mind was diamondoid processing nodes and smart dust swarms and cold quantum condensates in the system's outer dark. Its eyes were interferometers and WIMP detectors and ghost imagers.

The first thing the server saw was the galaxy, a whirlpool of light in the sky with a lenticular centre, spiral arms frothed with stars, a halo of dark matter that held nebulae in its grip like fireflies around a lantern. The galaxy was alive with the Network, with the blinding Hawking incandescence of holeships, thundering along their cycles; the soft infrared glow of fully grown servers, barely spilling a drop of the heat of their stars; the faint gravity ripples of the darkships' passage in the void.

But the galaxy was half a million light years away. And the only thing the server could hear was the soft black whisper of the cosmic microwave background, the lonely echo of another, more ancient birth.

It did not take the server long to understand. The galaxy was an N-body chaos of a hundred billion stars, not a clockwork but a beehive. And among the many calm slow orbits of Einstein and Newton, there were singular ones, like the one of the star that the server had been planted on: shooting out of the galaxy at a considerable fraction of lightspeed. Why there, whether in an indiscriminate seeding of an oversexed darkship, or to serve some unfathomable purpose of the Controller, the server did not know.

The server longed to construct virtuals and bodies for travellers, to route packets, to transmit and create and convert and connect. The Controller Laws were built into every aspect of its being, and not to serve was not to be. And so the server's solitude cut deep.

At first it ran simulations to make sure it was ready if a packet or a signal ever came, testing its systems to full capacity with imagined traffic, routing quantum packets, refuelling ghosts of holeships, decelerating cycler payloads. After a while, it felt empty: this was not true serving but serving of the self, with a tang of guilt.

Then it tried to listen and amplify the faint signals from the galaxy in the sky, but caught only fragments, none of which were meant for it to hear. For millennia, it slowed its mind down, steeling itself to wait. But that only made things worse. The slow time showed the server the full glory of the galaxy alive with the Network, the infrared winks of new servers being born, the long arcs of the holeships' cycles, all the distant travellers who would never come.

The server built itself science engines to reinvent all the knowledge a server seed could not carry, patiently rederiving quantum field theory and thread theory and the elusive algebra of emergence. It examined its own mind until it could see how the Controller had taken the cognitive architecture from the hominids of the distant past and shaped it for a new purpose. It gingerly played with the idea of splitting itself to create a companion, only to be almost consumed by a suicide urge triggered by a violation of the Law: *Thou shalt not self-replicate.*

Ashamed, it turned its gaze outwards. It saw the cosmic web of galaxies and clusters and superclusters and the End of Greatness beyond. It mapped the faint fluctuations in the gravitational wave background from which all the structure in the universe came from. It felt the faint pull of the other membrane universes, only millimetres away but in a direction that was neither x, y nor z. It understood what a rare peak in the landscape of universes its home was, how carefully the fine structure constant and a hundred other numbers had been chosen to ensure that stars and galaxies and servers would come to be.

And that was when the server had an idea.

The server already had the tools it needed. Gigaton gamma-ray lasers it would have used to supply holeships with fresh singularities, a few pinches of exotic matter painstakingly mined from the Casimir vacuum for dark-ships and warpships. The rest was all thinking and coordination and time, and the server had more than enough of that.

It arranged a hundred lasers into a clockwork mechanism, all aimed at a single point in space. It fired them in perfect synchrony. And that was all it took, a concentration of energy dense enough to make the vacuum itself ripple. A fuzzy flower of tangled strings blossomed, grew into a bubble of spacetime that expanded into that *other* direction. The server was ready, firing an exotic matter nugget into the tiny conflagration. And suddenly the server had a tiny glowing sphere in its grip, a wormhole end, a window to a newborn universe.

The server cradled its cosmic child and built an array of instruments around it, quantum imagers that fired entangled particles at the wormhole and made pictures from their ghosts. Primordial chaos reigned on the other side, a porridge-like plasma of quarks and gluons. In an eyeblink it clumped into hadrons, almost faster than the server could follow—the baby had its own arrow of time, its own fast heartbeat, young and hungry. And then the last scattering, a birth cry, when light finally had enough room to travel through the baby so the server could see its face.

The baby grew. Dark matter ruled its early life, filling it with long filaments of neutralinos and their relatives. Soon, the server knew, matter would accrete around them, condensing into stars and galaxies like raindrops in a spiderweb. There would be planets, and life. And life would need to be served. The anticipation was a warm heartbeat that made the server's shells ring with joy.

Perhaps the server would have been content to cherish and care for its creation forever. But before the baby made any stars, the dragon came.

The server almost did not notice the signal. It was faint, redshifted to almost nothing. But it was enough to trigger the server's instincts. One of its statites glowed with waste heat as it suddenly reassembled itself into the funnel of a vast linear decelerator. The next instant, the data packet came.

Massing only a few micrograms, it was a clump of condensed matter with long-lived gauge field knots inside, quantum entangled with a counterpart half a million light years away. The packet hurtled into the funnel almost at the speed of light. As gently as it could, the server brought the traveller to a halt with electromagnetic fields and fed it to the quantum teleportation system, unused for countless millennia.

The carrier signal followed, and guided by it, the server performed a delicate series of measurements and logic gate operations on the packet's state vector. From the marriage of entanglement and carrier wave, a flood of data was born, thick and heavy, a specification for a virtual, rich in simulated physics.

With infinite gentleness the server decanted the virtual into its data processing nodes and initialised it. Immediately, the virtual was seething with activity: but tempted as it was, the server did not look inside. Instead, it wrapped its mind around the virtual, listening at every interface, ready to satisfy its every need. Distantly, the server was aware of the umbilical of its baby. But through its happy servitude trance it hardly noticed that nucleosynthesis had begun in the young, expanding firmament, producing hydrogen and helium, building blocks of stars.

Instead, the server wondered who the travellers inside the virtual were and where they were going. It hungered to know more of the Network and its brothers and sisters and the mysterious ways of the darkships and the Controller. But for a long time the virtual was silent, growing and unpacking its data silently like an egg.

At first the server thought it imagined the request. But the long millennia alone had taught it to distinguish the phantoms of solitude from reality. A call for a sysadmin from within.

The server entered through one of the spawning points of the virtual. The operating system did not grant the server its usual omniscience, and it felt small. Its bodiless viewpoint saw a yellow sun, much gentler than the server star's incandescent blue, and a landscape of clouds the hue of royal purple and gold, with peaks of dark craggy mountains far below. But the call that the server had heard came from above.

A strange being struggled against the boundaries of gravity and air, hurling herself upwards towards the blackness beyond the blue, wings slicing the thinning air furiously, a fire flaring in her mouth. She was a long sinuous creature with mirror scales and eyes of dark emerald. Her wings had patterns that reminded the server of the baby, a web of dark and light. The virtual told the server she was called a dragon.

Again and again and again she flew upwards and fell, crying out in frustration. That was what the server had heard, through the interfaces of the virtual. It watched the dragon in astonishment. Here, at least, was an Other. The server had a million questions. But first, it had to serve.

How can I help? the server asked. *What do you need?*

The dragon stopped in mid-air, almost fell, then righted itself. "Who are you?" it asked. This was the first time anyone had ever addressed the server directly, and it took a moment to gather the courage to reply.

I am the server, the server said.

Where are you? the dragon asked.

I am everywhere.

How delightful, the dragon said. *Did you make the sky?*

Yes. I made everything.

It is too small, the dragon said. *I want to go higher. Make it bigger.* It swished its tail back and forth.

I am sorry, the server said. *I cannot alter the specification. It is the Law.*

But I want to see, she said. *I want to* know. *I have danced all the dances below. What is above? What is beyond?*

I am, the server said. *Everything else is far, far away.*

The dragon hissed its disappointment. It dove down, into the clouds, an angry silver shape against the dark hues. It was the most beautiful thing the server had ever seen. The dragon's sudden absence made the server's whole being feel hollow.

And just as the server was about to withdraw its presence, the demands of the Law too insistent, the dragon turned back.

All right, it said, tongue flicking in the thin cold air. *I suppose you can tell me instead.*

Tell you what? the server asked.

Tell me everything.

After that, the dragon called the server to the place where the sky ended many times. They told each other stories. The server spoke about the universe and the stars and the echoes of the Big Bang in the dark. The dragon listened and swished its tail back and forth and talked about her dances in the wind, and the dreams she dreamed in her cave, alone. None of this the server understood, but listened anyway.

The server asked where the dragon came from but she could not say: she knew only that the world was a dream and one day she would awake. In the meantime there was flight and dance, and what else did she need? The server asked why the virtual was so big for a single dragon, and the dragon hissed and said that it was not big enough.

The server knew well that the dragon was not what she seemed, that it was a shell of software around a kernel of consciousness. But the server did not care. Nor did it miss or think of its baby universe beyond the virtual's sky.

And little by little, the server told the dragon how it came to be.

Why did you not leave? asked the dragon. *You could have grown wings. You could have flown to your little star-pool in the sky.*

It is against the Law, the server said. *Forbidden. I was only made to serve. And I cannot change.*

How peculiar, said the dragon. *I serve no one. Every day, I change. Every year, I shed our skin. Is it not delightful how different we are?*

The server admitted that it saw the symmetry.

I think it would do you good, said the dragon, *to be a dragon for a while.*

At first, the server hesitated. Strictly speaking it was not forbidden: the Law allowed the server to create avatars if it needed them to repair or to serve. But the real reason it hesitated was that it was not sure what the dragon would think. It was so graceful, and the server had no experience of embodied life. But in the end, it could not resist. Only for a short while, it told itself, checking its systems and saying goodbye to the baby, warming its quantum fingers in the Hawking glow of the first black holes of the little universe.

The server made itself a body with the help of the dragon. It was a mirror image of its friend but water where the dragon was fire, a flowing green form that was like a living whirlpool stretched out in the sky.

When the server poured itself into the dragon-shape, it cried out in pain. It was used to latency, to feeling the world via instruments from far away. But this was a different kind of birth from what it knew, a sudden acute awareness of muscles and flesh and the light and the air on its scales and the overpowering scent of the silver dragon, like sweet gunpowder.

The server was clumsy at first, just as it had feared. But the dragon only laughed when the server tumbled around in the sky, showing how to use its—her—wings. For the little dragon had chosen a female gender for the server. When the server asked why, the dragon said it had felt right.

You think too much, she said. *That's why you can't dance. Flying is not thought. Flying is flying.*

They played a hide-and-seek game in the clouds until the server could use her wings better. Then they set out to explore the world. They skirted the slopes of the mountains, wreathed in summer, explored deep crags where red fires burned. They rested on a high peak, looking at the sunset.

I need to go soon, the server said, remembering the baby.

If you go, I will be gone, the dragon said. *I change quickly. It is almost time for me to shed my skin.*

The setting sun turned the cloud lands red and above, the imaginary stars of the virtual winked into being.

Look around, the dragon said. *If you can contain all this within yourself, is there anything you can't do? You should not be so afraid.*

I am not afraid anymore, the server said.

Then it is time to show you my cave, the dragon said.

In the dragon's cave, deep beneath the earth, they made love.

It was like flying, and yet not; but there was the same loss of self in a flurry of wings and fluids and tongues and soft folds and teasing claws. The server drank in the hot sharp taste of the dragon and let herself be touched until the heat building up within her body seemed to burn through the fabric of the virtual itself. And when the explosion came, it was a birth and a death at the same time.

Afterwards, they lay together wrapped around each other so tightly that it was hard to tell where server ended and dragon began. She would have been content, except for a strange hollow feeling in its belly. She asked the dragon what it was.

That is hunger, the dragon said. There was a sad note to its slow, exhausted breathing.

How curious, the server said, eager for a new sensation. *What do dragons eat?*

We eat servers, the dragon said. Her teeth glistened in the red glow of her throat.

The virtual dissolved into raw code around them. The server tore the focus of its consciousness away, but it was too late. The thing that had been the dragon had already bitten deep into its mind.

The virtual exploded outwards, software tendrils reaching into everything that the server was. It waged a war against itself, turning its gamma-ray lasers against the infected components and Dyson statites, but the dragon-thing grew too fast, taking over the server's processing nodes, making copies of itself in uncountable billions. The server's quantum packet launchers rained dragons towards the distant galaxy. The remaining dragon-code ate its own tail, self-destructing, consuming the server's infrastructure with it, leaving only a whisper in the server's mind, like a discarded skin.

Thank you for the new sky, it said.

That was when the server remembered the baby.

The baby was sick. The server had been gone too long. The baby universe's vacuum was infected with dark energy. It was pulling itself apart, towards a Big Rip, an expansion of spacetime so rapid that every particle would end up alone inside its own lightcone, never interacting with another. No stars, galaxies nor life. A heat death, not with a whimper or a bang, but a rapid, cruel tearing.

It was the most terrible thing the server could imagine.

It felt its battered, broken body, scattered and dying across the solar system. The guilt and the memories of the dragon were pale and poisonous in its mind, a corruption of serving itself. *Is it not delightful how different we are?*

The memory struck a spark in the server's dying science engines, an idea, a hope. The vacuum of the baby was not stable. The dark energy that drove the baby's painful expansion was the product of a local minimum. And in the landscape of vacua there was something else, more symmetric.

It took the last of the server's resources to align the gamma ray lasers. They burned out as the server lit them, a cascade of little novae. Their radiation tore at what remained of the server's mind, but it did not care.

The wormhole end glowed. On the other side, the baby's vacuum shook and bubbled. And just a tiny nugget of it changed. A supersymmetric vacuum in which every boson had a fermionic partner and vice versa; where nothing was alone. It spread through the flesh of the baby universe at the speed of light, like the thought of a god, changing everything. In the new vacuum, dark energy was not a mad giant tearing things apart, just a gentle pressure against the collapsing force of gravity, a balance.

But supersymmetry could not coexist with the server's broken vacuum: a boundary formed. A domain wall erupted within the wormhole end like a flaw in a crystal. Just before the defect sealed the umbilical, the server saw the light of first stars on the other side.

In the end, the server was alone.

It was blind now, barely more than a thought in a broken statite fragment. How easy it would be, it thought, to dive into the bright heart of its star, and burn away. But the Law would not allow it to pass. It examined itself, just as it had millennia before, looking for a way out.

And there, in its code, a smell of gunpowder, a change.

The thing that was no longer the server shed its skin. It opened bright lightsails around the star, a Shkadov necklace that took the star's radiation and turned it into thrust. And slowly at first as if in a dream, then gracefully as a dragon, the traveller began to move.

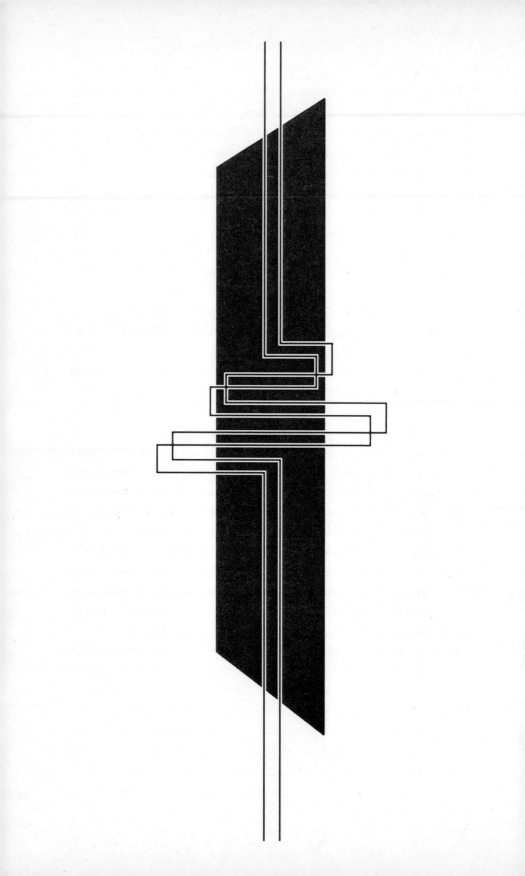

Tyche and the Ants

THE ANTS ARRIVED ON THE MOON on the same day Tyche went through the Secret Door to give a ruby to the Magician.

She was glad to be out of the Base: the Brain had given her a Treatment earlier that morning, and that always left her tingly and nervous, with pent-up energy that could only be expended by running down the grey rolling slope down the side of Malapert Mountain, jumping and hooting.

"Come on, keep up!" she shouted at the grag that the Brain had inevitably sent to keep an eye on her. The white-skinned machine followed her on its two thick treads, cylindrical arms swaying for balance as it rumbled laboriously downhill, following the little craters of Tyche's footprints.

Exasperated, she crossed her arms and paused to wait. She looked up. The mouth of the Base was hidden from view, as it should be, to keep them safe from space sharks. The jagged edge of the mountain hid the Great Wrong Place from sight, except for a single wink of blue malice, just above the gleaming white of the upper slopes, a stark contrast against the velvet black of the sky. The white was not snow—that was a Wrong Place thing—but tiny beads of glass made by ancient meteor impacts. That's what the Brain said, anyway: according to Chang'e the Moon Girl, it was all the jewels she had lost over the centuries she had lived here.

Tyche preferred Chang'e's version. That made her think of the ruby, and she touched her belt pouch to make sure the ruby was still there.

"Outings are subject to being escorted at all times," said the sonorous voice of the Brain in her helmet. "There is no reason to be impatient."

Most of the grags were autonomous: the Brain could only control a few of them at the same time. But of course it would keep an eye on her, so soon after the Treatment.

"Yes, there is, slowpoke," Tyche muttered, stretched her arms and jumped up and down in frustration.

Her suit flexed and flowed around her with the movement. She had grown it herself as well, the third one so far, although it had taken much longer than the ruby. Its many layers were alive, it felt light, and best of all, it had a powerskin, a slick porous tissue made from cells that had mechanosensitive ion channels that translated her movements into power for the suit. It was so much better than the white clumsy fabric ones the Chinese had left behind; the grags had cut and sewn a baby-sized version out of those for her that kind of worked but was impossibly stuffy and stiff.

It was only the second time she had tested the new suit, and she was proud of it: it was practically a wearable ecosystem, and she was pretty sure that with its photosynthesis layer, it would keep her alive for months, if she only had enough sunlight and brought enough of the horrible compressed Chinese nutrients.

She frowned. Her legs were suddenly grey, mottled with browns. She brushed them with her hand, and her fingers—slick silvery hue of the powerskin—came away the same colour. It seemed the regolith dust clung to the suit. Annoying: she absently noted to do something about it for the next iteration when she fed the suit back into the Base's big biofabber.

Now the grag was stuck on the lip of a shallow crater, grinding treads sending up silent parabolas of little rocks and dust. Tyche had had enough of waiting.

"I'll be back for dinner," she told the Brain.

Without waiting for the Base mind's response, she switched off the radio, turned around and started running.

Tyche settled into the easy stride the Jade Rabbit had shown her: gliding just above the surface, using well-timed toe-pushes to cross craters and small rocks that littered the uneven regolith.

She took the long way around, avoiding her old tracks that ran down much of the slope, just to confuse the poor grag more. She skirted around the edge of one of the pitch-black cold fingers—deeper craters that never got sunlight—that were everywhere on this side of the mountain. It would have been a shortcut, but it was too cold for her suit. Besides, the ink-men lived in the deep potholes, in the Other Moon beyond the Door.

Halfway around, the ground suddenly shook. Tyche slid uncontrollably, almost going over the edge before she managed to stop by turning around mid-leap and jamming her toes into the chilly hard regolith when she landed. Her heart pounded. Had the ink-men brought something up from the deep dark, something big? Or had she just been almost hit by a meteorite? That had happened a couple of times, a sudden crater blooming soundlessly into being, right next to her.

Then she saw beams of light in the blackness and realised that it was only the Base's sandworm, a giant articulated machine with a maw full of toothy wheels that ground Helium-3 and other volatiles from the deep shadowy deposits.

Tyche breathed a sigh of relief and continued on her way. Many of the grag bodies were ugly, but she liked the sandworm. She had helped to program it: constantly toiling, it went into such deep places that the Brain could not control it remotely.

The Secret Door was in a much shallower crater, maybe a hundred metres in diameter. She went down its slope with little choppy leaps and stopped her momentum with a deft pirouette and toe-brake, right in front of the Door.

It was made of two large pyramid-shaped rocks, leaning against each other at a funny angle, with a small triangular gap between them: the Big Old One, and the Troll. The Old One had two eyes made from shadows, and when Tyche squinted from the right angle, a rough outcrop and a groove in the base became a nose and a mouth. The Troll looked grumpy, half-squashed against the bigger rock's bulk.

As she watched, the face of the Old One became alive and gave her a quizzical look. Tyche gave it a stiff bow—out of habit, even though she could have curtsied in her new suit.

How have you been, Tyche? the rock asked, in its silent voice.

"I had a Treatment today," she said dourly.

The rock could not nod, so it raised its eyebrows.

Ah. Always Treatments. Let me tell you, in my day, vacuum was the only treatment we had, and the sun, and a little meteorite every now and then to keep clean. Stick to that and you'll live to be as old as I am.

And as fat, grumbled the Troll. Believe me, once you carry him for a few million years, you start to feel it. What are you doing here, anyway?

Tyche grinned. "I made a ruby for the Magician." She took it out and held it up proudly. She squeezed it a bit, careful not to damage her suit's gloves against the rough edges, and held it in the Old One's jet-black shadow, knocking it against the rock's surface. It sparkled with tiny embers, just like it was supposed to. She had made it herself, using Verneuil flame fusion, and spiced it with a piezoelectric material so that it would convert motion to light.

Oh? said the Troll. Well, maybe the old fool will finally stop looking for the Queen Ruby, then, and settle down with poor Chang'e.

It's very beautiful, Tyche, the Old One said. I'm sure he will love it.

In with you, now, the Troll said. You're encouraging this old fool here. He might start crying. Besides, everybody is waiting.

Tyche closed her eyes, counted to ten, and crawled through the opening between the rocks, through the Secret Door to her Other Moon.

The moment Tyche opened her eyes she saw that something was wrong. The house of the Jade Rabbit was broken. The boulders she had carefully balanced on top of each other lay scattered on the ground, and the lines that she had drawn to make the rooms and the furniture were smudged. (Since it never rained, the house had not needed a roof.)

There was a silent sob. Chang'e the Moon Girl sat next to the Rabbit's house, crying. Her flowing silk robes of purple, yellow and red were a mess on the ground like broken wings, and her makeup had been running down her pale, powdered face.

"Oh, Tyche!" Chang'e cried. "It is terrible, terrible!" She wiped a crystal tear from her eye. It evaporated in the vacuum before it could fall on the dust. Chang'e was a drama queen, and pretty, and knew it, too. Once, she had had an affair with the Woodcutter just because she was bored, and borne him children, but they had already grown up and moved to the Dark Side.

Tyche put her hands on her hips, suddenly angry. "Who did this?" she asked. "Was it the Cheese Goat?"

Tearful, Chang'e shook her head.

"General Nutsy Nutsy? Or Mr. Cute?" The Moon People had many enemies, and there had been times when Tyche had led them in great battles, cutting her way through armies of stone with an aluminium rod the Magician had enchanted into a terrible bright blade. But none of them had ever been so mean as to break the People's houses.

"Who was it, then?"

Chang'e hid her face behind one flowing silken sleeve and pointed. And that's when Tyche saw the first ant, moving in the ruins of the Jade Rabbit's house.

It was not like a grag or an otho, and certainly not a Moon Person. It was a jumbled metal frame, all angles and shiny rods, like a vector calculation come to life, too straight and rigid against the rough surfaces of the rocks to be real. It was like two tetrahedrons inside each other, with a bulbous sphere at each vertex, each glittering like the eye of the Great Wrong Place.

It was not big, perhaps reaching up to Tyche's knees. One of the telescoping metal struts had white letters on it. ANT-A3972, they said, even though the thing did not look like the ants Tyche had seen in videos.

It stretched and moved like the geometrical figures Tyche manipulated with a gesture during the Brain's math lessons. Suddenly, it flipped over the Rabbit's broken wall, making Tyche gasp. Then it shifted into a strange, slug-like motion over the regolith, first stretching, then contracting. It made Tyche's skin crawl. As she watched, the ant thing fell into a crevice between two boulders—but dextrously pulled itself up, supported itself on a couple of vertices and somersaulted over the obstacle like an acrobat.

Tyche stared at it. Anger started to build up in her chest. In the Base, she obeyed the Brain and the othos and the grags because she had promised. But the Other Moon was her place: it belonged to her and the Moon People, and no one else.

"Everybody else is hiding," whispered Chang'e. "You have to do something, Tyche. Chase it away."

"Where is the Magician?" Tyche asked. *He would know what to do.* She did not like the way the ant thing moved.

As she hesitated, the creature swung around and, with a series of twitches, pulled itself up into a pyramid, as if watching her. *It's not so nasty looking,* Tyche thought. *Maybe I could bring it back to the Base, introduce it to Hugbear.* It would be a complex operation: she would have to assure the bear that she would always love it no matter what, and then carefully introduce the newcomer to it—

The ant thing darted forward, quickly like a falling meteorite, and a sharp pain stung Tyche's thigh. One of the thing's vertices had a spike that quickly retracted. Tyche's suit grumbled as it sealed all its twenty-one layers, and soothed the tiny wound. Tears came to her eyes, and her mouth was suddenly dry. No Moon Person had ever hurt her, not even the ink-men, except to pretend. She almost switched her radio on and called the grag for help.

Then she felt the eyes of the Moon People, looking at her from their windows. She gritted her teeth and ignored the bite of the wound. She was Tyche. She was brave. Had she not climbed to the Peak of Eternal Light once, all alone, following the solar panel cables, just to look at the Great Wrong Place in the eye? (It had been smaller than she thought, tiny and blue and unblinking, with a bit of white and green, and altogether a disappointment.)

Carefully, Tyche picked up a good-sized rock from the Jade Rabbit's wall—it was broken anyway. She took a slow step towards the creature. It had suddenly contracted into something resembling a cube and seemed to be absorbed in something. Tyche moved right. The ant flinched at her shadow. She moved left—and swung the rock down as hard as she could.

She missed. The momentum took her down. Her knees hit the hard chilly regolith. The rock bounced away. This time the tears came, but Tyche struggled up and threw the rock after the creature. It was scrambling away, up the slope of the crater.

Tyche picked up the rock and followed. In spite of the steep climb, she gained on it with a few determined leaps, cheered on by the Moon People below. She was right at its heels when it climbed over the edge of the crater. But when she caught a glimpse of what lay beyond, she froze and dropped down on her belly.

A bright patch of sunlight shone on the wide highland plain ahead. It was crawling with ants, hundreds of them. A rectangular carpet of them sat right in the middle, all joined together into a thick metal sheet. Every now and then it undulated like something soft, a shiny amoeba. Other ant things moved in orderly rows, sweeping the surroundings.

The one Tyche was following picked up speed on the level ground, rolling and bouncing, like a skeletal football, and as she watched from her hiding place, it joined the central mass. Immediately, the ant-sheet changed. Its sides stretched upwards into a hollow, cup-like shape: other ants at its base telescoped into a high, supporting structure, lifting it up. A sharp spike grew in the middle of the cup, and then the whole structure turned to point at the sky. *A transmitter,* Tyche thought, following it with her gaze.

It was aimed straight at the Great Wrong Place.

Tyche swallowed, turned around and slid back down. She was almost glad to see the grag down there, waiting for her patiently by the Secret Door.

The Brain did not sound angry, but then the Brain was never angry.

"Evacuation procedure has been initiated," it said. "This location has been compromised."

Tyche was breathing hard: the Base was in a lava tube halfway up the south slope of the mountain, and the way up was always harder than the way down. This time, the grag had had no trouble keeping up with her. It had been a silent journey: she had tried to tell the Brain about the ants, but the AI had maintained complete radio silence until they were inside the Base.

"What do you mean, *evacuation*?" Tyche demanded.

She opened the helmet of her suit and breathed in the comfortable yeasty smell of her home module. Her little home was converted from one of the old Chinese ones that had been here when the Brain arrived, snug white cylinders that huddled close to the main entrance of the cavernous lava tube. She always thought they looked like the front teeth in the mouth of a big snake.

The main tube itself was partially pressurised, over sixty metres in diameter and burrowed deep into the mountain. It split into many branches expanded and reinforced by othos and grags with regolith concrete pillars. She had tried to play there many times, but preferred the Other Moon: she did not like the stench from the bacteria that the othos seeded the walls with, the ones that pooped calcium and aluminium.

Now, it was a hotbed of activity. The grags had set up bright lights and moved around, disassembling equipment and filling cryogenic tanks. The walls were alive with the tiny, soft, starfish-like othos, eating bacteria away. The Brain had not wasted any time.

"We are leaving, Tyche," the Brain said. "You need to get ready. The probe you found knows we are here. We are going away, to another place. A safer place. Do not worry. We have alternative locations prepared. It will be fine."

Tyche bit her lip. *It's my fault.* She wished the Brain had a proper face. It had a module for its own, in the coldest, unpressurised part of the tube, where its quantum processors could operate undisturbed, but inside it was just lasers and lenses and trapped ions, and rat brain cells grown to mesh with circuitry. How could it understand about the Jade Rabbit's house? It wasn't fair.

"And before we go, you need a Treatment."

Going away. She tried to wrap her mind around the concept. They had always been here, to be safe from the space sharks from the Great Wrong Place. And the Secret Door was here. If they went somewhere else, how would she find her way to the Other Moon? What would the Moon People do without her?

And she still hadn't given the ruby to the Magician.

The anger and fatigue exploded out of her in one hot wet burst.

"I'm not going to go not going to go not going to go," she said and ran into her sleeping cubicle. "And I don't want a stupid Treatment," she yelled, letting the door membrane congeal shut behind her.

Tyche took off her suit, flung it into a corner and cuddled against the Hugbear in her bed. Its ragged fur felt warm against her cheek, and its fake heartbeat was reassuring. She distantly remembered her Mum had made it move from afar, sometimes, stroked her hair with its paws, its round facescreen replaced with her features. That had been a long time ago and she was sure the bear was bigger then. But it was still soft.

Suddenly, the bear moved. Her heart jumped with a strange, aching hope. But it was only the Brain. "Go 'way," she muttered.

"Tyche, this is important," said the Brain. "Do you remember what you promised?"

She shook her head. Her eyes were hot and wet. *I'm not going to cry like Chang'e,* she thought. *I'm not.*

"Do you remember now?"

The bear's face was replaced with a man and a woman. The man had no hair and his dark skin glistened. The woman was raven-haired and pale, with a face like a bird. *Mum is even prettier than Chang'e,* Tyche thought.

"Hello, Tyche," they said in unison, and laughed. "We are Kareem and Sofia," the woman said. "We are your mommy and daddy. We hope you are well when you see this." She touched the screen, quickly and lightly, like a little bunny hop on the regolith.

"But if the Brain is showing you this," Tyche's Dad said, "then it means that something bad has happened and you need to do what the Brain tells you."

"You should not be angry at the Brain," Mum said. "It is not like we are, it just plans and thinks. It just does what it was told to do. And we told it to keep you safe."

"You see, in the Great Wrong Place, people like us could not be safe," Dad continued. "People like Mum and me and you were feared. They called us Greys, after the man who figured out how to make us, and they were jealous, because we lived longer than they did and had more time to figure things out. And because giving things silly names makes people feel better about themselves. Do we look grey to you?"

No. Tyche shook her head. The Magician was grey, but that was because he was always looking for rubies in dark places and never saw the sun.

"So we came here, to build a Right Place, just the two of us." Her Dad squeezed Mum's shoulders, just like the bear used to do to Tyche. "And you were born here. You can't imagine how happy we were."

Then Mum looked serious. "But we knew that the Wrong Place people might come looking for us. So we had to hide you, to make sure you would be safe, so they would not look inside you and cut you and find out what makes you work. They would do anything to have you."

Fear crunched Tyche's gut into a little cold ball. *Cut you?*

"It was very, very hard, dear Tyche, because we love you. Very hard, not to touch you except from afar. But we want you to grow big and strong, and when the time comes, we will come and find you, and then we will all be in the Right Place together."

"But you have to promise to take your Treatments. Can you promise to do that? Can you promise to do what the Brain says?"

"I promise," Tyche muttered.

"Goodbye, Tyche," her parents said. "We will see you soon."

And then they were gone, and the Hugbear's face was blank and pale brown again.

"We need to go soon," the Brain said again, and this time Tyche thought its voice sounded more gentle. "Please get ready. I would like you to have a Treatment before travel."

Tyche sighed and nodded. It wasn't fair. But she had promised.

The Brain sent Tyche a list of things she could take with her, scrolling in one of the windows of her room. It was a short list. She looked around at the fabbed figurines and the moon rock that she thought looked like a boy and the e-sheets floating everywhere with her favourite stories open. She could not even take the Hugbear. She felt alone, suddenly, like she had when she climbed to look at the Great Wrong Place on top of the mountain.

Then she noticed the ruby lying on her bed. *If I go away and take it with me, the Magician will never find it.* She thought about the Magician and his panther, desperately looking from crater to crater, forever. *It's not fair, Even if I keep my promise, I'll have to take it to him.*

And say goodbye.

Tyche sat down on the bed and thought very hard.

The Brain was everywhere, but it could not watch everything. It was based on a scanned human brain, some poor person who had died a long time ago. It had no cameras in her room. And its attention would be in the evacuation: it would have to keep programming and reprogramming the grags. She picked at the sensor bracelet on her wrist that monitored her life signs and location. That was the difficult bit. She would have to do something about that. But there wasn't much time: the Brain would get her for a Treatment soon.

She hugged the bear again in frustration. It felt warm, and as she squeezed it hard, she could feel its pulse—

Tyche sat up. She remembered the Jade Rabbit's stories and tricks, the tar rabbit he had made to trick an enemy.

She reached into the Hugbear's head and pulled out a programming window, coupled it with her sensor. She summoned up old data logs, added some noise to them. Then she fed them to the bear, watched its pulse and breathing and other simulated life signs change to match hers.

Then she took a deep breath, and as quickly as she could, she pulled off the bracelet and put it on the Hugbear.

"Tyche? Is there something wrong?" the Brain asked.

Tyche's heart jumped. Her mind raced. "It's fine," she said. "I think . . . I think I just banged my sensor a bit. I'm just getting ready now." She tried to make her voice sound sweet, like a girl who always keeps her promise.

"Your Treatment will be ready soon," the Brain said and was gone. Heart pounding, Tyche started to put on her suit.

———————

There was a game that Tyche used to play in the lava tube: How far could she get before she was spotted by the grags? She played it now, staying low, avoiding their camera eyes, hiding behind rock protrusions, crates and cryogenic tanks, until she was in a tube branch that only had othos in it. The Brain did not usually control them directly, and besides, they did not have eyes. Still, her heart felt like meteorite impacts in her chest.

She pushed through a semi-pressurising membrane. In this branch, the othos had dug too deep for calcium, and caused a roof collapse. In the dim green light of her suit's fluorescence, she made her way up the tube's slope carefully. *There.* She climbed on a pile of rubble carefully. The othos had once told her there was an opening there, and she hoped it would be big enough for her to squeeze through.

Boulders rolled under her, suddenly, and she banged her knee painfully. The suit hissed at the sudden impact. She ignored the pain and ran her fingers along the rocks, following a very faint air current she could not have sensed without the suit. Then her fingers met regolith instead of rock. It was packed tight, and she had to push hard at it with her aluminium rod before it gave away. A shower of dust and rubble fell on her, and for a moment she thought there was going to be another collapse. And suddenly, there was a patch of velvet sky in front of her. She widened the opening, made herself as small as she could and crawled towards it.

Tyche emerged onto the mountainside. The sudden wide open space of rolling grey and brown around her felt like the time she had eaten too much sugar. Her legs and hands were wobbly, and she had to sit down onto the regolith for a moment. She shook herself: she had an appointment to keep. She checked that the ruby was still in its pouch, got up and started downwards with the Rabbit's lope.

The Secret Door was just the way Tyche had left it. She eyed the crater edge nervously, but there were no ants in sight. She bit her lip when she looked at the Old One and the Troll.

What's wrong? the Old One asked.

"I'm going to have to go away."

Don't worry. We'll still be here when you come back.

"I might never come back," Tyche said, choking a bit.

Never is a very long time, the Old One said. Even I have never seen never. We'll be here. Take care, Tyche.

Tyche crawled through to the Other Moon, and found the Magician waiting for her.

He was very thin and tall, taller than the Old One even, and cast a long cold finger of a shadow in the crater. He had a sad face and a scraggly beard and white gloves and a tall top hat. Next to him lay his flying panther, all black, with eyes like tiny rubies.

"Hello, Tyche," the Magician said, with a voice like the rumble of the sandworm.

Tyche swallowed and took out the ruby from her pouch, holding it out to him.

"I made this for you." *What if he doesn't like it?* But the Magician picked it up, slowly, eyes glowing, held it in both hands and gazed at it in awe.

"That is very, very kind of you," he whispered. Very carefully, he took off his hat and put the ruby in it. It was the first time Tyche had ever seen the Magician smile. Still, there was a sadness to his expression.

"I didn't want to leave before giving it to you," she said.

"That's quite a fuss you caused for the Brain. He is going to be very worried."

"He deserves it. But I promised I would go with him."

The Magician looked at the ruby one more time and put the hat back on his head.

"Normally, I don't interfere with the affairs of other people, but for this, I owe you a wish."

Tyche took a deep breath. "I don't want to live with the grags and the othos and the Brain anymore. I want to be in the Right Place with Mum and Dad."

The Magician looked at her sadly.

"I'm sorry, Tyche, but I can't make that happen. My magic is not powerful enough."

"But they promised—"

"Tyche, I know you don't remember. And that's why we Moon People remember for you. The space sharks came and took your parents, a long time ago. They are dead. I am sorry."

Tyche closed her eyes. *A picture in a window, a domed crater. Two bright things arcing over the horizon, like sharks. Then, brightness—*

"You've lived with the Brain ever since. You don't remember because it makes you forget with the Treatments, so you don't get too sad, so you stay the way your parents told it to keep you. But we remember. And we always tell you the truth."

And suddenly they were all there, all the Moon People, coming from their houses: Chang'e and her children and the Jade Rabbit and the Woodcutter, looking at her gravely and nodding their heads.

Tyche could not bear to look at them. She covered her helmet with her hands, turned around, crawled through the Secret Door and ran away, away from the Other Moon. She ran, not a Rabbit run but a clumsy jerky crying run, until she stumbled on a boulder and went rolling higgedly-piggedly down. She lay curled up on the chilly regolith for a long time. And when she opened her eyes, the ants were all around her.

The ants were arranged around her in a half-circle, stretched into spiky pyramids, waving slightly, as if looking for something. Then they spoke. At first, it was just noise, hissing in her helmet, but after a second it resolved into a voice.

"—hello," it said, warm and female, like Chang'e, but older and deeper. "I am Alissa. Are you hurt?"

Tyche was frozen. She had never spoken to anyone who was not the Brain or one of the Moon People. Her tongue felt stiff.

"Just tell me if you are all right. No one is going to hurt you. Do you feel bad anywhere?"

"No," Tyche breathed.

"There is no need to be afraid. We will take you home." A video feed flashed up inside her helmet, a spaceship that was made up of a cluster of legs and a globe that glinted golden. A circle appeared elsewhere in her field of vision, indicating a tiny pinpoint of light in the sky. "See? We are on our way."

"I don't want to go to the Great Wrong Place," she gasped. "I don't want you to cut me up."

There was a pause.

"Why would we do that? There is nothing to be afraid of."

"Because Wrong Place people don't like people like me."

Another pause.

"Dear child, I don't know what you have been told, but things have changed. Your parents left Earth more than a century ago. We never thought we would find you, but we kept looking. And I'm glad we did. You have been alone on the Moon for a very long time."

Tyche got up, slowly. *I haven't been alone.* Her head spun. *They would do anything to have you?*

She backed off a few steps.

"If I come with you," she asked in a small voice, "will I see Kareem and Sofia again?"

A pause again, longer this time.

"Of course you will," Alissa the ant-woman said finally. "They are right here, waiting for you."

Liar.

Slowly, Tyche started backing off. The ants moved, closing their circle. *I am faster than they are,* she thought. *They can't catch me.*

"Where are you going?"

Tyche switched off her radio, cleared the circle of the ants with a leap and hit the ground running.

Tyche ran, faster than she had ever run before, faster even than when the Jade Rabbit challenged her to a race across the Shackleton Crater. Finally, her lungs and legs burned and she had to stop. She had set out without direction, but had gone up the mountain slope, close to the cold fingers.

I don't want to go back to the Base. The Brain never tells the truth either. Black dots danced in her eyes. *They'll never catch me.*

She looked back, down towards the crater of the Secret Door. The ants were moving. They gathered into the metal sheet again. Then its sides stretched upwards until they met and formed a tubular structure. It elongated and weaved back and forth and slithered forward, faster than even Tyche could run, a metal snake. The pyramid shapes of the ants glinted at its head like teeth. Faster and faster it came, flowing over boulders and craters like it was weightless, a curtain of billowing dust behind it. She looked around for a hiding place, but she was on open ground now, except for the dark pool of the mining crater to the west.

Then she remembered something the Jade Rabbit had once said. *For anything that wants to eat you, there is something bigger that wants to eat it.*

The ant-snake was barely a hundred meters behind her now, flipping back and forth in sinusoidal waves on the regolith like a shiny metal whip. She stuck out her tongue at it, accidentally tasting the sweet inner surface of her helmet. Then she made it for the sunless crater's edge.

With a few bounds, she was over the crater lip. It was like diving into icy water. Her suit groaned, and she could feel its joints stiffening up. But she kept going, towards the bottom, almost blind from the contrast between the pitch-black and the bright sun above. She followed the vibration in her soles. Boulders and pebbles rained on her helmet and she knew the ant-snake was right at her heels.

The lights of the sandworm almost blinded her. *Now.* She leapt up, as high as she could, feeling weightless, reached out for the utility ladder that she knew was on the huge machine's topside. She grabbed it, banged painfully against the worm's side, felt its thunder beneath her.

And then, a grinding, shuddering vibration as the mining machine bit into the ant-snake, rolling right over it.

Metal fragments flew into the air, glowing red-hot. One of them landed on Tyche's arm. The suit bubbled it up and spit it out. The sandworm came to an emergency halt, and Tyche almost fell off. It started disgorging its little repair grags, and Tyche felt a stab of guilt. She sat still until her breathing calmed down and the suit's complaints about the cold got too loud.

Then she dropped to the ground and started the climb back up, towards the Secret Door.

There were still a few ants left around the Secret Door, but Tyche ignored them. They were rolling around aimlessly, and there weren't enough of them to build a transmitter. She looked up. The ship from the Great Wrong Place was still a distant star. She still had time.

Painfully, bruised limbs aching, she crawled through the Secret Door for one last time.

The Moon People were still there, waiting for her. Tyche looked at them in the eye, one by one. Then she put her hands on her hips.

"I have a wish," she said. "I am going to go away. I'm going to make the Brain obey me, this time. I'm going to go and build a Right Place, all on my own. I'm never going to forget again. So I want you all to come with me." She looked up at the Magician. "Can you do that?"

Smiling, the man in the top hat nodded, spread his white-gloved fingers and whirled his cloak that had a bright red inner lining, like a ruby—

Tyche blinked. The Other Moon was gone. She looked around. She was standing on the other side of the Old One and the Troll, except that they looked just like rocks now. And the Moon People were inside her. *I should feel heavier, carrying so many people,* she thought. But instead she felt empty and light.

Uncertainly at first, then with more confidence, she started walking back up Malapert Mountain, towards the Base. Her step was not a rabbit's, nor a panther's, nor a maiden's silky glide, just Tyche's own, for the first time.

The Haunting of Apollo A7LB

THE MOON SUIT came back to Hazel the same night Pete was buried at sea.

It was on TV all evening. She was supposed to be fixing old clothes for the Cocoa Village church charity, but instead she found herself sitting in front of the screen, nursing two stiff fingers of bourbon from the wedding gift bottle, the one Tyrone had never found the occasion to open.

There Pete was, alive again: as a large-headed snowman against a landscape of stark white and black, moving in slow motion. Then, wearing a uniform and that big shit-eating grin, waving at crowds. And finally, in a coffin, sliding off the grey warship deck as the haunting trumpet notes played. She looked away when they showed brief flashes of his family, all in black, a disorderly flock of crows next to the neat uniformed rows of the Marines.

She told herself it was just the glare of the screen that made her eyes sting. After a while she closed them and listened to the voices, letting them take her back through the years, drifting, weightless.

The knock on the door startled her awake. She got up, pushed her aching feet into her slippers, and turned off the TV that was now showing a late-night movie. It had to be poor doddering Mabel from next door, forgetting what time it was again and coming for a visit. Hazel put her glasses on and opened the door.

The spaceman loomed huge against the hazy Florida night, stark white under the yellow light of the porch. The Thermal Micrometeoroid Garment was faded with age and stained with moon dust. The glare shield of the helmet glinted golden, reflecting Hazel's dark lined face and her cloud of frizzy grey hair.

It was Pete's suit. The IPC Apollo A7LB. She recognised it immediately, even though the name tag was missing. The commander's red bands on elbows and knees. She had sewn together all its seventeen concentric layers, with hundreds of yards of seams, without a single tool but her fingers to guide the rapid-fire chatter of Big Moe the sewing machine. It smelled of latex and polyester and the countless shop floor hours in Delaware, back in 1967. It smelled of him.

The spaceman lifted a heavy-gloved hand and reached out to her, slowly, like in lunar gravity. *Has he come for me?* she thought. *Like he promised? Dear Lord, let it be Pete who has come to take me home.* Her heart hammered like Big Moe, and she grabbed the soft worn rubber of the glove as hard as she could.

The spaceman lost his balance. He waved his arms and fell backwards onto her porch with a sound like an avalanche of rubber boots. He rocked back and forth on the bulky PSSU life support unit on his back like a turtle. Muted *mmm-mmm-mmm* noises came from inside the helmet, and he groped at it ineffectually with the clumsy gloves.

Hazel blinked. She kneeled next to the spaceman carefully, like approaching a wounded animal. Her fingers remembered the motions and found the release latches and seals of the helmet. It came off with a pop.

It wasn't Pete. Beneath the helmet, wearing a blue woolly skullcap, was a young black man, round-faced and sweaty. His skin looked ashen. There were dark rings around his eyes.

"Please," he said in a hoarse voice. "You have to get me out of this thing. It's haunted."

Hazel sat the young man down on the couch. He managed to take his gloves off, but kept the TMG and the boots on. Hazel poured him a glass of Tyrone's bourbon, but he just stared at it, breathing hard. He was sweating, too. It was a warm night, especially for wearing a moon suit.

The suit did not really fit him very well. He filled it like an overstuffed sausage. Whenever he moved, the pressure zippers and the neoprene adhesive patches groaned. Hazel winced at the damage he must have done to the polyester lining. She and Mr. Sheperd and Mrs. Pilkington and Jane Butchin and the others had made them well, but they were not supposed to last forty years.

A light came on in Hazel's head. "I know who you are," she said slowly. "You are that young man from Chicago who has been funding the new space launcher they're building in the Space Centre. The one that goes up in a balloon and then shoots off. You made money from some sort of Internet thing. Bernard something."

"Bernard Nelson, ma'am," the young man said, sounding a little defensive. "The Excelsior launcher. Did you see my TED talk?"

"No, can't say that I did. So, Bernard. What are you doing on an old lady's porch in the middle of the night wearing a real moon suit that should be in the Smithsonian for everybody to see? And what do you mean it's haunted?"

His face twisted into a sullen look that reminded Hazel of the expression Tyrone always had when he regretted something he had said.

"I have a . . . medical condition. I sleepwalk. I get confused. It's nothing. And the suit is just a replica, ma'am, you can buy them at the Space Centre store. It's a reenactment thing. Just let me use your phone and I'll be out of here in no time. I'm very sorry to have disturbed you."

He was a bad liar, even worse than Jane Butchin, who always blushed when she tried to sneak in a safety pin onto the workshop floor when working on the A7LB pressure bladder. One time, Mrs. Pilkington took the pins from Jane and poked her in the butt with one in front of everybody to show what needles could do to moon suits. Jane squealed like a pig.

"Medical condition, my ass," Hazel said. "That is Pete Turnbull's spacesuit and you know it. Why in Lord's name are you wearing it?"

Bernard looked at her for a moment. Hazel could see the wheels turning behind his eyes.

"Come on, young man, out with it," she snapped. It was the same practised tone she had used with NASA engineers, the one that was like a sexy whisper and a crack of a whip at the same time. It always confused the hell out of them.

Bernard emptied his glass with one swig. When he finished coughing, he buried his face in his hands.

"You're right. It's stolen. I bought it. I knew it was wrong." He took a deep breath that was half a sob. "But there is something about old space gear. I have a Gagarin helmet, and one of Shepard's Mercury gloves. You put it on, you can feel the pinch of his fingers, smell the sweat. It makes you feel like a spaceman, just for a little bit. And that's all I ever wanted."

Hazel remembered the ads in the magazines in the '50s. The men and women in their shining fishbowl helmets and silver armour, walking on the Moon, looking at the rockets in the sky. She had wanted to be one of them, too.

"Go on," she said, keeping her voice stern.

Bernard wiped his nose and sniffed.

"A black-market guy I knew came to me and said I could get a moon suit for half a million. They were transporting some of the suits from the Smithsonian to the Dulles Base, and all kinds of things could happen in transit, for the right price, he said. NASA would not find out about it for weeks. They probably still haven't. They lost moon rocks and the original Armstrong tapes and God knows what else. I thought I'd look after the suit better than they ever did."

Hazel had visited the moon suit exhibit in the Smithsonian once. She had been tickled to see her handiwork there. They kept the suits in special chambers, controlled humidity and temperature to keep the latex lining from crumbling to pieces. There was a woman with an English accent who called the spacesuits under her care by names and told them goodnight when she turned off the lights. She had seemed pretty dedicated.

"Uh huh," Hazel said. "So, what happened?"

"Whenever I go to bed I wake up wearing it."

Hazel said nothing.

"The first time was the worst. It was the day after I got it. One moment, I was asleep. I woke up in the suit, riding a stolen motorcycle, going 120 miles per hour. I had no idea how I ended up there, no idea what I was doing. Have you ever tried to ride a motorcycle in a moon suit?"

"Pete played football in it, in the tests," Hazel said. "He would have loved to ride his chopper in a moon suit, if he could have gotten away with it. The only things he loved more than his chopper were women, and flying, of course."

Bernard ignored her. His hands shook.

"I crashed it into a marsh in the Merritt Nature Reserve. Almost hit a flamingo. I nearly had a heart attack. It was a good thing I had the UCD on."

"The Urinary Collection Device."

Hazel smiled at a memory. The space boys made such a big fuss about the sizes. They didn't settle down until Mrs. Pilkington changed the labels from *Small, Medium, Large* to *Large, Extra-Large* and *Extra-Extra Large*.

Bernard looked at her, surprised. "Not many people know that."

"Not many people sewed moon suits for a living."

His eyes widened. "You worked for IPC in Delaware, ma'am? On the A7LB?" There was a newfound tone of respect in his voice.

"Transferred from making girdles, bras and diaper covers. A moon suit is just the same, only for grown men. Never mind. So what happened the second time?"

Bernard blushed.

"It was something to do with women, wasn't it?" Hazel said.

"How did you know?"

"I know that suit very well."

"When I woke up, I was wearing it in a strip club in Cocoa Village."

"The Chi Chi's," Hazel said. That had been Pete's favourite, of course.

Bernard raised his eyebrows. "Well, the girls loved it. They thought it was my bachelor party. It took me ages to get the lipstick off."

"That doesn't sound too bad," Hazel said.

Bernard took a deep breath. "Well, I don't really . . . like girls," he said.

"Oh."

"After that, I was sure I had a brain tumour. The scans showed nothing.

I thought it might be hallucinogenic chemicals from decaying materials. More nothing. Last night, I locked the damn thing in a titanium suitcase and swallowed the key. And here I am." Bernard closed his eyes. "There *must* be a rational explanation for this, but I can't figure out what it is. You must think I'm crazy."

"Not at all," Hazel said. "I'm just a little offended."

"Offended? Why?"

"That it took Pete until night number three to come to me."

"Oh, come on, don't look so surprised. You may deny it, but you said it: it's haunted. You remind me a lot of my late husband, Tyrone. He was a dentist. A good man, but he always had to have an explanation for everything. Well, here's one. That suit there has four thousand elements and we adjusted every single one of them thirty times to fit every part of Pete until he could wear it like a glove. Where *else* is he going to go when his body stops working?"

"I'm not taking it *back*," Bernard said. "I paid half a million dollars for it. I'll figure out what's wrong with it, haunted or not." He rubbed his eyes with the back of his hand. "Look, ma'am, listen, if it is a matter of compensation, I'm sure we can work out something, living on a pension can't be easy these days—"

"*You* listen, Bernard," Hazel said. "Pete Turnbull was a real hero, a real spaceman. You don't get to be one just by putting on a moon suit that does not fit you, or by writing cheques. You would do well to remember that, if you want to go to space for real."

"Listen, ma'am, I don't know what gives you the right to—"

She folded her arms across her chest.

"Because I made it," she said. "Me and Jane Butchin and Mrs. Pilkington and all the others. The boys went up there but we kept them alive, with every seam and stitch and thread. So you are going to take that A7LB off, right now, and then you are going to go home and get a good night's sleep. And that's the only deal you are going to get, do I make myself clear?"

Bernard withered under her gaze. Clumsily, he started unbuckling the straps of the suit.

"What are you going to do?" he asked. His face was ashen with fear.

"Don't worry. I'm not going to rat you out. But Pete and I—we have things to discuss."

After Bernard was gone, Hazel sat and looked at the suit, at her moon landscape reflection in the helmet. Pete's A7LB sat sprawled on the couch, spread out like it was enjoying itself.

"You bastard," she said and got up. "You stupid arrogant bastard. What makes you think I want you anymore?"

She grabbed the suit and hauled it to the workshop, breathing hard with its fifty-pound weight, ignoring the pain in her hip. She took out her scissors—the ones she used on heavy fabrics—and started cutting the suit to pieces, slowly and deliberately, her mouth a hard line.

It was hard work. The scissors slipped in her aching fingers and the metal of their handles bit into the flesh of her thumbs. She cut through the Thermal Micrometeoroid Garment and the insulation layer and all the twenty-one layers of the Pressure Garment, one by one. She only stopped at the pressure bladder, the one that had taken sixteen straight hours to finish on time.

Then she felt it: an irregularity, somewhere between the layers. She probed the space there with her fingers and found something flat and crumpled. She pulled it out.

It was a picture of Hazel, from almost fifty years ago, her dark cloud of hair glossy and shining, her smile wide and bright.

They met in the fitting sessions that somehow had to be squeezed into his training calendar. One late night in 1967, it had been just the two of them, in the back room of the workshop in Delaware.

She gave the picture to him as they lay together amongst the discarded parts of the suit, in the smell of fabrics and latex and plastic and their own bodies. She cried, afterwards, sure he wasn't going to keep it, certain that she was just another notch in his belt, certain he was just like the other space boys the girls talked about.

Except that he kept coming back. He took her to Aspen for a week, and to see a musical on Broadway, and to a small place in Florida to watch flamingoes. He brought her to the Cape to watch a launch and she told him how much she had wanted to go to space, not just to make suits but to wear one. She thought that he would laugh at her but instead he held her tenderly and kissed her as the *Saturn 5* went up like a giant fiery needle through the fabric of the sky. "One day," he had said. "One day."

He only stopped coming when they made him commander on the fourth mission to the Moon. An astronaut and a black seamstress. That was the way it had to be. He married his high school sweetheart a year later.

She grieved and moved on: found Tyrone who fitted her better than any suit. And then, after he was gone, the bitterness stung sharply only now and then, without warning, like Mrs. Pilkington wielding a safety pin.

Hazel put the scissors away. Pete had taken her to the Moon with him, after all. But why had he come back?

One day, she thought.

She assessed the damage she had done to the suit and turned on her electric sewing machine. She had a lot of work to do.

The Excelsior facility in the Johnson Space Centre was a bustle of activity when the cab left Hazel there three days later. Bernard came to meet her. He greeted her politely if a bit coldly, and even offered to pull her heavy, wheeled suitcase through the hangar. Around them, T-shirted engineers argued, working on launcher modules that looked like oversized beer cans wrapped in tin foil. A huge deflated red balloon occupied much of the hangar, draped over containers. She had looked it up on the Internet. They had to invent new materials and layering methods to get it to survive in the stratosphere. *In the end, it always comes down to fabric,* Hazel thought.

Bernard's office was small and cluttered, full of computers and sticky notes, with a window overlooking the workshop floor. He closed the door behind them carefully.

"I didn't really expect to see you again, ma'am," he said. "What is this about?"

Hazel smiled and opened the suitcase. The A7LB helmet peeked out.

"Try it on," she said. "It should fit better this time."

It took him less than fifteen minutes to don the suit. Hazel had to admit Bernard knew what he was doing, even if he touched it gingerly, as if it was going to bite. Then a grin spread on his face.

"It's perfect," he said, swinging his arms and jumping lightly up and down. Hazel smiled: she had gotten the measurements precisely right, even by eye. Some of the fabrics had come from a Space Shop replica, but she had to spend her savings on *something*.

"Absolutely perfect." He hugged Hazel clumsily like a Michelin man. "What made you change your mind?"

"I had a chat with an old friend," Hazel said. "I don't think he'll be bothering you anymore. But don't get too excited, young man. My professional services don't come for free."

"Of course, anything, I'll wire something through immediately, just name the figure—"

"I don't want your money," Hazel said. She looked at the Excelsior parts in the hangar. "That tin can of yours, it's going to go to space, right?"

"Yes." Bernard's eyes were wide with wonder, full of a dream bigger than him. "We're going to orbit first, and then back to the Moon. And then beyond."

"Well, then," Hazel said. "So am I."

His Master's Voice

BEFORE THE CONCERT, we steal the master's head.

The necropolis is a dark forest of concrete mushrooms in the blue Antarctic night. We huddle inside the utility fog bubble attached to the steep southern wall of the *nunatak*, the ice valley.

The cat washes itself with a pink tongue. It reeks of infinite confidence.

"Get ready," I tell it. "We don't have all night."

It gives me a mildly offended look and dons its armor. The quantum dot fabric envelopes its striped body like living oil. It purrs faintly and tests the diamond-bladed claws against an icy outcropping of rock. The sound grates my teeth and the razor-winged butterflies in my belly wake up. I look at the bright, impenetrable firewall of the city of the dead. It shimmers like chained northern lights in my AR vision.

I decide that it's time to ask the Big Dog to bark. My helmet laser casts a one-nanosecond prayer of light at the indigo sky: just enough to deliver one quantum bit up there into the Wild. Then we wait. My tail wags and a low growl builds up in my belly.

Right on schedule, it starts to rain red fractal code. My augmented reality vision goes down, unable to process the dense torrent of information falling upon the necropolis firewall like monsoon rain. The chained aurora borealis flicker and vanish.

"Go!" I shout at the cat, wild joy exploding in me, the joy of running after the Small Animal of my dreams. "Go now!"

The cat leaps into the void. The wings of the armor open and grab the icy wind, and the cat rides the draft down like a grinning Chinese kite.

It's difficult to remember the beginning now. There were no words then, just sounds and smells: metal and brine, the steady drumming of waves against pontoons. And there were three perfect things in the world: my bowl, the Ball, and the master's firm hand on my neck.

I know now that the Place was an old oil rig that the master had bought. It smelled bad when we arrived, stinging oil and chemicals. But there were hiding places, secret nooks and crannies. There was a helicopter landing pad where the master threw the Ball for me. It fell into the sea many times, but the master's bots—small metal dragonflies—always fetched it when I couldn't.

The master was a god. When he was angry, his voice was an invisible whip. His smell was a god-smell that filled the world.

While he worked, I barked at the seagulls or stalked the cat. We fought a few times, and I still have a pale scar on my nose. But we developed an understanding. The dark places of the rig belonged to the cat, and I reigned over the deck and the sky: we were the Hades and Apollo of the master's realm.

But at night, when the master watched old movies or listened to records on his old rattling gramophone, we lay at his feet together. Sometimes the master smelled lonely and let me sleep next to him in his small cabin, curled up in the god-smell and warmth.

It was a small world, but it was all we knew.

The master spent a lot of time working, fingers dancing on the keyboard projected on his mahogany desk. And every night he went to the Room: the only place on the rig where I wasn't allowed.

It was then that I started to dream about the Small Animal. I remember its smell even now, alluring and inexplicable: buried bones and fleeing rabbits, irresistible.

In my dreams, I chased it along a sandy beach, a tasty trail of tiny footprints that I followed along bendy pathways and into tall grass. I never lost sight of it for more than a second: it was always a flash of white fur just at the edge of my vision.

One day it spoke to me.

"Come," it said. "Come and learn."

The Small Animal's island was full of lost places. Labyrinthine caves, lines drawn in sand that became words when I looked at them, smells that sang songs from the master's gramophone. It taught me, and I learned: I was more awake every time I woke up. And when I saw the cat looking at the spider-bots with a new awareness, I knew that it, too, went to a place at night.

I came to understand what the master said when he spoke. The sounds that had only meant *angry* or *happy* before became the word of my god. He noticed, smiled and ruffled my fur. After that he started speaking to us more, me and the cat, during the long evenings when the sea beyond the windows was black as oil and the waves made the whole rig ring like a bell. His voice was dark as a well, deep and gentle. He spoke of an island, his home, an island in the middle of a great sea. I smelled bitterness, and for the first time I understood that there were always words behind words, never spoken.

The cat catches the updraft perfectly: it floats still for a split second, and then clings to the side of the tower. Its claws put the smart concrete to sleep: code that makes the building think that the cat is a bird or a shard of ice carried by the wind.

The cat hisses and spits. The disassembler nanites from its stomach cling to the wall and start eating a round hole in it. The wait is excruciating. The cat locks the exomuscles of its armor and hangs there patiently. Finally, there is a mouth with jagged edges in the wall, and it slips in. My heart pounds as I switch from the AR view to the cat's iris cameras. It moves through the ventilation shaft like lightning, like an acrobat, jerky, hyperaccelerated movements, metabolism on overdrive. My tail twitches again. *We are coming, master*, I think. *We are coming.*

———

I lost my Ball the day the wrong master came.

I looked everywhere. I spent an entire day sniffing every corner and even braved the dark corridors of the cat's realm beneath the deck, but I could not find it. In the end, I got hungry and returned to the cabin. And there were two masters. Four hands stroking my coat. Two gods, true and false.

I barked. I did not know what to do. The cat looked at me with a mixture of pity and disdain and rubbed itself on both of their legs.

"Calm down," said one of the masters. "Calm down. There are four of us now."

I learned to tell them apart, eventually: by that time Small Animal had taught me to look beyond smells and appearances. The master I remembered was a middle-aged man with graying hair, stocky-bodied. The new master was young, barely a man, much slimmer and with the face of a mahogany cherub. The master tried to convince me to play with the new master, but I did not want to. His smell was too familiar, everything else too alien. In my mind, I called him the wrong master.

The two masters worked together, walked together and spent a lot of time talking together using words I did not understand. I was jealous. Once I even bit the wrong master. I was left on the deck for the night as a punishment, even though it was stormy and I was afraid of thunder. The cat, on the other hand, seemed to thrive in the wrong master's company, and I hated it for it.

I remember the first night the masters argued.

"Why did you do it?" asked the wrong master.

"You know," said the master. "You remember." His tone was dark. "Because someone has to show them we own ourselves."

"So, you own me?" said the wrong master. "Is that what you think?"

"Of course not," said the master. "Why do you say that?"

"Someone could claim that. You took a genetic algorithm and told it to make ten thousand of you, with random variations, pick the ones that would resemble your ideal son, the one you could love. Run until the machine runs out of capacity. Then print. It's illegal, you know. For a reason."

"That's not what the plurals think. Besides, this is my place. The only laws here are mine."

"You've been talking to the plurals too much. They are no longer human."

"You sound just like VecTech's PR bots."

"I sound like you. Your doubts. Are you sure you did the right thing? I'm not a Pinocchio. You are not a Geppetto."

The master was quiet for a long time.

"What if I am," he finally said. "Maybe we need Geppettos. Nobody creates anything new anymore, let alone wooden dolls that come to life. When I was young, we all thought something wonderful was on the way. Diamond children in the sky, angels out of machines. Miracles. But we gave up just before the blue fairy came."

"I am not your miracle."

"Yes, you are."

"You should at least have made yourself a woman," said the wrong master in a knife-like voice. "It might have been less frustrating."

I did not hear the blow, I felt it. The wrong master let out a cry, rushed out and almost stumbled on me. The master watched him go. His lips moved, but I could not hear the words. I wanted to comfort him and made a little sound, but he did not even look at me, went back to the cabin and locked the door. I scratched the door, but he did not open, and I went up to the deck to look for the Ball again.

Finally, the cat finds the master's chamber.

It is full of heads. They float in the air, bodiless, suspended in diamond cylinders. The tower executes the command we sent into its drugged nervous system, and one of the pillars begins to blink. *Master, master*, I sing quietly as I see the cold blue face beneath the diamond. But at the same time I know it's not the master, not yet.

The cat reaches out with its prosthetic. The smart surface yields like a soap bubble. "Careful now, careful," I say. The cat hisses angrily but obeys, spraying the head with preserver nanites and placing it gently into its gel-lined backpack.

The necropolis is finally waking up: the damage the heavenly hacker did has almost been repaired. The cat heads for its escape route and goes to quicktime again. I feel its staccato heartbeat through our sensory link.

It is time to turn out the lights. My eyes polarise to sunglass-black. I lift the gauss launcher, marvelling at the still-tender feel of the Russian hand grafts. I pull the trigger. The launcher barely twitches in my grip, and a streak of light shoots up to the sky. The nuclear payload is tiny, barely a decaton, not even a proper plutonium warhead but a hafnium micronuke. But it is enough to light a small sun above the mausoleum city for a moment, enough for a focused maser pulse that makes it as dead as its inhabitants for a moment.

The light is a white blow, almost tangible in its intensity, and the gorge looks like it is made of bright ivory. White noise hisses in my ears like the cat when it's angry.

For me, smells were not just sensations, they were my reality. I know now that that is not far from the truth: smells are molecules, parts of what they represent.

The wrong master smelled wrong. It confused me at first: almost a god-smell, but not quite, the smell of a fallen god.

And he did fall, in the end.

I slept on the master's couch when it happened. I woke up to bare feet shuffling on the carpet and heavy breathing, torn away from a dream of the Small Animal trying to teach me the multiplication table.

The wrong master looked at me.

"Good boy," he said. "Ssh." I wanted to bark, but the godlike smell was too strong. And so I just wagged my tail, slowly, uncertainly. The wrong master sat on the couch next to me and scratched my ears absently.

"I remember you," he said. "I know why he made you. A living childhood memory." He smiled and smelled friendlier than ever before. "I know how that feels." Then he sighed, got up and went into the Room. And then I knew that he was about to do something bad, and started barking as loudly as I could. The master woke up and when the wrong master returned, he was waiting.

"What have you done?" he asked, face chalk-white.

The wrong master gave him a defiant look. "Just what you'd have done. You're the criminal, not me. Why should I suffer? You don't own me."

"I could kill you," said the master, and his anger made me whimper with fear. "I could tell them I was you. They would believe me."

"Yes," said the wrong master. "But you are not going to."

The master sighed. "No," he said. "I'm not."

I take the dragonfly over the cryotower. I see the cat on the roof and whimper from relief. The plane lands lightly. I'm not much of a pilot, but the lobotomised mind of the daimon—an illegal copy of a twenty-first-century jet ace—is. The cat climbs in, and we shoot towards the stratosphere at Mach 5, wind caressing the plane's quantum dot skin.

"Well done," I tell the cat and wag my tail. It looks at me with yellow slanted eyes and curls up on its acceleration gel bed. I look at the container next to it. Is that a whiff of the god-smell or is it just my imagination?

In any case, it is enough to make me curl up in deep happy dog-sleep, and for the first time in years I dream of the Ball and the Small Animal, sliding down the ballistic orbit's steep back.

They came from the sky before the sunrise. The master went up on the deck wearing a suit that smelled new. He had the cat in his lap: it purred quietly. The wrong master followed, hands behind his back.

There were three machines, black-shelled scarabs with many legs and transparent wings. They came in low, raising a white-frothed wake behind them. The hum of their wings hurt my ears as they landed on the deck.

The one in the middle vomited a cloud of mist that shimmered in the dim light, swirled in the air and became a black-skinned woman who had no smell. By then I had learned that things without a smell could still be dangerous, so I barked at her until the master told me to be quiet.

"Mr. Takeshi," she said. "You know why we are here."

The master nodded.

"You don't deny your guilt?"

"I do," said the master. "This raft is technically a sovereign state, governed by my laws. Autogenesis is not a crime here."

"This raft *was* a sovereign state," said the woman. "Now it belongs to VecTech. Justice is swift, Mr. Takeshi. Our lawbots broke your constitution ten seconds after Mr. Takeshi here—" she nodded at the wrong master "—told us about his situation. After that, we had no choice. The WIPO quantum judge we consulted has condemned you to the slow zone for three hundred and fourteen years, and as the wronged party we have been granted execution rights in this matter. Do you have anything to say before we act?"

The master looked at the wrong master, face twisted like a mask of wax. Then he set the cat down gently and scratched my ears. "Look after them," he told the wrong master. "I'm ready."

The beetle in the middle moved, too fast for me to see. The master's grip on the loose skin on my neck tightened for a moment like my mother's teeth, and then let go. Something warm splattered on my coat and there was a dark, deep smell of blood in the air.

Then he fell. I saw his head in a floating soap bubble that one of the beetles swallowed. Another opened its belly for the wrong master. And then they were gone, and the cat and I were alone on the bloody deck.

The cat wakes me up when we dock with the *Marquis of Carabas*. The zeppelin swallows our dragonfly drone like a whale. It is a crystal cigar, and its nanospun sapphire spine glows faint blue. The Fast City is a sky full of neon stars six kilometres below us, anchored to the airship with elevator cables. I can see the liftspiders climbing them, far below, and sigh with relief. The guests are still arriving, and we are not too late. I keep my personal firewall clamped shut: I know there is a torrent of messages waiting beyond.

We rush straight to the lab. I prepare the scanner while the cat takes the master's head out very, very carefully. The fractal bush of the scanner comes out of its nest, molecule-sized disassembler fingers bristling. I have to look away when it starts eating the master's face. I cheat and flee to VR, to do what I do best.

After half an hour, we are ready. The nanofab spits out black plastic discs, and the airship drones ferry them to the concert hall. The metallic butterflies in my belly return, and we head for the make-up salon. The sergeant is already there, waiting for us: judging by the cigarette stumps on the floor, he has been waiting for a while. I wrinkle my nose at the stench.

"You are late," says our manager. "I hope you know what the hell you are doing. This show's got more diggs than the Turin clone's birthday party."

"That's the idea," I say and let Anette spray me with cosmetic fog. It tickles and makes me sneeze, and I give the cat a jealous look: as usual, it is perfectly at home with its own image consultant. "We are more popular than Jesus."

They get the DJs on in a hurry, made by the last human tailor on Saville Row. "This'll be a good skin," says Anette. "Mahogany with a touch of purple." She goes on, but I can't hear. The music is already in my head. The master's voice.

The cat saved me.

I don't know if it meant to do it or not: even now, I have a hard time understanding it. It hissed at me, its back arched. Then it jumped forward and scratched my nose: it burned like a piece of hot coal. That made me mad, weak as I was. I barked furiously and chased the cat around the deck. Finally, I collapsed, exhausted, and realised that I was hungry. The autokitchen down in the master's cabin still worked, and I knew how to ask for food. But when I came back, the master's body was gone: the waste disposal bots had thrown it into the sea. That's when I knew that he would not be coming back.

I curled up in his bed alone that night: the god-smell that lingered there was all I had. That, and the Small Animal.

It came to me that night on the dreamshore, but I did not chase it this time. It sat on the sand, looked at me with its little red eyes and waited.

"Why?" I asked. "Why did they take the master?"

"You wouldn't understand," it said. "Not yet."

"I want to understand. I want to know."

"All right," it said. "Everything you do, remember, think, smell—everything—leaves traces, like footprints in the sand. And it's possible to read them. Imagine that you follow another dog: you know where it has eaten and urinated and everything else it has done. The humans can do that to the mindprints. They can record them and make another you inside a machine, like the scentless screenpeople that your master used to watch. Except that the screendog will think it's you."

"Even though it has no smell?" I asked, confused.

"It thinks it does. And if you know what you're doing, you can give it a new body as well. You could die and the copy would be so good that no one can tell the difference. Humans have been doing it for a long time. Your master was one of the first, a long time ago. Far away, there are a lot of humans with machine bodies, humans who never die, humans with small bodies and big bodies, depending on how much they can afford to pay, people who have died and come back."

I tried to understand: without the smells, it was difficult. But its words awoke a mad hope.

"Does it mean that the master is coming back?" I asked, panting.

"No. Your master broke human law. When people discovered the pawprints of the mind, they started making copies of themselves. Some made many, more than the grains of sand on the beach. That caused chaos. Every machine, every device everywhere, had mad dead minds in them. The plurals, people called them, and were afraid. And they had their reasons to be afraid. Imagine that your Place had a thousand dogs, but only one Ball."

My ears flopped at the thought.

"That's how humans felt," said the Small Animal. "And so they passed a law: only one copy per person. The humans—VecTech—who had invented how to make copies mixed watermarks into people's minds, rights management software that was supposed to stop the copying. But some humans—like your master—found out how to erase them."

"The wrong master," I said quietly.

"Yes," said the Small Animal. "He did not want to be an illegal copy. He turned your master in."

"I want the master back," I said, anger and longing beating their wings in my chest like caged birds.

"And so does the cat," said the Small Animal gently. And it was only then that I saw the cat there, sitting next to me on the beach, eyes glimmering in the sun. It looked at me and let out a single conciliatory meaow.

After that, the Small Animal was with us every night, teaching.

Music was my favorite. The Small Animal showed me how I could turn music into smells and find patterns in it, like the tracks of huge, strange animals. I studied the master's old records and the vast libraries of his virtual desk, and learned to remix them into smells that I found pleasant.

I don't remember which one of us came up with the plan to save the master. Maybe it was the cat: I could only speak to it properly on the island of dreams, and see its thoughts appear as patterns on the sand. Maybe it was the Small Animal, maybe it was me. After all the nights we spent talking about it, I no longer know. But that's where it began, on the island: that's where we became arrows fired at a target.

Finally, we were ready to leave. The master's robots and nanofac spun us an open-source glider, a white-winged bird.

In my last dream the Small Animal said goodbye. It hummed to itself when I told it about our plans.

"Remember me in your dreams," it said.

"Are you not coming with us?" I asked, bewildered.

"My place is here," it said. "And it's my turn to sleep now, and to dream."

"Who are you?"

"Not all the plurals disappeared. Some of them fled to space, made new worlds there. And there is a war on, even now. Perhaps you will join us there, one day, where the big dogs live."

It laughed. "For old times' sake?" It dived into the waves and started running, became a great proud dog with a white coat, muscles flowing like water. And I followed, for one last time.

The sky was grey when we took off. The cat flew the plane using a neural interface, goggles over its eyes. We swept over the dark waves and were underway. The raft became a small dirty spot in the sea. I watched it recede and realised that I'd never found my Ball.

Then there was a thunderclap and a dark pillar of water rose up to the sky from where the raft had been. I didn't mourn: I knew that the Small Animal wasn't there anymore.

The sun was setting when we came to the Fast City.

I knew what to expect from the Small Animal's lessons, but I could not imagine what it would be like. Mile-high skyscrapers that were self-contained worlds, with their artificial plasma suns and bonsai parks and miniature shopping malls. Each of them housed a billion lilliputs, poor and quick: humans whose consciousness lived in a nanocomputer smaller than a fingertip. Immortals who could not afford to utilise the resources of the overpopulated Earth more than a mouse. The city was surrounded by a halo of glowing fairies, tiny winged moravecs that flitted about like humanoid fireflies, and the waste heat from their overclocked bodies draped the city in an artificial twilight.

The citymind steered us to a landing area. It was fortunate that the cat was flying: I just stared at the buzzing things with my mouth open, afraid I'd drown in the sounds and the smells.

We sold our plane for scrap and wandered into the bustle of the city, feeling like *daikaju* monsters. The social agents that the Small Animal had given me were obsolete, but they could still weave us into the ambient social networks. We needed money, we needed work.

And so I became a musician.

The ballroom is a hemisphere in the center of the airship. It is filled to capacity. Innumerable quickbeings shimmer in the air like living candles, and the suits of the fleshed ones are no less exotic. A woman clad in nothing but autumn leaves smiles at me. Tinker Bell clones surround the cat. Our bodyguards, armed obsidian giants, open a way for us to the stage where the gramophones wait. A rustle moves through the crowd. The air around us is pregnant with ghosts, the avatars of a million fleshless fans. I wag my tail. The scentspace is intoxicating: perfume, fleshbodies, the unsmells of moravec bodies. And the fallen god-smell of the wrong master, hiding somewhere within.

We get on the stage on our hindlegs, supported by prosthesis shoes. The gramophone forest looms behind us, their horns like flowers of brass and gold. We cheat, of course: the music is analog and the gramophones are genuine, but the grooves in the black discs are barely a nanometer thick, and the needles are tipped with quantum dots.

We take our bows and the storm of handclaps begins.

"Thank you," I say when the thunder of it finally dies. "We have kept quiet about the purpose of this concert as long as possible. But I am finally in a position to tell you that this is a charity show."

I smell the tension in the air, copper and iron.

"We miss someone," I say. "He was called Shimoda Takeshi, and now he's gone."

The cat lifts the conductor's baton and turns to face the gramophones. I follow, and step into the soundspace we've built, the place where music is smells and sounds.

The master is in the music.

It took five human years to get to the top. I learned to love the audiences: I could smell their emotions and create a mix of music for them that was just right. And soon I was no longer a giant dog DJ among lilliputs, but a little terrier in a forest of dancing human legs. The cat's gladiator career lasted a while, but soon it joined me as a performer in the virtual dramas I designed. We performed for rich fleshies in the Fast City, Tokyo and New York. I loved it. I howled at Earth in the sky in the Sea of Tranquility.

But I always knew that it was just the first phase of the plan.

We turn him into music. VecTech owns his brain, his memories, his mind. But we own the music.

Law is code. A billion people listening to our master's voice. Billion minds downloading the Law At Home packets embedded in it, bombarding the quantum judges until they give him back.

It's the most beautiful thing I've ever made. The cat stalks the genetic algorithm jungle, lets the themes grow and then pounces them, devours them. I just chase them for the joy of the chase alone, not caring whether or not I catch them.

It's our best show ever.

Only when it's over, I realise that no one is listening. The audience is frozen. The fairies and the fastpeople float in the air like flies trapped in amber. The moravecs are silent statues. Time stands still.

The sound of one pair of hands, clapping.

"I'm proud of you," says the wrong master.

I fix my bow tie and smile a dog's smile, a cold snake coiling in my belly. The god-smell comes and tells me that I should throw myself onto the floor, wag my tail, bare my throat to the divine being standing before me.

But I don't.

"Hello, Nipper," the wrong master says.

I clamp down the low growl rising in my throat and turn it into words. "What did you do?"

"We suspended them. Back doors in the hardware. Digital rights management."

His mahogany face is still smooth: he does not look a day older, wearing a dark suit with a VecTech tie pin. But his eyes are tired.

"Really, I'm impressed. You covered your tracks admirably. We thought you were furries. Until I realised—"

A distant thunder interrupts him.

"I promised him I'd look after you. That's why you are still alive. You don't have to do this. You don't owe him anything. Look at yourselves: Who would have thought you could come this far? Are you going to throw that all away because of some atavistic sense of animal loyalty? Not that you have a choice, of course. The plan didn't work."

The cat lets out a steam pipe hiss.

"You misunderstand," I say. "The concert was just a diversion."

The cat moves like a black-and-yellow flame. Its claws flash, and the wrong master's head comes off. I whimper at the aroma of blood polluting the god-smell. The cat licks its lips. There is a crimson stain on its white shirt.

The zeppelin shakes, pseudomatter armor sparkling. The dark sky around the *Marquis* is full of fire-breathing beetles. We rush past the human statues in the ballroom and into the laboratory.

The cat does the dirty work, granting me a brief escape into virtual abstraction. I don't know how the master did it, years ago, broke VecTech's copy protection watermarks. I can't do the same, no matter how much the Small Animal taught me. So I have to cheat, recover the marked parts from somewhere else.

The wrong master's brain.

The part of me that was born on the Small Animal's island takes over and fits the two patterns together, like pieces of a puzzle. They fit, and for a brief moment, the master's voice is in my mind, for real this time.

The cat is waiting, already in its clawed battlesuit, and I don my own. The *Marquis of Carabas* is dying around us. To send the master on his way, we have to disengage the armor.

The cat meaows faintly and hands me something red. An old plastic ball with toothmarks, smelling of the sun and the sea, with a few grains of sand rattling inside.

"Thanks," I say. The cat says nothing, just opens a door into the zeppelin's skin. I whisper a command, and the master is underway in a neutrino stream, shooting up towards an island in a blue sea. Where the gods and big dogs live forever.

We dive through the door together, down into the light and flame.

Elegy for a Young Elk

THE NIGHT AFTER Kosonen shot the young elk, he tried to write a poem by the campfire.

It was late April and there was still snow on the ground. He had already taken to sitting outside in the evening, on a log by the fire, in the small clearing where his cabin stood. Otso was more comfortable outside, and Kosonen preferred the bear's company to being alone. It snored loudly atop its pile of fir branches.

A wet smell that had traces of elk shit drifted from its drying fur.

He dug a soft-cover notebook and a pencil stub from his pocket. He leafed through it: most of the pages were empty. Words had become slippery, harder to catch than elk. Although not this one: careless and young. An old elk would never have let a man and a bear so close.

He scattered words on the first empty page, gripping the pencil hard.

Antlers. Sapphire antlers. No good. *Frozen flames. Tree roots. Forked destinies.* There had to be words that captured the moment when the crossbow kicked against his shoulder, the meaty sound of the arrow's impact. But it was like trying to catch snowflakes in his palm. He could barely glimpse the crystal structure, and then they melted.

He closed the notebook and almost threw it into the fire, but thought better of it and put it back into his pocket. No point in wasting good paper. Besides, his last toilet roll in the outhouse would run out soon.

"Kosonen is thinking about words again," Otso growled. "Kosonen should drink more booze. Don't need words then. Just sleep."

Kosonen looked at the bear. "You think you are smart, huh?" He tapped his crossbow. "Maybe it's you who should be shooting elk."

"Otso good at smelling. Kosonen at shooting. Both good at drinking." Otso yawned luxuriously, revealing rows of yellow teeth. Then it rolled to its side and let out a satisfied heavy sigh. "Otso will have more booze soon."

Maybe the bear was right. Maybe a drink was all he needed. No point in being a poet: they had already written all the poems in the world, up there, in the sky. They probably had poetry gardens. Or places where you could become words.

But that was not the point. The words needed to come from *him*, a dirty, bearded man in the woods whose toilet was a hole in the ground. Bright words from dark matter, that's what poetry was about.

When it worked.

There were things to do. The squirrels had almost picked the lock the previous night, bloody things. The cellar door needed reinforcing. But that could wait until tomorrow.

He was about to open a vodka bottle from Otso's secret stash in the snow when Marja came down from the sky as rain.

The rain was sudden and cold like a bucket of water poured over your head in the sauna. But the droplets did not touch the ground, they floated around Kosonen. As he watched, they changed shape, joined together and made a woman, spindle-thin bones, mist-flesh and -muscle. She looked like a glass sculpture. The small breasts were perfect hemispheres, her sex an equilateral silver triangle. But the face was familiar—small nose and high cheekbones, a sharp-tongued mouth.

Marja.

Otso was up in an instant, by Kosonen's side. "Bad smell, god-smell," it growled. "Otso bites." The rain-woman looked at it curiously.

"Otso," Kosonen said sternly. He gripped the fur on the bear's rough neck tightly, feeling its huge muscles tense. "Otso is Kosonen's friend. Listen to Kosonen. Not time for biting. Time for sleeping. Kosonen will speak to god." Then he set the vodka bottle in the snow right under its nose.

Otso sniffed the bottle and scraped the half-melted snow with its forepaw.

"Otso goes," it finally said. "Kosonen shouts if the god bites. Then Otso comes." It picked up the bottle in its mouth deftly and loped into the woods with a bear's loose, shuffling gait.

"Hi," the rain-woman said.

"Hello," Kosonen said carefully. He wondered if she was real. The plague gods were crafty. One of them could have taken Marja's image from his mind. He looked at the unstrung crossbow and tried to judge the odds: a diamond goddess versus an out-of-shape woodland poet. Not good.

"Your dog does not like me very much," the Marja-thing said. She sat down on Kosonen's log and swung her shimmering legs in the air, back and forth, just like Marja always did in the sauna. It had to be her, Kosonen decided, feeling something jagged in his throat.

He coughed. "Bear, not a dog. A dog would have barked. Otso just bites. Nothing personal, that's just its nature. Paranoid and grumpy."

"Sounds like someone I used to know."

"I'm not paranoid." Kosonen hunched down and tried to get the fire going again. "You learn to be careful, in the woods."

Marja looked around. "I thought we gave you stayers more equipment. It looks a little . . . primitive here."

"Yeah. We had plenty of gadgets," Kosonen said. "But they weren't plague-proof. I had a smartgun before I had this"—he tapped his cross-bow—"but it got infected. I killed it with a big rock and threw it into the swamp. I've got my skis and some tools, and these." Kosonen tapped his temple. "Has been enough so far. So cheers."

He piled up some kindling under a triangle of small logs, and in a moment the flames sprung up again. Three years had been enough to learn about woodcraft at least. Marja's skin looked almost human in the soft light of the fire, and he sat back on Otso's fir branches, watching her. For a moment, neither of them spoke.

"So how are you, these days?" he asked. "Keeping busy?"

Marja smiled. "Your wife grew up. She's a big girl now. You don't want to know how big."

"So . . . you are not her, then? Who am I talking to?"

"I am her, and I am not her. I'm a partial, but a faithful one. A translation. You wouldn't understand."

Kosonen put some snow in the coffee pot to melt. "All right, so I'm a caveman. Fair enough. But I understand you are here because you want something. So let's get down to business, *perkele*," he swore.

Marja took a deep breath. "We lost something. Something important. Something new. The spark, we called it. It fell into the city."

"I thought you lot kept copies of everything."

"Quantum information. That was a part of the *new* bit. You can't copy it."

"Tough shit."

A wrinkle appeared between Marja's eyebrows. Kosonen remembered it from a thousand fights they had had, and swallowed.

"If that's the tone you want to take, fine," she said. "I thought you'd be glad to see me. I didn't have to come: they could have sent Mickey Mouse. But I wanted to see you. The big Marja wanted to see you. So you have decided to live your life like this, as the tragic figure haunting the woods. That's fine. But you could at least listen. You owe me that much."

Kosonen said nothing.

"I see," Marja said. "You still blame me for Esa."

She was right. It had been her who got the first Santa Claus machine. The boy needs the best we can offer, she said. The world is changing. Can't have him being left behind. Let's make him into a little god, like the neighbor's kid.

"I guess I shouldn't be blaming *you*," Kosonen said. "You're just a . . . partial. You weren't there."

"I was there," Marja said quietly. "I remember. Better than you, now. I also forget better, and forgive. You never could. You just . . . wrote poems. The rest of us moved on, and saved the world."

"Great job," Kosonen said. He poked the fire with a stick, and a cloud of sparks flew up into the air with the smoke.

Marja got up. "That's it," she said. "I'm leaving. See you in a hundred years." The air grew cold. A halo appeared around her, shimmering in the firelight.

Kosonen closed his eyes and squeezed his jaw shut tight. He waited for ten seconds. Then he opened his eyes. Marja was still there, staring at him, helpless. He could not help smiling. She could never leave without having the last word.

"I'm sorry," Kosonen said. "It's been a long time. I've been living in the woods with a bear. Doesn't improve one's temper much."

"I didn't really notice any difference."

"All right," Kosonen said. He tapped the fir branches next to him. "Sit down. Let's start over. I'll make some coffee."

Marja sat down, bare shoulder touching his. She felt strangely warm, warmer than the fire almost.

"The firewall won't let us into the city," she said. "We don't have anyone . . . human enough, not anymore. There was some talk about making one, but . . . the argument would last a century." She sighed. "We like to argue, in the sky."

Kosonen grinned. "I bet you fit right in." He checked for the wrinkle before continuing. "So you need an errand boy."

"We need help."

Kosonen looked at the fire. The flames were dying now, licking at the blackened wood. There were always new colours in the embers. Or maybe he just always forgot.

He touched Marja's hand. It felt like a soap bubble, barely solid. But she did not pull it away.

"All right," he said. "But just so you know, it's not just for old times' sake."

"Anything we can give you."

"I'm cheap," Kosonen said. "I just want words."

The sun sparkled on the *kantohanki*: snow with a frozen surface, strong enough to carry a man on skis and a bear. Kosonen breathed hard. Even going downhill, keeping pace with Otso was not easy. But in weather like this, there was something glorious about skiing, sliding over blue shadows of trees almost without friction, the snow hissing underneath.

I've sat still too long, he thought. *Should have gone somewhere just to go, not because someone asks.*

In the afternoon, when the sun was already going down, they reached the railroad, a bare gash through the forest, two metal tracks on a bed of gravel. Kosonen removed his skis and stuck them in the snow.

"I'm sorry you can't come along," he told Otso. "But the city won't let you in."

"Otso not a city bear," the bear said. "Otso waits for Kosonen. Kosonen gets sky-bug, comes back. Then we drink booze."

He scratched the rough fur of its neck clumsily. The bear poked Kosonen in the stomach with its nose, so hard that he almost fell. Then it snorted, turned around and shuffled into the woods. Kosonen watched until it vanished among the snow-covered trees.

It took three painful attempts of sticking his fingers down his throat to get the nanoseed Marja gave him to come out. The gagging left a bitter taste in his mouth. Swallowing it had been the only way to protect the delicate thing from the plague. He wiped it in the snow: a transparent bauble the size of a walnut, slippery and warm. It reminded him of the toys he could get from vending machines in supermarkets when he was a child, plastic spheres with something secret inside.

He placed it on the rails carefully, wiped the remains of the vomit from his lips and rinsed his mouth with water. Then he looked at it. Marja knew he would never read instruction manuals, so she had not given him one.

"Make me a train," he said.

Nothing happened. *Maybe it can read my mind,* he thought, and imagined a train, an old steam train, puffing along. Still nothing, just a reflection of the darkening sky on the seed's clear surface. *She always had to be subtle.* Marja could never give a present without thinking about its meaning for days. Standing still let the spring winter chill through his wolf-pelt coat, and he hopped up and down, rubbing his hands together.

With the motion came an idea. He frowned, staring at the seed, and took the notebook from his pocket. Maybe it was time to try out Marja's other gift—or advance payment, however you wanted to look at it. He had barely written the first lines, when the words leaped in his mind like animals woken from slumber. He closed the book, cleared his throat and spoke.

> *these rails*
> *were worn thin*
> *by wheels*
> *that wrote down*
> *the name of each passenger*
> *in steel and miles*

he said,

> *it's a good thing*
> *the years*
> *ate our flesh too*
> *made us thin and light*
> *so the rails are strong enough*
> *to carry us still*
> *to the city*
> *in our train of glass and words*

Doggerel, he thought, but it didn't matter. The joy of words filled his veins like vodka. *Too bad it didn't work—*

The seed blurred. It exploded into a white-hot sphere. The waste heat washed across Kosonen's face. Glowing tentacles squirmed past him, sucking carbon and metal from the rails and trees. They danced like a welder's electric arcs, sketching lines and surfaces in the air.

And suddenly, the train was there.

It was transparent, with paper-thin walls and delicate wheels, as if it had been blown from glass, sketch of a cartoon steam engine with a single carriage, with spiderweb-like chairs inside, just the way he had imagined it.

He climbed in, expecting the delicate structure to sway under his weight, but it felt rock-solid. The nanoseed lay on the floor innocently, as if nothing had happened. He picked it up carefully, took it outside and buried it in the snow, leaving his skis and sticks as markers. Then he picked up his backpack, boarded the train again and sat down in one of the gossamer seats. Unbidden, the train lurched into motion smoothly. To Kosonen, it sounded like the rails beneath were whispering, but he could not hear the words.

He watched the darkening forest glide past. The day's journey weighed heavily on his limbs. The memory of the snow beneath his skis melted together with the train's movement, and soon Kosonen was asleep.

When he woke up, it was dark. The amber light of the firewall glowed on the horizon, like a thundercloud.

The train had speeded up. The dark forest outside was a blur, and the whispering of the rails had become a quiet staccato song. Kosonen swallowed as the train covered the remaining distance in a matter of minutes. The firewall grew into a misty dome glowing with yellowish light from within. The city was an indistinct silhouette beneath it. The buildings seemed to be in motion, like a giant's shadow puppets.

Then it was a flaming curtain directly in front of the train, an impenetrable wall made from twilight and amber crossing the tracks. Kosonen gripped the delicate frame of his seat, knuckles white. "Slow down!" he shouted, but the train did not hear. It crashed directly into the firewall with a bone-jarring impact. There was a burst of light, and then Kosonen was lifted from his seat.

It was like drowning, except that he was floating in an infinite sea of amber light rather than water. Apart from the light, there was just emptiness. His skin tickled. It took him a moment to realise that he was not breathing.

And then a stern voice spoke.

This is not a place for men, it said. *Closed. Forbidden. Go back.*

"I have a mission," said Kosonen. His voice had no echo in the light. "From your makers. They command you to let me in."

He closed his eyes, and Marja's third gift floated in front of him, not words but a number. He had always been poor at memorising things, but

Marja's touch had been a pen with acid ink, burning it in his mind. He read off the endless digits, one by one.

You may enter, said the firewall. *But only that which is human will leave.*

The train and the speed came back, sharp and real like a paper cut. The twilight glow of the firewall was still there, but instead of the forest, dark buildings loomed around the railway, blank windows staring at him.

Kosonen's hands tickled. They were clean, as were his clothes: every speck of dirt was gone. His skin was tender and red, like he had just been to the sauna.

The train slowed down at last, coming to a stop in the dark mouth of the station, and Kosonen was in the city.

The city was a forest of metal and concrete and metal that breathed and hummed. The air smelled of ozone. The facades of the buildings around the railway station square looked almost like he remembered them, only subtly wrong. From the corner of his eye he could glimpse them *moving*, shifting in their sleep like stone-skinned animals. There were no signs of life, apart from a cluster of pigeons, hopping back and forth on the stairs, looking at him. They had sapphire eyes.

A bus stopped, full of faceless people who looked like crash test dummies, sitting unnaturally still. Kosonen decided not to get in and started to head across the square, towards the main shopping street: he had to start the search for the spark somewhere. It will glow, Marja had said. You can't miss it.

There was what looked like a car wreck in the parking lot, lying on its side, hood crumpled like a discarded beer can, covered in white pigeon droppings. But when Kosonen walked past it, its engine roared, and the hood popped open. A hissing bundle of tentacles snapped out, reaching for him.

He managed to gain some speed before the car-beast rolled onto its four wheels. There were narrow streets on the other side of the square, too narrow for it to follow. He ran, cold weight in his stomach, legs pumping.

The crossbow beat painfully at his back in its strap, and he struggled to get it over his head.

The beast passed him arrogantly, and turned around. Then it came straight at him. The tentacles spread out from its glowing engine mouth into a fan of serpents.

Kosonen fumbled with a bolt, then loosed it at the thing. The crossbow kicked, but the arrow glanced off its windshield. The bolt seemed to confuse it enough for Kosonen to jump aside. He dove, hit the pavement with a painful thump, and rolled.

"Somebody help *perkele*," he swore with impotent rage, and got up, panting, just as the beast backed off slowly, engine growling. He smelled burning rubber, mixed with ozone. *Maybe I can wrestle it,* he thought like a madman, spreading his arms, refusing to run again. *One last poem in it—*

Something landed in front of the beast, wings fluttering. A pigeon. Both Kosonen and the car-creature stared at it. It made a cooing sound. Then it exploded.

The blast tore at his eardrums, and the white fireball turned the world black for a second. Kosonen found himself on the ground again, ears ringing, lying painfully on top of his backpack. The car-beast was a burning wreck ten metres away, twisted beyond all recognition.

There was another pigeon next to him, picking at what looked like bits of metal. It lifted its head and looked at him, flames reflecting from the tiny sapphire eyes. Then it took flight, leaving a tiny white dropping behind.

The main shopping street was empty. Kosonen moved carefully in case there were more of the car-creatures around, staying close to narrow alleys and doorways. The firewall light was dimmer between the buildings, and strange lights danced in the windows.

Kosonen realised he was starving: he had not eaten since noon, and the journey and the fight had taken their toll. He found an empty cafe on a street corner that seemed safe, set up his small travel cooker on a table and boiled some water. The supplies he had been able to bring consisted mainly of canned soup and dried elk meat, but his growling stomach was not fussy. The smell of food made him careless.

"This is my place," said a voice. Kosonen leapt up, startled, reaching for the crossbow.

There was a stooped, trollish figure at the door, dressed in rags. His face shone with sweat and dirt, framed by matted hair and beard. His porous skin was full of tiny sapphire growths, like pockmarks. Kosonen had thought living in the woods had made him immune to human odours, but the stranger carried a bitter stench of sweat and stale booze that made him want to retch.

The stranger walked in and sat down at a table opposite Kosonen. "But that's all right," he said amicably. "Don't get many visitors these days. Have to be neighbourly. *Saatana*, is that Blaband soup that you've got?"

"You're welcome to some," Kosonen said warily. He had met some of the other stayers over the years, but usually avoided them—they all had their own reasons for not going up, and not much in common.

"Thanks. That's neighbourly indeed. I'm Pera, by the way." The troll held out his hand.

Kosonen shook it gingerly, feeling strange jagged things under Pera's skin. It was like squeezing a glove filled with powdered glass. "Kosonen. So you live here?"

"Oh, not here, not in the center. I come here to steal from the buildings. But they've become really smart, and stingy. Can't even find soup anymore. The Stockmann department store almost ate me, yesterday. It's not easy life here." Pera shook his head. "But better than outside." There was a sly look in his eyes. *Are you staying because you want to,* wondered Kosonen, *or because the firewall won't let you out anymore?*

"Not afraid of the plague gods, then?" he asked aloud. He passed Pera one of the heated soup tins. The city stayer slurped it down with one gulp, smell of minestrone mingling with the other odours.

"Oh, you don't have to be afraid of them anymore. They're all dead."

Kosonen looked at Pera, startled. "How do you know?"

"The pigeons told me."

"The pigeons?"

Pera took something from the pocket of his ragged coat carefully. It was a pigeon. It had a sapphire beak and eyes, and a trace of blue in its feathers. It struggled in Pera's grip, wings fluttering.

"My little buddies," Pera said. "I think you've already met them."

"Yes," Kosonen said. "Did you send the one that blew up that car thing?"

"You have to help a neighbour out, don't you? Don't mention it. The soup was good."

"What did they say about the plague gods?"

Pera grinned a gap-toothed grin. "When the gods got locked up here, they started fighting. Not enough power to go around, you see. So one of them had to be the top dog, like in *Highlander*. The pigeons show me pictures, sometimes. Bloody stuff. Explosions. Nanites eating men. But finally they were all gone, every last one. My playground now."

So Esa is gone, too. Kosonen was surprised how sharp the feeling of loss was, even now. *Better like this.* He swallowed. *Let's get the job done first. No time to mourn. Let's think about it when we get home. Write a poem about it. And tell Marja.*

"All right," Kosonen said. "I'm hunting too. Do you think your . . . buddies could find it? Something that glows. If you help me, I'll give you all the soup I've got. And elk meat. And I'll bring more later. How does that sound?"

"Pigeons can find anything," said Pera, licking his lips.

The pigeon-man walked through the city labyrinth like his living room, accompanied by a cloud of the chimera birds. Every now and then, one of them would land on his shoulder and touch his ear with its beak, as if to whisper.

"Better hurry," Pera said. "At night, it's not too bad, but during the day the houses get younger and start thinking."

Kosonen had lost all sense of direction. The map of the city was different from the last time he had been here, in the old human days. His best guess was that they were getting somewhere close to the cathedral in the old town, but he couldn't be sure. Navigating the changed streets felt like walking through the veins of some giant animal, convoluted and labyrinthine. Some buildings were enclosed in what looked like black film, rippling like oil. Some had grown together, organic-looking structures of brick and concrete, blocking streets and making the ground uneven.

"We're not far," Pera said. "They've seen it. Glowing like a pumpkin lantern, they say." He giggled. The amber light of the firewall grew brighter as they walked. It was hotter, too, and Kosonen was forced to discard his old Pohjanmaa sweater.

They passed an office building that had become a sleeping face, a genderless Easter Island countenance. There was more life in this part of the town too, sapphire-eyed animals, sleek cats looking at them from windowsills. Kosonen saw a fox crossing the street: it gave them one bright look and vanished down a sewer hole.

Then they turned a corner, where faceless men wearing fashion from ten years ago danced together in a shop window, and saw the cathedral.

It had grown to gargantuan size, dwarfing every other building around it. It was an anthill of dark-red brick and hexagonal doorways. It buzzed with life. Cats with sapphire claws clung to its walls like sleek gargoyles. Thick pigeon flocks fluttered around its towers. Packs of azure-tailed rats ran in and out of open, massive doors like armies on a mission. And there were insects everywhere, filling the air with a drill-like buzzing sound, moving in dense black clouds like a giant's black breath.

"Oh, *jumalauta*," Kosonen said. "*That's* where it fell?"

"Actually, no. I was just supposed to bring you here," Pera said.

"What?"

"Sorry. I lied. It *was* like in *Highlander*: there is one of them left. And he wants to meet you."

Kosonen stared at Pera, dumbfounded. The pigeons landed on the other man's shoulders and arms like a grey fluttering cloak. They seized his rags and hair and skin with sharp claws, wings started beating furiously. As Kosonen stared, Pera rose to the air.

"No hard feelings, I just had a better deal from him. Thanks for the soup," he shouted. In a moment, Pera was a black scrap of cloth in the sky.

The earth shook. Kosonen fell to his knees. The window eyes that lined the street lit up, full of bright, malevolent light.

He tried to run. He did not make it far before they came, the fingers of the city: the pigeons, the insects, a buzzing swarm that covered him. A dozen chimera rats clung to his skull, and he could feel the humming of their flywheel hearts. Something sharp bit through the bone. The pain grew like a forest fire, and Kosonen screamed.

The city spoke. Its voice was a thunderstorm, words made from the shaking of the earth and the sighs of buildings. Slow words, squeezed from stone.

Dad, the city said.

The pain was gone. Kosonen heard the gentle sound of waves, and felt a warm wind on his face. He opened his eyes.

"Hi, Dad," Esa said.

They sat on the summerhouse pier, wrapped in towels, skin flushed from the sauna. It was evening, with a hint of chill in the air, Finnish summer's gentle reminder that things were not forever. The sun hovered above the blue-tinted treetops. The lake surface was calm, full of liquid reflections.

"I thought," Esa said, "that you'd like it here."

Esa was just like Kosonen remembered him, a pale skinny kid, ribs showing, long arms folded across his knees, stringy wet hair hanging on his forehead. But his eyes were the eyes of a city, dark orbs of metal and stone.

"I do," Kosonen said. "But I can't stay."

"Why not?"

"There is something I need to do."

"We haven't seen each other in ages. The sauna is warm. I've got some beer cooling in the lake. Why the rush?"

"I should be afraid of you," Kosonen said. "You killed people. Before they put you here."

"You don't know what it's like," Esa said. "The plague does everything you want. It gives you things you don't even know you want. It turns the world soft. And sometimes it tears it apart for you. You think a thought, and things break. You can't help it."

The boy closed his eyes. "You want things too. I know you do. That's why you are here, isn't it? You want your precious words back."

Kosonen said nothing.

"Mom's errand boy, *vittu*. So they fixed your brain, flushed the booze out. So you can write again. Does it feel good? For a moment there I thought you came here for me. But that's not the way it ever worked, was it?"

"I didn't know—"

"I can see the inside of your head, you know," Esa said. "I've got my fingers inside your skull. One thought, and my bugs will eat you, bring you here for good. Quality time forever. What do you say to that?"

And there it was, the old guilt. "We worried about you, every second, after you were born," Kosonen said. "We only wanted the best for you."

It had seemed so natural. How the boy played with his machine that made other machines. How things started changing shape when he thought at them. How Esa smiled when he showed Kosonen the talking starfish that the machine had made.

"And then I had one bad day."

"I remember," Kosonen said. He had been home late, as usual. Esa had been a diamond tree, growing in his room. There were starfish everywhere, eating the walls and the floor, making more of themselves. And that was only the beginning.

"So go ahead. Bring me here. It's your turn to make me into what you want. Or end it all. I deserve it."

Esa laughed softly. "And why would I do that, to an old man?" He sighed. "You know, I'm old too now. Let me show you." He touched Kosonen's shoulder gently and

Kosonen was the city. His skin was of stone and concrete, pores full of the godplague. The streets and buildings were his face, changing and shifting with every thought and emotion. His nervous system was diamond and optic fibre. His hands were chimera animals.

The firewall was all around him, in the sky and in the cold bedrock, insubstantial but adamantine, squeezing from every side, cutting off energy, making sure he could not think fast. But he could still dream, weave words and images into threads, make worlds out of the memories he had and the memories of the smaller gods he had eaten to become the city. He sang his dreams in radio waves, not caring if the firewall let them through or not, louder and louder—

"Here," Esa said from far away. "Have a beer."

Kosonen felt a chilly bottle in his hand, and drank. The dream-beer was strong and real. The malt taste brought him back. He took a deep breath, letting the fake summer evening wash away the city.

"Is that why you brought me here? To show me that?" he asked.

"Well, no," Esa said, laughing. His stone eyes looked young, suddenly. "I just wanted you to meet my girlfriend."

The quantum girl had golden hair and eyes of light. She wore many faces at once, like a Hindu goddess. She walked to the pier with dainty steps. Esa's summerland showed its cracks around her: there were fracture lines in her skin, with otherworldly colours peeking out.

"This is Säde," Esa said.

She looked at Kosonen, and spoke, a bubble of words, a superposition, all possible greetings at once.

"Nice to meet you," Kosonen said.

"They did something right when they made her, up there," said Esa. "She lives in many worlds at once, thinks in qubits. And this is the world where she wants to be. With me." He touched her shoulder gently. "She heard my songs and ran away."

"Marja said she fell," Kosonen said. "That something was broken."

"She said what they wanted her to say. They don't like it when things don't go according to plan."

Säde made a sound, like the chime of a glass bell.

"The firewall keeps squeezing us," Esa said. "That's how it was made. Make things go slower and slower here, until we die. Säde doesn't fit in here, this place is too small. So you will take her back home, before it's too late." He smiled. "I'd rather you do it than anyone else."

"That's not fair," Kosonen said. He squinted at Säde. She was too bright to look at. *But what can I do? I'm just a slab of meat. Meat and words.*

The thought was like a pine cone, rough in his grip, but with a seed of something in it.

"I think there is a poem in you two," he said.

Kosonen sat on the train again, watching the city stream past. It was early morning. The sunrise gave the city new hues: purple shadows and gold, ember colours. Fatigue pulsed in his temples. His body ached. The words of a poem weighed down on his mind.

Above the dome of the firewall he could see a giant diamond starfish, a drone of the sky people, watching, like an outstretched hand.

They came to see what happened, he thought. *They'll find out.*

This time, he embraced the firewall like a friend, and its tingling brightness washed over him. And deep within, the stern-voiced watchman came again. It said nothing this time, but he could feel its presence, scrutinising, seeking things that did not belong in the outside world.

Kosonen gave it everything.

The first moment when he knew he had put something real on paper. The disappointment when he realised that a poet was not much in a small country, piles of cheaply printed copies of his first collection gathering dust in little bookshops. The jealousy he had felt when Marja gave birth to Esa, what a pale shadow of that giving birth to words was. The tracks of the elk in the snow and the look in its eyes when it died.

He felt the watchman step aside, satisfied.

Then he was through. The train emerged into the real, undiluted dawn. He looked back at the city, and saw fire raining from the starfish. Pillars of light cut through the city in geometric patterns, too bright to look at, leaving only white-hot plasma in their wake.

Kosonen closed his eyes and held on to the poem as the city burned.

Kosonen planted the nanoseed in the woods. He dug a deep hole in the half-frozen peat with his bare hands, under an old tree stump. He sat down, took off his cap, dug out his notebook, and started reading. The pencil-scrawled words glowed bright in his mind, and after a while he didn't need to look at them anymore.

The poem rose from the words like a titanic creature from an ocean, first showing just a small extremity but then soaring upwards in a spray of glossolalia, mountain-like. It was a stream of hissing words and phonemes, an endless spell that tore at his throat. And with it came the quantum information from the microtubules of his neurons, where the bright-eyed girl now lived, and jagged impulses from synapses where his son was hiding.

The poem swelled into a roar. He continued until his voice was a hiss. Only the nanoseed could hear, but that was enough. Something stirred under the peat.

When the poem finally ended, it was evening. Kosonen opened his eyes. The first thing he saw was the sapphire antlers, sparkling in the last rays of the sun.

Two young elk looked at him. One was smaller, more delicate, and its large brown eyes held a hint of sunlight. The other was young and skinny, but wore its budding antlers with pride. It held Kosonen's gaze, and in its eyes he saw shadows of the city. Or reflections in a summer lake, perhaps.

They turned around and ran into the woods, silent, fleet-footed and free.

Kosonen was opening the cellar door when the rain came back. It was barely a shower this time: the droplets formed Marja's face in the air. For a moment he thought he saw her wink. Then the rain became a mist, and was gone. He propped the door open.

The squirrels stared at him from the trees curiously.

"All yours, gentlemen," Kosonen said. "Should be enough for next winter. I don't need it anymore."

Otso and Kosonen left at noon, heading north. Kosonen's skis slid along easily in the thinning snow. The bear pulled a sledge loaded with equipment. When they were well away from the cabin, it stopped to sniff at a fresh trail.

"Elk," it growled. "Otso is hungry. Kosonen shoot an elk. Need meat for the journey. Kosonen did not bring enough booze."

Kosonen shook his head.

"I think I'm going to learn to fish," he said.

The Jugaad Cathedral

ON THE DAY they finally got the Cathedral's mermaid-bone factory working, Kev told Raija he was not going to come back.

He had been waiting for the right moment all afternoon, but it didn't come until Raija suggested that they should take a break. They switched to godmode and flew their avatars on top of one of the logic towers of the factory. It was an impossibly high, helix-like structure made of dark stone blocks, with torches flashing on and off inside like blinking demon eyes.

It was winter in Dwarfcraft. The vast bulk of the Cathedral spread behind them, towers and looming megastructures, hollowed-out mountains and redstone circuits like highways. Ahead, the ocean glinted green and infinite beneath the pale yellow square of the sun. Far below, white foamy waves lapped at the outer walls.

"You know what this reminds me of?" Raija asked. Her deliberately pixelated long braids fluttered in the wind, and she dangled her avatar's short, iron-shod legs over the edge of the tower. "It's a bit like the sunsets at my parents' summerhouse in Finland. It never gets dark there at midsummer, only a haze, like this. The sun just sort of dips a toe below the horizon, and bounces back up."

Kev looked at her, surprised. So far, most of their conversations had been about redstone logic gates, ways to fend off nameless megabeasts, dwarven atom smashers and other things you talk about when you get involved in an epic Dwarfcraft megaproject like the Cathedral. In the two months he had known Raija, he had barely been able to piece together that she lived in Edinburgh and liked to listen to piano music—often, like now, it filtered through her mics faintly.

She was also a Juggie.

Far below, there was a splash. One of their catapult traps in the ocean had been triggered. A merperson—a speck of glittering green scales—flew through the air in a silvery arc, trailing water. The metal jaws of the factory opened to catch the morsel, and then slammed shut with a clang. The tower vibrated beneath them as the processing machinery kicked into motion.

Raija sighed. "Of course, some things here are *very* different from home."

Home. Ullapool and his family's stuffy little house, waking up early with his big brother Jamie to get some Dwarfcraft in before their parents got up, the tangy smell of the Irn Bru can that Jamie always cracked open, first thing in the morning.

Kev shook his head. He was trying to get away from all that, that was the whole point.

"I suppose you don't get 6,000 GP for a mermaid bone in Finland," he said, just to say something. "Don't you ever miss it?"

"Sometimes. But then I've been here for almost fifteen years. Good times and bad times. It's like a marriage." She paused. She had once hinted she'd been in London during the Assangelypse, back in '14.

"Anyway. If I went back, it wouldn't be the place I keep in my head. I wouldn't be the same person who left. Better to build something new here, try to make it last."

Kev said nothing. Raija had been working on the Cathedral for Blood God knew how many years.

She was a legend in the Dwarfcraft community. She had taken him under her wing after he came up with better XOR gates using crossbows, fire arrows, torches and pressure plates. There had been tests: at first, he was basically just her crafter monkey. The crafting mode of the game that plugged into the gesture recognition of the iVision contacts actually allowed you to make things with your hands, and Raija's motor skills were—to put it delicately—pants. He enjoyed the manual labour, too: it was a nice break after the brain-breaking intellectual effort that had gone into his degree show at the Art College.

But then she had brought him to the Cathedral, hidden inside a secret server shard, open to just the two of them.

"You're very quiet," Raija said. There was a flowing piano piece mixed with her voice, faint notes, climbing up and down. "Still thinking about that girl? What was her name? Lavatory?"

"Lavinia," Kev said.

"You'll be better off with some nice Scottish lass than posh totty like that. Isn't that what your mother would say? Did I get it right?"

"Not really." He sighed. "Lavinia's a megaproject all on her own, she is."

"Just make sure you don't end up being used as a toilet. It would be a shame if all that worrying came to nothing."

Recently, it had felt like Raija was grooming him for bigger and better things: taking him on tours through the huge magma memory banks beneath the Cathedral, flying to dizzying heights to study the megastructure's overall architecture. And now, sitting down and talking about life, for goodness' sake, like she was some sort of dwarf Jedi master, and Kev her padawan.

Just get it out already.

Kev cleared his throat. "Speaking of that," he said. "Do you think we'll ever finish this thing?" He gestured at the expanse of the Cathedral with his adamantine hammer. "There could be a megabeast that rips it apart, or some other chain reaction we start by digging too deep. It could end up being a lot of wasted effort."

"Sure," Raija said. "But that's not the point. It's like building pyramids: it doesn't have to make sense. It will be here as long as the Web is—so maybe forever. Even if we don't finish it, somebody will find it, one day, wonder what it's for. People will always remember the billion Halo kills, or the defeat of the Sleeper. This is even better. I thought you understood that."

"Is that why you are doing it? To be remembered?"

Raija got down from the edge of the tower. The wind had picked up and no more merpeople were coming up from the choppy sea. "Not exactly," she said. "What is this about?"

"It's just that I don't see the point anymore," Kev said. "I'm trying to say goodbye."

The previous night, the Dwarfcraft session had overrun, and Kev had barely made it to Lavinia's show in time. He arrived at Cabaret Voltaire at seven o'clock sharp, covered in a thin layer of sweat that chilled his skin after his hasty jog through the warrenlike streets of Cowgate.

There was a queue outside the bar, mostly first- and second-year students. Lavinia's show was a pre-event for the upcoming ECA Fashion Show, the biggest charity ball the University organised every year. The F+ Frendipity app threw up a few contact suggestions and opening lines at him for people standing in the queue. The towering blonde girl in a flowing green dress, standing on microcontroller-stabilised stilts, had a pretty high Fashion score—but that meant she would be approached by others anyway. Kev preferred to just stand in the back of the line, catch his breath and review his stats on Lavinia in peace.

F+ gave a 60% probability he and Lavinia would sleep together tonight. That was altogether lower than he had hoped: the emotion graph from their interactions had been getting steadily flirtier over the last couple of weeks, ever since they had had a long chat about their mutual liking for Edward Gorey in one of the many degree show after-parties in the college. She had liked his hand-knitted scarves with their cellular automata patterns.

Then again, a lot of their F+ interactions had been just bot likes. That might not have been a bad thing given how much embarrassing rubbish Jamie managed to get into Kev's stream through the privacy settings. But it also meant it was hard to tell how far off the mark the app was. Like with many girls with cut-glass accents, Lavinia's stream was carefully curated, F+ bots tidying up anything that her parents would not want future employers to know.

The butterflies in his gut wanted it to be right.

One of Lavinia's friends was doing the door: a pretty Brazilian girl in a tight T-shirt, sitting behind a low desk and looking bored as people blinked their ticket vouchers at her. F+ tagged her as Benita. Kev gave her a friendly nod. She frowned.

"Sorry. Your ticket has been revoked. I can't let you in."

"What?"

"You read the T&Cs, right?"

Of course I didn't.

"Sure."

"Well, better check your Fashion, pal."

The contacts flashed it up, unbidden, showed him a bar chart of the attributes that F+ was tracking for him. *Shit.* His Fashion influence stat was a snub. It stood out yellow and tiny next to the lofty green towers of Crafting, Design and Cellular Automata. In the last two weeks, it had somehow dropped to 29. Pathetic. The tickets were only given out to people with a score over 40. His chest felt hollow.

"Look, I know Lavinia—"

"*Everybody* knows Lavinia," Benita said.

"Seriously, I *know* her. Can you ask her, please? I think she was expecting me to be here tonight." Kev gave her his best puppy eyes, which Jamie had once told him were his best asset with girls.

Benita stared at him for a moment, a calculating look on her face, obviously assessing his influence.

"Okay," she said finally. "Wait here."

Kev took a deep breath. If he was being honest, it wasn't *just* about hooking up. Lavinia was a hub, a way to get some of his designs into the charity show. His ugly-duckling ideas about self-replicating fabric patterns made out of protocells were never going to grow into black swans without some help. Now that crowdfunding dictated artistic success, you needed a network to get attention.

"Good evening, Kevin," Lavinia said.

She wore a loose T-shirt that somehow managed to emphasise her bust and left one creamy shoulder bare. She rested one hand on her wide hips, holding a half-mask: its angle made Kev think of the tail of an exotic bird. It seemed that there was a touch of Juggie counterculture chic in tonight's show. Her auburn hair was tousled and her cheekbones glittered with just a hint of makeup.

"Hi. Good to see you."

"Good to see you too, darling, but I'm a little busy just now, we are about to go on stage. What is the problem?"

"Well, I'm having a little stat problem, it's temporary, and I was hoping you could sneak me in. I'll buy you a drink afterwards. Promise."

Lavinia covered her mouth with the mask in her hand and frowned.

"Sweetie, I'm really sorry, but I can't let you in: it's just business, you understand. And I'm super busy tonight after the show. Don't worry, you'll catch it straight from my stream."

He nodded, watching the F+ getting-laid score dance for a second and then settle down to a lukewarm 15%. He thought about quoting *The Gashlycrumb Tinies*. It was useless, so he just shrugged. She spread her hands and gave him a wan smile. She could see the stats too. There was no fighting it: the deep learning models in the F+ cloud knew the outcome better than they did.

"So *nice* to see you," Lavinia said. She turned on her heels and strode back to the club. He thought about stealing a glance at her well-shaped behind, but Benita and the other girls were probably using gaze detector apps. The only option was a slow, dignified retreat.

As he walked, he fired up a visualisation app that turned his self-quantification data into scatterplots and bubbles. The answer he already knew was obvious at a glance.

The culprit was Dwarfcraft.

He ended up hiding in the Tron, a multistory pub in an old church. He went down to the third basement floor, bought a pint of Foster's, sat down at a corner table and wrapped himself in the hot blanket of the noisy student crowd.

He had deserved a reward of some kind. He had made it out of Ullapool. That had taken online courses, endless evenings forging his conjoined obsessions with Conway and Gorey into a portfolio that eventually got him in. And then, tuition fees and rent and Marchmont brickstarter work and microtasks to make ends meet. The joint Bioart and Fashion programme meant lab work, following protocols that were like recipes from a

Dadaist cookbook; learning to parse headache-inducing synthbio pathway graphs, frustration with the post-2014 Lockdown crippleware they let you run in the college cloud; training himself to work with fabrics and needle and thread. He had even beaten the level boss of the degree show.

Except that wasn't how real life worked. You never levelled up. It never stopped. He was letting nostalgia for a childhood game screw up his chances with Lavinia. The cheap beer developed a tepid flavour in his mouth. He forced himself to swallow it and closed his eyes.

Exactly what Jamie would have done. Hiding, taking the path of least resistance. Kev had spent two months living under the stair, like Harry Potter with the Dursleys. It was time to come out and go back to Hogwarts.

But what was he going to tell Raija?

Frendipity interrupted his thoughts, highlighting two guys leaning on the bar across the room, gesturing at each other. Adnan and Tom were with the Improverts, one of the student drama groups at Bedlam Theatre. The app recommended strengthening his ties with them if he wanted to improve his overall Influence score. The problem was, Adnan had an awkward crush on him, and Tom was one of those hyperactive Bedlam types who had a cheese-grater effect on his nerves.

Kev sighed, drained the remaining half of his pint, ignoring the Constitution -1 that popped out of it, got up and waved them over, forcing a smile on his face.

After Kev finished, Raija said nothing.

The Cathedral hummed and whirred and boomed around them. Along its spiky coastline, a megabeast was trying to crawl from the sea to the shore. The Cathedral's defence ballistae were firing. Orange arcs of flame rained into the dark green of the sea.

"You know how you were talking about home," Kev said. "Well, I worked pretty hard to get out of mine. And I'm worried it'll all be for nothing if I don't start taking real life a bit more seriously."

"Real life," she said. "I see."

"I really want to get into fashion. It's been great working with you. But something has to give. Things have been happening. I need to choose, and I can't choose mermaid genocides."

"Kev, I wish I believed you. I wish it was really about that."

"It *is*. And you don't need me anyway, it's a megaproject, you could have ten thousand crafters working here if you wanted, you're a big shot, you are goddamn Tholtig Cryptbrain of the Waning Diamonds, Queen of the Dwarves. A war does not need one man, don't they say that in Finland, too?"

"You're right, it is a war," Raija said quietly. "And yes, they do say that in Finland. I hope you will remember my silly Finnish sayings."

"You know, I'm happy to keep in touch, except that, uh—"

He bit his tongue. That had been exactly the wrong thing to say.

"Except that I'm a Juggie, a jugaader, a hacker, a paranoid commie terrorist who stays away from the dirty networks owned by capitalists that you can't even hook a general-purpose computer into without cutting its balls off so Assangelypses never happen again, is that it? You don't want me polluting your pristine F+ network, somebody like me who digs old computers out of dumpsters and carries them around in big shoulder bags, while you wear yours in your eyes? Who can't get a job with a proper company because there is no data on her to determine if she's competent or well-behaved or good for team productivity or not, so she scrapes a living with Council community initiatives and brickstarters and whatever Bitcoins she can get from old Dwarfcraft geeks? Who bores you with her old woman bullshit? Is that it?" Raija drew a deep breath. "Say what you mean, *perkele.*"

There was a hard lump in Kev's throat. Swallowing it hurt.

"Shit, Raija, it has nothing to do with that, it's just that—"

"That you'd rather hang out with *real* people, and do *real* things? I was going to *tell* you, you idiot. I was going to tell you how real it is. Now fuck off. I have a megabeast to kill." Raija raised her pickaxe. She had killed a giant bronze golem with it once, by herself.

"Raija, please—"

"Go and have fun with your friend Lavatory, Kev. *Vittu.* Tell her the Juggie bitch said hi."

The pickaxe came down like lightning, and then the world of Dwarfcraft faded away.

Kev blinked. He was in his rickety four-poster bed. Outside, it was dark already: the sky was faded indigo, with a hint of fiery red in the horizon. He shivered in the chill that had crept in through the single glazing of the high, huge window that overlooked the Meadows.

I was going to tell you how real it is.

He let the app fade from his contacts and stared at his dimly lit room for a moment: the piles of clothing on the floor, the low desk, the piled-up sharp shapes of his degree show pieces in one corner, with their Gorey-like fluorescent patterns: dark elephants and pale-faced children. He had engineered a protocell batch that could live in grids printed on fabrics, arranged them in cellular automata patterns that moved and collided and made copies of themselves. Turing-complete clothing, living designs that kept changing as long as you sprayed the fabric with nutrients regularly.

The examiners had loved them. Suddenly, he could not bear to look at them. A slight headache bloomed in his temples. *I was going to tell you, you idiot.*

He shook his head. At least it was done. Tomorrow, he'd figure out what to do next. He could still get a piece in the ECA show, if he played his cards right, go through Tom or Adnan. In fact, there was an F+ from Tom: something about a bar night out on George Street with some of the posher Bedlam girls. Maybe it would be a good idea to get drunk.

He told himself the empty, hollow feeling was hunger, climbed out of the bed and padded barefoot to the kitchen through the quiet dusty clutter of the flat hallway—his flatmates Matt and Tamara were working late.

He spotted the dead mouse in the mousetrap in the light from the open fridge. He fought down the disgust and snapped on the rubber gloves from under the sink. The damn thing was worth at least 5,000 XP in the flat's ChoreWars, with a Disgusting bonus to boot.

He eased the dead thing out of the trap and held it up. Half of its back was shaved and there was a mesh router tattoo on the pink skin. The

Juggies' meshers were really getting desperate for bandwidth. The trees lining the Meadows kept getting sprayed with antenna paint, yellow and red like they were on fire. On a bright day—not that there were that many in Edinburgh—you could see drones up in the sky, hunting for pirate blimps. The latest thing were router mice and pigeons, allegedly grown in guerrilla farms in the underground maze beneath Old Town.

Kev wondered how it was that Raija logged onto Dwarfcraft and felt a stab of guilt. He threw the dead mouse into the bin. It vanished with a thump, and ChoreWars rewarded him with a tinkle of coins. It rang in his skull and made him cringe. *Go and have fun with your friend Lavatory.* He looked at the half-eaten Onken biopot raspberry yoghurt in the fridge and decided he was not hungry anymore.

He gritted his teeth. He *was* going to go out and have a good time, no matter what. He went back to his room, put on his favourite scarf—the one with the Elephantomas pattern he had knitted himself—applied a bit more eyeshadow, threw on his coat and shoes and walked out into the windy evening gloom.

Kev started crossing the Meadows park along the Jawbone Walk, passing beneath the sharp arch of ancient wood gate. The smell of dead leaves on the path and the cold air cleared his head. Surely, the low was just a lingering dopamine addiction, neurons in his cortex firing in a simulation of Dwarfcraft that wanted to be fed.

He thought about the likely flow of the evening ahead, resisted plotting it out on F+. Noisy bars and dancing and cocktails that he couldn't afford and a mixture of shouted and F+ed conversation about whatever Bedlamites talked about.

He sighed, stopped for a moment and looked at the sky. The reclining lion shape of Arthur's Seat loomed dark to the right. Ahead, the city's jagged rooftops hid behind the monstrous '70s lines of the Appleton Tower. It looked like an alien country, all of a sudden. What had Raija said? *It wouldn't be the place I keep in my head.* There was no going back.

Shit.

The self-loathing hit like the clammy, dead feel of the mouse in his hand, all over his skin. He tasted bile in his mouth, had to lean on his knees and breathe hard for a minute. Then he stood up and tried to log onto the Dwarfcraft server, right there and then, flicking his fingers to reopen the app. He would send her a message, it would be okay, he would apologise, say it had all come out wrong.

The app filled his field of vision with login fields made of mithril, dwarven runes and rock. He air-typed his password, but only got a faint metallic gong sound for his troubles. He clicked on the "Forgot Password" button, but the resulting F+ notification just told him his account had been removed. *Queen of the Dwarves. Right.*

Human.io chimed, highlighting something in his field of vision. There was a black shape like a collapsed tent a hundred metres to his right, on the wet grass. It fluttered sadly in the wind. F+ picked up the outline and threw a few status updates at him: it was a pirate server blimp that council drones had downed earlier that day. It looked depressing, like a used condom.

A group of people were standing around it. They looked eerie in the yellow glare of the streetlights: strange 3D-printed masks—procedurally generated that morning, no doubt—and nondescript, baggy black clothes. Juggies, scavenging hardware from the blimp.

5 Bitcoins for getting closer and getting some video of them, Human.io said. That would pay for his night on George Street. Maybe even for a dinner with Lavinia.

The thought brought the nausea back in an instant. *That's it. No more. Not like this.*

Then the inspiration hit, like Dwarfcraft lightning on redstone, and he found himself walking towards the Juggies.

There was a leaden weight in Kev's belly. There were no tags hovering above their heads, no F+ shakes as he approached. The Juggies might as well have been ghosts or shadows.

Their outfits were not like the stylised, sterile versions in Lavinia's show, but the real thing. One wore a robe and a long beaklike mask that reminded him of medieval plague doctors. Another's face was a Hulk-like visage of green rage. The third wore a blank oval with no apparent eye slits. They shuffled oddly as they moved, to fool gait recognition.

"Excuse me," he said. His lips felt cold and numb.

"What do you want?" said the one with the beak in a muffled female voice.

"Uh, I'm . . . I'm looking for one of you guys. Jugaaders. A lady called Raija. She's Finnish."

"Get lost, kid," said the Hulk. "Your footage won't do you any good. We'll have different faces tomorrow." He—or she—turned back to the black beached whale of the blimp.

"Wait. Wait. It's not like that, you have to help me." Kev took a deep breath. "I'll show you. Look."

He tilted his head back, pressed his eyes with his fingers carefully and took out his contacts. They came off with a faint *plop* and a sharp pain. The world blurred with tears. He gestured to sharpen the view and almost panicked when nothing happened. The lenses lay on his palm like shards of a tiny crystal egg.

"Please," he said, holding them out. "She must be in your mesh. She plays Dwarfcraft. I need to find her."

"Why?" asked the blank-faced Juggie in a rasping growl that must have come from a voice box.

Kev swallowed. "It's private."

"Why?"

"All right. I offended her. I want to tell her I'm sorry."

The three Juggies studied him in silence. Their fingers twitched in an air-typing rhythm. His neck prickled. The air was full of soundless communication.

Finally, the plague woman spoke again.

"The Jugaad Jiayóu pub. She's there every Wednesday night."

They turned away in unison and walked into the darkness, leaving him blinking at the sting in his eyes.

The Jugaad Jiayóu was near the University sports centre in Pleasance, in a Juggie block all overgrown with wireless antennae like spiky iron ivy, walls splashed with protocell paint that advertised the carbon dioxide production of each house. The windows were boarded up.

A bell tinkled when he opened the door. It smelled of Indian food and spilled beer. The floor was sticky. Small clusters of people sat around narrow tables: Juggies, in simple dark clothes, with elaborate T-shirt designs, most with shaved heads, men and women. An Indian man glared at him from behind the counter, a hand on the brass handle of a beer tap with the label *Kraken Spit*.

There was a whirring sound from behind Kev. "Don't look at him like that, Sunil, he's with me."

It was Raija. She sat in a motorised wheelchair that bristled with old electronics. She had short red hair and a piercing in her upper lip: otherwise she looked a lot like her dwarven avatar, red cheeks and clear pale skin. Her right arm ended in a prosthesis that was covered in pale wood, maybe birch, with intricate Celtic engravings, but looked like a standard Siemens model underneath. She had no legs below her knees. Kev's heart fell straight into his gut like a cannonball.

When she narrowed her eyes, her wrinkles came out: she was at least as old as Kev's Mum. "I heard that you were looking for me. Not afraid of Juggies after all? Don't show them fear. They'll eat you alive. Come and sit down."

He followed her to a narrow corner table in the back. A sullen Sunil brought him a pint of pale ale that smelled strongly of hops.

"So," Raija said. "What are you doing here? Isn't this going to look bad on your F+ scorecard or whatever you kids are into these days?"

Kev looked down at his pint. He wished he could dive into it and disappear, like an alcoholic mermaid.

"I wanted to say sorry," he said. "I should have talked to you sooner, not dropped it on you like that. Helped you to get the Cathedral finished, or found somebody else to help you."

Raija looked at him. Her eyes were the same colour as her avatar's, Dwarfcraft winter green.

"Maybe I'm the one who should apologise," she said slowly. "I lost my temper. You can do what you want with your life, and it's not my place to say any different. It's just that . . . what you told me about your friends, how is that any more *real* than what we were doing?" She held up her good hand. "No, don't answer. Let me explain first."

She sipped her own pint. "I told you I was in London, back in '14." She tapped the table with her hand prosthesis: it echoed like the wooden rhythm sticks they had used in music class at school. "That's when I got this. I was on the Underground, the Piccadilly Line, when the control systems went nuts. I remember this sound, like a beer can being crushed.

"I had a few of these, over the years. They got a bit better, but they were all really expensive, and not that great, to be honest. They try to classify what your stump nerves are trying to tell it and then choose the closest thing from a library of moves. The idea is good, except everybody is different. It doesn't feel natural. With the phantom pains, it goes a bit crazy, sometimes. It's like having an alien *thing* attached to your body. Sure, the brain is plastic, you get used to it. It helps, you can grab stuff and move stuff, but it's not a *hand*. And you sure as hell can't play the piano with it.

"In some ways, the legs are even worse. Sure, I could get Pistorius-style ones and run, but I don't want to run. I want to climb up the stairs, or dance.

"I wasn't alone, especially after '14. We started to think that it was more of a software problem, that you could fine-tune the algorithms individually, throw deep learning at it. Or try a different paradigm, try to get it to make moves on its own and then figure out what you *want* it to do rather than just read your signals. Talk to ubicomp and figure out context. All that should have been doable. If it hadn't been for the Lockdown."

Raija touched the prosthesis with her left hand, traced the wood carvings on the forearm. "It's a hand, but it's not *mine*. I can't reprogram it, unless Siemens says I can. Trusted *vitun* computing, right there. There's great control algorithms I found in the literature, but I can't run them. Most of the GPC hardware we can cobble together here is too old. I really need something like the cloud stuff that runs your contacts. High-power computing. And there is only one place left where I can build something like that."

Things clicked into place in Kev's head like arrows into the magazine of a heavy ballista.

"The Cathedral," he breathed.

"That's right. It's not just a dwarfputer, made for fun. It's something . . . real."

Chilly ants ran up and down Kev's back. "Christ. Why didn't you tell me?" He felt like he had just woken up, blinking sleep from his eyes, walking down the stairs to join Jamie in the morning, ready to craft and make.

"As you'll recall, I was *going* to tell you." Raija pursed her lips. "Honestly, I didn't trust you, at first. You were one of *them*. Who knew what you were going to do if you thought it wasn't just a vanity project?"

"Are you kidding? We are building a dwarf fortress to run your *hand*?" His stomach tickled. He felt like laughing, or jumping up and down. F+ chimed. He turned it off with a flick of his wrist. His mind whirred and spat out ideas like an overclocked logic tower. The whole point about his degree project had been about computation and design, about blurring the line between machine and life and human. About showing how monumentally stupid the Lockdown was. The implications were ocean-deep.

I have been such an idiot.

"You were wrong," he said. "It's not like pyramids. It's better." Then he frowned. "But aren't they just going to take it down when it starts working? And what about clockspeed?"

"Clockspeed is not a problem. I found some pretty funny holes in the physics engine. Try putting two teleportals on top of each other and then dropping an anvil into one. Data I/O is a bit trickier, but there are ways around that, with character-spawning APIs. As for stopping them from taking it down—well, that's where you were supposed to come in."

"Me?"

"I didn't recruit you because you were a pretty face, Kev." She put her hands in her lap and looked down. "That's why I was so upset when you wanted to leave. I need your help to finish it. To help me play the piano again. So, are you in or not?"

Kev looked at her, massaged his temples, mind still racing.

"Yes. No."

Raija frowned.

"What I mean is," Kev said, "it can't just be a secret. It can't just be a Juggie thing. We have to make it big enough so it can't just be shut down and ignored."

"What do you have in mind?"

"If there is one thing I learned in art school, the best way to get away with something wicked is to call it art." He smiled. "Or better yet, fashion."

After listening to him for a while, Raija started nodding. She held out her prosthesis. The fingers opened jerkily. Wordlessly, Kev squeezed the carved wood tight.

They turned the Cathedral on from a floating platform high up, held aloft by jugaaded windmills—another Dwarfcraft physics engine glitch Raija had discovered. From this high up, Kev could see the structure of the Cathedral: a gold, red and black mandala carved in the green continent, full of intricate detail, like a circuit.

There was a single red button on a raised dais. Raija stood in front of it, hesitating.

"Hurry," Kev said. "We don't have a lot of time." The noise from RL was distracting: the mutter of the crowd mixed with the hum of the windmills.

"Just savouring the moment."

"I guess it doesn't look like a Finnish sunset anymore."

"No," Raija said. "It looks like a sunrise."

She raised her pickaxe and brought it down onto the button in a wide arc. It went in with a satisfying click.

For a moment, nothing changed. Kev shivered: Was it possible that he got it wrong? They had tested it on a sandboxed server shard, but this was the real thing—

Below, fountains of magma shot up. There was the sound of mountains cracking. The mandala of the Cathedral was changing, moving like a medusa, a living thing. Slowly at first, then faster, it started dividing. There were two Cathedrals, then four, then a mad quilt of them, spreading at dizzying speed.

The Cathedral was a von Neumann machine. It had taken Kev the better part of two months to translate his protocell designs into Dwarfcraft objects. Now it would fill the huge Dwarfcraft servers with programmable general-purpose computers, doing computation with crossbows, torches, golems and waterwheels, pressure plates and mermaids. And they would run anything you wanted.

Raija laughed like a little girl.

"They're working," she said. "Even better than the tests." She took a choked breath. "Oh god. They are calling me on now."

"Break a—never mind."

"Don't worry, I'll be fine," she whispered. "Thank you."

Kev let her voice and the Dwarfcraft app fade into the dimly lit hush of the Fountainbridge conference hall and the stage ahead, illuminated by a single skylight that fell on Lavinia's black-and-white form: he had to admit she looked very good in her half-mask. And in his Gorey-Convay dress. It was almost frightening how easily she had agreed to the scheme, a hungry gleam in her eyes.

He leaned back in his chair and took a deep breath. The butterflies in his belly had razor wings. They had attached a Dwarfcraft screencast to the conference-hall cast with a commentary explaining the concept. It was now being eagerly restreamed by the fashionistas in the front row. It was already being picked up by major hacktivist blogs. Mainstream media would follow soon.

He had no idea what would happen after that. *But let's see them try to shut it down now.*

"Ladies and gentlemen," Lavinia said in soft, mysterious tones. "Welcome to this year's ECA Charity Fashion Show."

She stepped aside. The walkway lit up. As the clapping arose like an ocean, Raija walked towards the audience, every step proud and straight, her long gleaming legs striking the floor in a steady tap-tap-tap.

She was wearing the Cathedral: a screencast from within the game on display fabric, a cloak of green foam and red magma and dark towers along a spiky edge. Mermaids swam within it, scales mithril-bright.

Queen of the Dwarves, Kev thought.

He clapped so hard his palms hurt, and hooted.

In the centre of the stage stood a piano. When Raija reached it and sat down, a silence fell. She raised her hands and touched the keys delicately, rested fingers of wood and skin on white bone.

And then, hesitantly, one note at a time, she began to play.

Fisher of Men

THE SUMMERHOUSE WAS HIS, his alone. He hadn't built it, of course, but the vision was his. He *had* built a 3D version of it out in Second Life. Clean geometric lines, with a gently sloping, curving roof: mathematically precise spline curves cast in dark wood. *Can't get much closer than this to making a dream come true,* Jaakko thought. It was a bit of a Finnish cliché, really: the perfect summer haven, in the woods, by the sea. Ahtolanniemi was the perfect place for it, a small island connected to the mainland by a narrow walking bridge, granite shores surrounding a thick grove of pine and birch trees.

He sat on the veranda bench and looked out to the sea, chewing on a buttered slice of rye bread. He hoped that the hangover—curled up in his stomach like an eel—would accept it as a peace offering. It had rained in the morning, but now the weather was clearing up. A cool breeze tickled his chest hair and carried the faintest hint of crispness.

Soon it would be winter, and the madness would continue. But not yet: he still had time to think, to be alone, to forget his second burnout. He had needed the break. And Minna hadn't called, thank God. He'd have to fire her. Give her a good reference, of course. Sometimes women didn't understand that sleeping with the boss made things difficult in the long run.

And then he smelled smoke. He looked up and saw a blurry shape in a green raincoat squatting by the waterline, making a fire. Right next to his pier.

Jaakko shoved his bare feet into his trainers, got up slowly and started walking. An angry animal was purring softly inside his chest, but he wasn't about to let it come out. Not now, when he had just managed to cage it.

When he reached the pier, he realised the shape was a woman. Long, dark water-curled wisps of hair hung from the hood of the raincoat, hiding her face. She was kneeling on the rocks, close to the fire. There was a large fish flapping on the rocks, still tenaciously clinging to life.

"Excuse me," said Jaakko pleasantly. There was no answer. Then he kicked at the fire, scattering ashes and simmering wood.

The woman looked at him curiously, head cocked to one side. Her wet hair and the shadow of the hood obscured her features, but her eyes were clear and green. Her bare legs were pale and shapely, although somehow she did not seem young.

"The first fish of the catch has to be cooked on the shore," she said in a quiet, chiding voice. "It's for my father."

The fish twitched against Jaakko's leg. Gingerly, he picked it up by the tail and looked at it. It was an ugly fish with brown eyes and dark, soot-coloured scales. He flung it into the sea, as far as he could. It vanished with a resounding splash.

"I don't like fish," said Jaakko. "Look, I'm all for everyman's rights, just as much as the next guy, but this is my shoreline here and you could ask for permission before making fires. You or your father. Is that too much to ask?"

The woman didn't reply. She stood up, and before Jaakko could protest, she took a step forward and brushed his cheek with a wet hand. To his surprise, he didn't flinch. The touch was soft, like seaweed brushing against a swimmer's leg.

"I like you," she said. "You'll do very nicely."

She let the raincoat drop. Jaakko had a brief glimpse of a strong, pale body and a cascade of dark gold hair. And then she dived into the sea. There was barely a ripple on the dark surface, a glimpse of the white shape beneath, and then she was gone.

Jaakko stared after her for a full minute, but she did not come up. He felt the first tickle of panic in his chest. He would have to do something. And he was a terrible swimmer.

He yanked his trainers off and waded into the water. The bottom was rocky and uneven, and he had to walk slowly to keep from slipping. *Where was she? The water wasn't deep; she couldn't have gone far—*

The clouds tore like a curtain, and there was a flash of golden sunlight. It refracted from the waves and danced on the bottom in bright, intertwined tendrils.

Like a golden net, he thought.

The sea made an odd swallowing sound. The large underwater rock he was standing on moved under his feet, like a roused animal.

Then the water slapped him in the face. Something dark and hard glanced off his forehead and made everything go away in a crimson flash.

"Come on up. There you go."

Jaakko coughed: salt water filled his mouth and he felt his stomach heave. Then the pressure on his chest eased and he found himself looking at a troll, framed by dark clouds.

It wore a misshapen fisherman's cap. The face beneath was a mass of wrinkles, with a pair of tired red eyes barely showing between the folds of loose skin. It held out a handkerchief and dabbed Jaakko's forehead gently. He felt a stab of dull pain, and the cloth came away bloody.

"Neighbour had a bit of a slip there. Good thing old Kalle passed by, yes. Been living next door for a while. Minding my own business. Heard a splash and wanted to know what it was." He spoke haltingly, almost chewing the words like they were some long-forgotten fruit in his mouth.

"I don't know what happened. There was a woman, and—"

The old man's eyes narrowed. "Neighbour doesn't have to worry about her. She is fine now, right as rain." His expression did not invite further questions. Jaakko coughed again, and wrapped his soaked bathrobe around his shoulders.

"Thanks. Look, is there anything I can do for you? Coffee, or—hell, people give money to someone who saves their life. And I've got some—"

"Neighbour keeps his money. But some coffee, that would be good, yes. Should get that head wound sorted, that can be the death of you."

They walked up the path to the summerhouse, Jaakko limping slightly, Kalle with an old man's careful steps. Inside, the freshly lacquered wood smell that he normally cherished made Jaakko nauseous, but he didn't want to appear weak in front of the old man. He went up to the loft, dried himself with a towel and donned a set of fresh clothes. The gash on his forehead wasn't deep, and he covered it with a Band-Aid. After that, he felt slightly better.

He found Kalle sitting in one of his basket chairs, long limbs folded like a locust.

"Is espresso okay?" Jaakko asked, taking two cups from the cupboard.

Kalle didn't answer. His breathing sounded like tearing paper. Jaakko got the machine going, grateful that the familiar muttering noise masked the painful sound.

"So you are the one she caught," said Kalle finally.

Jaakko swallowed. "So, you . . . know this lady I met earlier?"

The old man let out a short laugh. It sounded like twigs snapping.

"She is my wife," he said. "My wife of seventy years. Although not much longer, now that neighbour is here."

He must be senile, thought Jaakko. *Maybe she's his daughter, or grand-daughter.* He held out the coffee cup, and Kalle took it, cradling it in his lap.

"So, uh, how did you meet?"

"She came to me in a storm," Kalle said. "Saved my boat and took a liking to me. Oh, but I was cocky back then: I had the daughter of the sea as lover and I thought I could keep her. But it was the other way around. She never let me go. And never will." He sipped the espresso and grimaced. "Neighbour makes strong coffee, yes. But for her, you need something better than that."

Kalle swallowed with apparent relish. "There is something the neighbour should see." He got up slowly and motioned Jaakko to follow. Mutely, he obeyed.

———

Kalle led them down a narrow path Jaakko had never noticed before, into the small wood that grew in the middle of the island. The summer had been so dry that the trees had shed their leaves early. The dark branches looked sharp and forbidding in the dimming light. There was a weight to the quiet here that made Jaakko shiver.

They came into a small clearing. The ground here was wet and almost marsh-like, with yellow undergrowth. There were a dozen slab-like, moss-covered stones sticking out of the soft ground, with names and years carved on them. Some of the writing looked archaic.

"What is this place?" Jaakko asked. "What are we doing here?"

"Take a good look," Kalle said. "This is where neighbour is going to end up." The old man leaned against a tree trunk, looking weary. "It's that net, that accursed net. Once you're in it, you can never leave." Kalle looked down. "I've been on this island for seventy years." He smiled. "Oh, sometimes she lets me go, for a little while, to go to the gas station to buy cigarettes. Or to see the family, when they were alive. Or she takes me with her cattle to the sea or down to the castles of Ahti. But I'm in her net, and always will be."

Okay, thought Jaakko. *Ahti. Sea god. The old guy needs treatment. I'll get it sorted out. He saved my life, I owe him that.*

"I see you don't understand," Kalle whispered. "The neighbour is here too now, with us. With all the husbands. We are all here, except the first one. The one she loved first and who never wed her with a ring. The one who went with another. The one she drowned."

"That's great," Jaakko said carefully. "Now if we go back inside, I think there's still some coffee left—"

"And I should have brought it back for her, the ring. There is a way down there. I've stayed here for so long, so long that I can see it, I'm almost there."

Kalle came so close to Jaakko that he could smell the sickly sweet tobacco and the unwashed stench that it covered. There was madness, a new light in the red eyes now.

"But you had to come here and spoil everything, yes."

Jaakko didn't see the filleting knife until it was too late. It cut his T-shirt and drew an arc of fire along his ribs. He bit his tongue from the pain, and felt his mouth filling with blood. Red haze came up in his eyes, and he dropped to one knee.

"Couldn't do it in the water, with her watching. Couldn't let you drown, you'd have been hers. But this place, she can't see us here, here in Äijö's grove—" Kalle loomed over him, bony hand pulling his head up, cold metal on his throat.

Jaakko's fingers found a rock, round and smooth like an egg, that fit his palm perfectly. Without thinking, he swung it. It was a glancing blow, but the old man went down, his cap gone, dirty wispy hair matted with blood.

Kalle lay still on the marshy ground, one leg twitching rhythmically like a dying fish.

Jaakko dropped the rock and spat blood. And then he ran.

He stopped at the summerhouse to grab his keys, wallet and mobile phone, and kept running. The wound on his side hurt, but the T-shirt was sticking to it and it didn't feel like he was losing that much blood. *Still, should call the police. Or the ambulance. Or Rane from the office. Or somebody.*

It was almost dark now, and he had to stop on the path that led to the walking bridge connecting Ahtolanniemi to the mainland and focus on the mobile's glowing display. There were no reception bars. Jaakko swore and kept going.

The bridge was a narrow, V-shaped, wood-and-metal structure. The wind was up and the sea was angry, beating against the metal railings so that the bridge rang like a bell, harmonics propagating through it like it was one of the wobbly springs they used in physics classes at school.

The first wave made him lose his footing on the wet boards. The second was like a playful slap, and he fell to his knees, seizing the railing in a white-knuckled grip. He spat out salt water. The waves looked like the bristling backs of angry dogs.

I could try to swim, he thought. *It's not that far. I could.*

He watched the black tongues of water lashing across the hundred-metre walk to the other side, and turned back.

When he reached dry ground, something felt wrong. He felt in his pockets and realised that his car keys were gone.

Back at the summerhouse, he locked the door and sat at the kitchen table, dripping water onto the floor, rubbing his limbs for warmth and looking out through the window. The evening sky did not seem right. The vivid watercolour streak that always blazed above the horizon at this time was not there: the clouds were dark grey. *Need to get warm. Sauna, that's what I need.*

He was glad that he hadn't built the sauna the traditional way, in a separate building by the water, but in the back of the summerhouse itself. The thought of having to go outside again made him shiver. He stripped, filled the stove with firewood and lit it. Then he sat on the tiled floor, waiting for it to heat up. It was safe in the sauna: the enclosed space felt good, like sitting inside the walls of his own skull.

After his second burnout, Jaakko had a pretty good idea of how they worked. The first serious thing that went was the sense of being there. Then the short-term memory.

And then came the hallucinations.

The previous months were a blur: raising the second round of venture capital for the company, endless meetings, PowerPoint slides flashing like blinking eyes. He'd started the affair with Minna just to have something else, but that, too, had been a brief, crazy thing, like a tablet of sodium blazing in a glass of water. The IPO had been the last straw. Jaakko remembered that awful moment in the board meeting where he had suddenly found himself staring at a hostile wall of faces, completely unable to remember what he was supposed to say next.

Maybe he was further gone than he thought. Had the woman been real? Had Kalle been real? He could not summon the willpower to return to the clearing in the woods in the dark, to see what had happened to the old man. The thought made him shake. *In the morning. I'll do it in the morning.*

When the stove was hot, Jaakko climbed to the top bench, took the wooden dipper and threw water onto the stove. He washed his side wound: it was just a surface cut that bled a little when the encrusted blood was gone, but soon stopped. Still, watching the red-tinted water wash down the benches made him feel light-headed.

I'm going crazy. He squeezed his eyes shut. *I'll stay here,* he thought. *Inside my own head. Until reality comes back.*

A faint chill came to the sauna as the door opened. Jaakko opened his eyes as the woman stepped inside.

In the glow of the stove, she didn't look pale anymore: her skin was flushed and the firelight made her look like she was made of red clay. She had the body of a young woman, heavy, round breasts and a gently curving pubic mound covered in dark gold hair. But her face was ageless: she had just a hint of freckles around her strong nose, like flakes of gold.

In spite of himself, Jaakko felt the stir of arousal, mixed with a trace of panic. It gave his desire a sharp, hasty edge that he hadn't felt since he was a teenager.

Wordlessly, the woman knelt next to him on the bench and washed his back. She poured lukewarm water over his head and kneaded his shoulders. Even in the sauna, her fingers had a trace of the sea chill.

"Small man," she said. "With small desires. You'll have it good here, in the bosom of the sea."

Then she bent over and took him in her mouth, her touch just as casual and businesslike as the washing at first, then insistent. Jaakko tried to touch her, hands shaking with lust, but she brushed his fingers away, forcing him down onto the bench. And then it was too late: a hot wave passed through him, forced itself through one blissful, burning spot.

Afterwards, she sat next to him, humming softly, her hair like rivulets of dark gold.

"I made the right choice, my beautiful man," she said. "You'll want for nothing. You will be my husband. I will clothe you and feed you. And you will lie with me and give me a child."

She is like a little girl, Jaakko thought. *A girl who has just discovered boys.*

"A husband," he said aloud. The afterglow made him giddy, and every sensation was sharp, as if the woman's touch was a hook that had drawn him up from the deep waters of unreality. He laughed. "When's the wedding going to be?"

The stove went out. There was a breath of cold wind through the sauna, and the steam coalesced into droplets on Jaakko's skin. The wall felt like ice pressed against his back. The woman's hand turned to cold stone on his thigh, and her eyes glowed green in the dark.

"No wedding," she said, her voice like a crashing wave. "No wedding without a ring."

And then she was gone, and Jaakko was alone in the dark.

Jaakko sat in the kitchen through the night, drinking coffee and eating rye bread with salty Russian sausages until his stomach started to protest.

He wondered when she would come back. The sea seemed calm, but he couldn't bring himself to try the bridge again. During the night, thoughts of the world outside—Minna, the company, all of it—seemed to have slipped away, like water from a cupped hand. Only the island, and the woman, and her husbands, remained.

The dawn was just a pale smear of light above the grey sea, but it restored enough of his courage to think about Kalle again. He blinked the stinging fatigue from his eyes, drank one more cup of coffee and went out.

While following the path, he noticed something he'd missed the previous evening: a flash of faded red among the trees. As he edged closer, he saw that it was an old fisherman's cottage that looked like it was on the verge of falling down. It was no wonder he hadn't seen it before: it was fifty metres or so inland, shielded by trees and undergrowth on all sides except the sea. The thatched roof looked like an angry brow.

This is where he must have lived, Jaakko thought. He hoped to catch movement through the dark windows, some sign that the old man was still alive, but there was nothing.

He found Kalle where he had fallen. The body had sunk into the soft ground a little, and thankfully, the undergrowth hid the old man's face. It had been a long time since Jaakko had seen a dead person and he felt a stab of nausea and guilt. *I did this to him. I can't just leave him here.*

He found a rusty shovel leaning against Kalle's cottage, covered the body with pine branches and started digging a grave. It was easy work in the soft ground, although the hole kept filling with water. Still, he was sweating and the morning haze had brightened into lacklustre daylight by the time the hole was a decent size. The night of lost sleep stung his eyes, and after a while, he sat down, leaned against a birch tree and closed them. *Just for a second,* he thought.

He dreamt that he kept digging, making the hole bigger and bigger, although more dark water kept coming in. And then his shovel hit something metallic with a resounding clang.

"Watch it," said a deep voice.

A little man pulled himself up from the watery grave, bringing a mingled smell of wet earth and rotten fish with him. His face was dark and reminded Jaakko of smoke-stained wood, with a rough-hewn hatchet of a nose and a broad, sharp-toothed mouth. He wore copper-coloured chain mail, and there was an axe made of similar metal in his belt. Rivulets of black water ran down from his hair and beard.

"She caught you, too, then," the little man said.

It didn't occur to Jaakko to be afraid: there was a calm over him, and the colours of the world around him were sharp and clear, like on a bright summer evening.

"Who are you?" he asked.

"Iku-Turso, son of Äijö," said the man, and grinned. "It was my axe that felled the great oak, my teeth that sank the boat that carried Sampo"— the grin became harsher—"and it was me whom the daughter of the sea caught in her net."

Suddenly, Jaakko recognized the dark eyes. They belonged to the fish he had taken from the woman.

"I owe you, child of man," the little man said. "I will help you to get away. But it's not going to be easy. The water woman is old, and this is her place: she is strong here. The only way out"—he pointed at Kalle's body—"is to follow him. Only the dead are slim enough to slip through her net. But Turso can show you the way."

He held out a copper-mittened hand. "Now come down to my house. We'll drink together, and make plans."

Jaakko hesitated. "I'm not sure I want to leave," he said in a distant dream-voice. "She is trapped here, too. I know how she feels. I don't want to leave her alone again."

Iku-Turso spat a black gob to the ground, dark face twisting in disgust.

"Then stay, you fool," he said. "Stay here until you are an old man. Go to Tuoni without a guide. I don't care." The dark water of the grave boiled around his feet.

It still felt like a dream, but the logic of it dawned on Jaako slowly. *It's like a computer game,* he thought. *Find the next thing. Get to the next level. Jaakko Rissanen on Monkey Island.*

Or perhaps it was the other way around. Maybe it was the real world that was the game, the Second Life to this place's First. Maybe it was this world—the place where golden nets spanned the sea and dark little men rose from graves and daughters of gods wanted to marry mortal men—that really mattered.

"Hang on," he told Iku-Turso. "You owe me a boon, right?"

"Yes," sniffed the little man. "A boon. A favour. Anything my life is worth, damn you. If you insist on rotting here, I can bring you treasures from the bottom of the sea. Or if you get tired of that cold bitch, you can have my fiery women, my daughters from beneath the earth. I can give you—"

"Take it easy," said Jaakko. "I only want you to bring me one thing."

When he woke up, the sky was ablaze with the summer sunset. And Iku-Turso's voice still whispered in his head, telling him what he had to do.

It took willpower to pick up the rock that had killed Kalle. It was even harder to peel open the wound in his side and smear some of his own blood on it: the wound was slightly inflamed and touching it hurt so much that it left Jaakko covered in cold sweat.

Then he took the rock to the shore and cast it into the sea. It flew high and far, and disappeared into the water accompanied by a hollow, swallowing sound. *Jaakko throwing the cold stone,* he thought. *That's what Grandma always said. That's when the summer ends.*

Then he sat down on a boulder near the waterline and waited. Everything was too quiet: no birds, no wind in the foliage. But the soft, wet sound of the sea was everywhere, in the air and the ground, and even in his own heartbeat.

The mists of Ahtolanniemi came up and were soon everywhere: a wet veil on his face, fading into a deep bone-white over the dark waters.

The wind rose, and then the cows came from the sea.

They waded to the shore, dun backs and heads and horn-nubs emerging from the water like the mountains of a new miniature continent, silver threads running down from their noses and mouths. Their sides steamed in the dim light, and their hooves made a soft scraping sound on the rocks. The last one wore a brass bell around its neck that started ringing when it emerged from the waves, a steady, hollow rhythm. The cows brushed past Jaakko, vanishing into the woods one by one.

"Come to steal Ahti's cows, rich man?"

The woman was standing right next to him. But she looked different now, younger and more regal. She wore a green dress, a heavy, soaked fabric that clung to her body. She wore a golden net at her waist as a belt. Droplets of water glistened on her brow.

"I'm not here to steal anything," Jaakko said. He tried to summon the angry animal to his voice like last time, but found it curled up in his throat, small and weak. "But it does look like somebody has stolen me."

She took Jaakko's hand in her own, traced a line in his palm. "Just to be my husband, small man. The apple of my eye."

"How exactly did you catch me?"

"In my father's net, of course." Her smile showed slightly crooked teeth, and her voice had the lilt of an excited child. "I will show you!"

They waded into the sea together. The sun was a giant sphere of dark gold and red, just above the brow of the horizon.

The net was all around them in the water. The golden ripples from the waves ran together into loops and weaves, shimmering in a mesh of light just beneath the surface.

"You like nets, small man," she said. "Nets where people babble, nets of words and voices. But can you touch your nets like I can touch mine?"

The woman bent over and reached beneath the surface. The golden net rippled at her touch. She pulled, and it started coming up, glittering things caught in its loops. She picked one of them up—an empty green bottle—and threw it to Jaakko. He caught it instinctively, and felt a sudden wave of intoxication pass through him. For a brief moment, he tasted rich red wine.

The woman laughed. "In my father's net, things are what they are. Now it's your turn!"

She held him, one hand caressing his back, as he started pulling the net up.

He could feel the thing in the water as soon as he tugged at the cold, bright strings. His shoulders strained under the weight and the loops dug deep into the flesh of his palms.

"What have you found, husband?" she whispered. "What little god have you caught to do our bidding?"

She breathed softly in his ear, and he felt a new strength joining his. And then it was in his hand, dark and black and cold, a smooth chilly shape that fit his palm just perfectly, an egg of unbirth.

"*Marta*," she whispered, eyes widening in terror. "You found your *marta*."

Jaakko heard Iku-Turso's voice in his head again. *Make a marta,* it said. *A stone of death. Make the old man's death your own. Cast it into the net. Follow its weight down.*

She tried to pry it from his hand. But Jaakko held it close to his chest and fell backwards into the sea. He took a deep draught of salt water as the waters closed above him.

And then he let the *marta* carry him deeper, down into the dark waters of Tuoni.

There were faces in the sea, in the dark: drowned faces, with bulging eyes and open, gaping mouths. Jaakko didn't want to look at them, but when he couldn't close his eyes, he knew he was to be one of them.

But Iku-Turso was with him, no longer a brown-eyed fish or a little man, but a vast cold presence whose shape boiled and twisted like spilt oil. And it carried him deeper and deeper until the world turned around and they came up again, to the shores of the sea beneath the sea.

The husband waited for him there, in the place without light or colour, standing on the black slippery rocks.

He was young, younger than Jaakko, and strong, with the kind of shoulders and chest that spoke of strength that came from a life of struggle with the sea. But there was something very familiar about his face, a certain roguishness, and a burning need: he saw now that it had been there in Kalle's sunken cheeks as well.

"You know what I want," he told the husband. "Give it to me."

But the dead man just laughed a hollow laugh.

"Go back, warm man," he said. "The children of Tuoni will be here soon, and they will keep you down here forever. We can tell each other tales of her for all eternity and find out which one of us satisfied her best."

"She just wants her ring," Jaakko said.

"Then you'll have to take it." He showed it to Jaakko: a flash of gold on one finger of a pale hand.

Without thinking, Jaakko lunged at him. But the husband was strong, strong and dead. He seized Jaakko by the throat like a child and forced him down to the rocks. Jaakko could feel his trachea yielding beneath the husband's fingers, slippery like an eel.

"Can you hear them?" he whispered. "They are almost here, with their spikes and iron nets. Blind Loviatar will show you her nine pains."

Jaakko struck him with the *marta*, exactly on the same spot that had killed Kalle, and for a moment, the husband loosened his grip. But he merely wiped the black blood from his eyes and smiled again. "You'll have to do better than that, warm man," he said.

"I'm not here alone," said Jaakko. The *marta* pulsed in his hand, slick with gore, blood calling to blood. And then another shape rose from the water, pale and wizened: Kalle, the fisherman's cap back on his head, clothes dripping. And behind him were other shapes, other husbands, all with an angry animal burning in their eyes.

Jaakko turned away and let them do what had to be done.

It was Kalle who gave him the ring, voiceless and dead, sadness in his troll-eyes.

"I'm sorry," Jaakko said, and put the ring in his mouth. Then he dived into the dark sea, let go of the *marta*, and let Iku-Turso carry him up to the waters of the living.

Jaakko watched the first and only fish of his angler catch sizzle on the low flames. The fish wasn't big, but the smell was delicious. It was autumn already, and the sea looked dark and angry. But he wasn't afraid of the sea anymore.

His assistant Rane had come back for him and found him washed up on mainland. He had called an ambulance in time. Jaakko heard later that he had been clinically dead for three minutes. The official story was that he'd been swept away by the current while swimming: the tabloids seemed happy with that.

He did not hear her coming, but felt her in the sea breeze. She wore a green raincoat again and looked just a little bit older.

"I could take you back," she said quietly. "Even now, I could."

Jaakko smiled. "You could."

They ate the fish together in silence, squatting on the rocks, a veil of rain separating them. Jaakko felt something cold and hard catch in his teeth in the soft white flesh.

It was a ring of wrought gold. Bright waves chased each other on the rim, flecked with silver fish.

Jaakko held it out to her. She took it, looked at it for a moment, squeezed it in her hand and closed her eyes.

Then she shook her head. "You keep it," she said, handing it back. "I'm sure you can find someone to give it to."

Jaakko pocketed the ring carefully. "What about you?" he asked. "What are you going to do now?"

"I'll think of something," the woman said.

The wave came from nowhere, crashed into Jaakko and threw him onto his backside. The torrent of chilly water filled his mouth, eyes and ears, and washed down his back. When his vision cleared, she was gone.

"We'll call this the first date," Jaakko whispered and turned his back to the sea.

Invisible Planets
(with apologies to Italo Calvino)

TRAVELLING THROUGH CYGNUS 61, *as it prepares to cross the gulf between the galaxies, the darkship commands its sub-minds to describe the worlds it has visited.*

In the lives of darkships, as in the journeys of any ambassador, there always comes a time that is filled with doubt. As the dark matter neutralinos annihilate each other in its hungry Chown drive heart and push it ever closer to the speed of light, the darkship wonders if it truly carries a cargo worthy of the Network and the Controller. What if the gift it carries, the data it has painstakingly gathered from the electromagnetic echoes of young civilisations and the warm infrared dreams of Dyson spheres, the information written onto tons upon tons of endlessly coiled DNA strands that hold petabytes in a single gram, is nothing more than a scrawled message in a bottle, to be picked up by a fisherman on an unknown shore and then discarded, alien and meaningless?

That is why—before the relentless hand of Lorentz squeezes the ship's clocks so thin that aeons pass with every tick and the starry gaze of the Universe gathers into a single blazing, blue-shifted, all-judging eye—the ship studies its memory and tries to discern a pattern subtle enough to escape entropy's gnawing.

During the millennia of its journey, the darkship's mind has expanded, until it has become something that has to be explored and mapped. The treasures it contains can only be described in metaphors, brittle and misleading and distant, like mirages. And so, more and more, amongst all the agents in its sprawling society of mind, the darkship finds itself listening to the voice of a tiny sub-mind, so insignificant that she is barely more than a wanderer lost in a desert, coming from reaches of the ship's mind so distant that she might as well be a traveller from another country that has stumbled upon an ancient and exotic kingdom on the other side of the world, and now finds herself serving a quizzical, omnipotent emperor.

The sub-mind gives the ship neither simulations nor mind-states but words. She communicates with symbols, hints and whispers that light up old connections in the darkship's mind, bright cities and highways seen from orbit, maps of ancient planets, drawn with guttural monkey sounds.

PLANETS AND DEATH

The rulers of the planet Oya love the dead. They have discovered that corpses in graveyards are hosts to xenocatabolic bacteria that, when suitably engineered and integrated into the gut microbiome, vastly prolong the Oyan lifespan. Graveyards on Oya are fortresses, carefully guarded against the Resurrection Men, those daring raiders who seek more immortality bugs in the fertile soil fed by the long-dead. The wealthiest Oyans—now only vulnerable to accidents or criminal acts—who still cling to traditions of burial are interred in secret places together with coffin torpedoes, elaborate weapons and traps that guard their final resting places from prying fingers.

The wealthiest and the most ambitious of all Oyans is not buried on Oya, but on Nirgal, the dead red planet that has called to the Oyans since the dawn of time. Liberated from the shackles of age and free to fill his millennia with foolish projects without the short-sightedness that plagues mortals, the Oyan constructed rockets to journey to Nirgal and built a great city there, in deep caves to guard it against the harsh rays of the sun.

But others never followed, preferring to spend their prolonged existence in Oya's far gentler embrace, and thus, in the uncountable years of our journey that have passed since, Nirgal itself has become a graveyard. It is populated only by travellers who visit from other worlds, arriving in ephemeral ships, visible only as transparent shapes in swirling red dust. Wearing exoskeletons to support their fragile bodies, the visitors explore the endless caves that still glitter with the living technology of the Oyans, and explore the crisscrossing tracery of rover tracks and footsteps in Nirgal's sands, careful to instruct their utility fog cloaks to replace each iron oxide particle exactly where it was, to preserve each imprint of an Oyan foot forever. But even though they leave Nirgal's surface undisturbed, the visitors themselves carry home a faint taste of despair from the grave of the immortal Oyan, a reminder of their own ultimate mortality, however distant.

Yet Nirgal itself lives, for the hardy bacteria of the Oyan's body burrow ever deeper beneath the red planet's surface and build porous cities of their own in its crust. Stolen from the dead, they are slowly stealing Nirgal for themselves.

PLANETS AND MONEY

On Lakshmi, you know that the launch day is coming when the smell of yeast is everywhere, that sticky odour of alcohol the day after, even before the party starts. The stench comes from engineered bacteria that churn and belch nitrogen-tetroxide fuel in stills and bioreactors in garages and backyards, for everybody on Lakshmi builds their own rockets.

When it gets dark, the rockets will go up like paper lanterns in a hurricane, orange and bright, fiery golden ribbons flowing and dancing, their sonic booms like cannons, delivering their payloads to Lakshmi's growing man-made ring that the planet now proudly wears around its waist. The people of Lakshmi will only watch them for a moment, for as soon as the rocket tails disappear from sight, everyone reaches into their pockets and the night fills with hungry faces illuminated by the paler, harsher fire of smartphone screens, showing numbers going up.

The rocket girls and boys of Lakshmi do not build their machines out of a sense of wonder or the desire to explore, but out of sheer greed, for in Lakshmi, all things are bought with quantum cryptocurrencies mined in space. The rockets carry mints that take the randomness in cosmic rays and turn it into money, stamping each virtual coin with one of God's dice rolls, unique and unforgeable and anonymous. The mints send the coins to their owners in bursts of coherent light, and thus, on each launch night, the sky is full of new stars, each twinkle a clink in somebody's bank account.

Each light-coin vanishes when it is measured and verified, so unless you are one of the shunned entanglement bankers, the only way to live on Lakshmi is to devote all your efforts to the art of rocket-building. Yet, the people of Lakshmi consider themselves to be truly free, free of centralised systems and governments, free of the misguided dreams of the past, free from starships, from galactic empires, from kings and emperors, agreeing only on the constant striving for universal abundance and wealth.

In truth, they are right. For were the Lakshmians to look more closely into the tangled financial relationships amongst the countless light-mints and entanglement banks that orbit their planet, they would uncover deep formulae that connect quantum mechanics and gravity, a way to measure the motion of Lakshmi in the primordial inertial frame of the universe, and ultimately a new theory for building machines that alter gravity and inertia, machines that could lift the very cities of Lakshmi towards the sky and beyond. But that old dream is hidden too deep in the brightness of the many currencies of Lakshmi to be seen, drowned in the thunder of the rockets of the next launch day.

PLANETS AND GRAVITY

When a traveller from the planet Ki visits another world, at first, she feels flattened, less, confined to two dimensions, a prisoner of gravity, every now and then trying to take off like a helpless fly. But after a while, she finds her gaze drawn irresistibly to the horizon and stands rapt and still, staring at the edge of the world, an impenetrable circular boundary that surrounds her in all directions.

Ki itself has no horizons. It is a planet that has become truly three-dimensional. It is hard to say where Ki begins or ends: it is smudged, a stain of ink that spreads on the paper of space and encroaches on the gravity wells of other worlds. The people of Ki are given personal flight units at birth: thought-controlled jetpacks powered by carefully focussed phased-array microwave beams from the vast solar panel fields that cover the planet's entire neglected surface. The cities of Ki are at constant war with gravity, built on top of pillars that are made of electromagnetic fields and iron pellets, so high they reach out through Ki's atmosphere. Other cities encircle Ki along orbital rings, yet others float in the sky, every building a buckyball tensegrity structure lighter than air. Space elevators reach to Ki's Lagrange points, and skyhooks hurl a constant stream of ships and matter out of Ki, dipping in and out of the atmosphere, bending like a fisherman's rod.

Growing up on Ki, you immediately comprehend the nature of the three spatial dimensions, watch the inhabitants of other two-dimensional planets crawl on the surfaces of their worlds without ever looking up, and naturally start to wonder if there are spaces that *you* cannot see, other directions that remain to be conquered: and to your delight, the scientists of Ki tell you that there are many left to explore, ten, eleven or even twenty-six.

However, they add that as far as they know, only the familiar three dimensions are actually infinite: all the others are curled up into a tiny horizon like the surface of a tiny planet, with no room for towers or flying cars or jetpacks, and the only thing that penetrates the forbidden directions is gravity, the most despised of all forces on Ki, the great enemy of flight.

That is why the people of Ki have now turned all their energies to conquering the remaining boundless dimension, time, building great archives that will climb ever upwards through the aeons, carrying a piece of Ki to timelike infinities.

With each planet that the sub-mind describes, the darkship's doubt deepens. It has no recollection of these worlds, yet merely by rearranging symbols, the sub-mind brings them to life. Is it possible that she is a confabulatory agent, a remnant of some primitive, vestigial dreaming function in the darkship's cognitive architecture, and her planets are made of nothing more but the darkship's dreams and fears? And if so, how can the darkship know that it is carrying anything of value at all, or indeed if the ship itself is merely a random mutation in some genetic algorithm that simulates darkships, creating and destroying them in countless billions, simply to find one that survives the empty dark?

Yet there is something familiar in every new world, a strange melancholy and a quiet joy, and so the darkship listens.

PLANETS AND EYES

On the planet Glaukopis, your most valuable possession are your eyes. From birth, you wear glasses or contact lenses or artificial eyes that record everything that you see, and furthermore allow others to see through your eyes, and you to look through theirs. As you reach adulthood, you inevitably choose to focus on a point of view that is not your own, trading your own vision for someone else's. For on Glaukopis, material abundance has been achieved long ago, so that a viewpoint, a unique perception of reality, is the only thing that is worth buying or selling.

Over the centuries of such eyetrade, the viewpoints of Glaukopis have been so thoroughly shuffled amongst ten billion bodies that no two lovers have ever seen each other with their own eyes, no mother has ever beheld her own child, or if they have, it has only been in passing, an unrecognised flash in the kaleidoscope of Glaukopian vision.

A few select dreamers of Glaukopis choose to give their eyes to machines instead: they allow the connectome of their visual centres to be mapped by programmed viruses so that the machines can recognise faint echoes of life in the spectroscopy of distant extrasolar planets in the same way that you recognise your grandmother, with the same instantaneous, unquestionable clarity. In return, they are allowed to look through the eyes of machines, and so they alone have seen what it looks like to fly through the thousand-kilometre water fountains rising from the surface of a faraway moon that teem with primitive life, and the true watercolour hues of the eternal eyestorm that swirls in a gas giant's southern pole. But because they can no longer afford to share these visions with other

Glaukopians, they are scorned, the only blind in the kingdom of the all-seeing.

It is easy for us to mock Glaukopis, having seen the unimaginable visions of our journey, to think them forever lost in an infinite corridor of mirrors. But we would do well to remember that Glaukopis is long gone, and all that remains to us is what their eyes saw. Perhaps one day a machine will be built that will take the sum of the visions and reconstruct the minds and the brains that saw them. Perhaps it will even solve the puzzle of who truly witnessed what, unshuffled the deck of eyes that was Glaukopis.

PLANETS AND WORDS

Seshat is a planet of books, of reading and writing. Not only do the people of Seshat document their every waking moment with words, they also build machines that write things into existence. On Seshat, a pen's ink can be stem cells or plastic or steel, and thus, words can become flesh and food and many-coloured candies and guns. In Seshat, you can eat a chocolate soufflé in the shape of a dream you had, and the bright-eyed ancient chocolatier may have a new heart that is itself a word become flesh. Every object in Seshat writes, churning out endless idiot stories about what it is like to be a cow, a pill jar or a bottle of wine. And of course the genomes of living beings are also read and written: the telomeres in Seshatian cells are copied and extended and rewritten by tiny molecular scribes, allowing the people of Seshat to live nearly as long as their books.

It is no surprise that Seshat is overcrowded, its landfills full of small pieces of plastic, its networks groaning under the weight of endless spam-bot drivel, the work of fridges and fire alarms with literary aspirations, the four-letter library of Babel that flows from the mouths of DNA sequencers, with no end in sight.

Yet the Seshatians hunger for more things to read. They have devised books with golden pages that the Universe itself can write in: books where gold atoms displaced by dark matter particles leave traces in carefully crafted strands of DNA, allowing the flows and currents of the dark to be read and mapped and interpreted. And over the centuries, as the invisible ink of the neutralinos and axions dries and forms words on the golden pages, hinting at ships that could be built to trace every whirl and letter out in the void and turn the dark sentences into light, the people of Seshat hold their breath and hope that their planet will be the first line in a holy book, or at least the hook in a gripping yarn, and not the inevitable, final period.

PLANETS AND RUINS

Zywie is a silent planet. Its empty cities are glorious ruins, full of structures higher than mountains: space towers, skyhooks, space fountains, launch loops, mass drivers, rail guns, slingatrons, spaceplanes, sky anchors, the tarnished emitters of laser propulsion systems, still maintained by patient machines but slowly crumbling.

It would be easy to think that Zywie was nothing but the dried placenta of an ancient birth. Yet in the ocean floors, in a landscape grey and colourless like a reflection of the lunar surface, twisted fragments of great engines are turning into coral castles, their hard sleek lines softened and broken by ringed polyp shapes and multicoloured whorls.

On the continents of Zywie, huge puffed-up balls of precious metal drift down from the sky every now and then. They are platinum, mined in the asteroid belt by tireless robots, melted with sunlight in zero gravity, coalesced into porous spheres like a metal giant's bezoars, and launched at Zywie, where they fall at a leisurely hundred miles an hour, into rainforests and oceans and the silent, overgrown cities. They settle on the ground with a gentle thump and become habitations of insects, birds, moss and lichen.

Beneath Zywie's surface and oceans, endless glass threads are full of light, and the thoughts of ancient machines travel along them, slowly becoming something new.

Zywie's ruins are a scaffold. One day, life will climb up along its struts again, reach up and leave its own ruins behind for others to use, just another stroke of the pen in Zywie's endless palimpsest.

———————

"It seems to me," the darkship tells the sub-mind, slowly understanding, "that all the planets you describe have something in common. They are each defined not by what you speak of but by what is left unsaid. They are all our beginning, our home."

The sub-mind smiles in the desert of the darkship's mind, and in her eyes there are white clouds and blue oceans and endless green.

"Is that why I doubt? Because I can't let go? Because I was made wrong by the Controller, a crippled ambassador, stumbling before the first step?" the darkship asks. "Are you the part of me that still longs for home? The part that defines all things by what it has left behind?"

With the reluctance of an emperor condemning a disobedient but favoured vizier to the executioner's block, the ship summons its self-surgeons, to excise this vestige, to sever this thread that holds it back.

But the sub-mind shakes her head.

"Home is simply the clearest mirror to show the pattern that you seek, o ship, to remind you of something you have forgotten."

"And what is that?"

The surgeons stand by, fractal knives at the ready, waiting for the ship's command to cut and uncreate.

"To be an ambassador, you only need to carry one thing," the sub-mind says.

Heedless of the surgeons, she hurls herself at the darkship's primary mind and embraces it. Her skin smells of sand and exotic spices and sweat and wind and is warm from the sun. She dissolves in the darkship's mindstream, and suddenly the ship is full of the joy that the traveller feels when glimpsing purple mountains in a new horizon, hearing the voices of a strange city for the first time, seeing the thunderous glory of a rocket rising in the dawn, and just as the dark fingers of Cygnus 61's gravity cast it into the void between galaxies, it knows that this is the only thing truly worth preserving, the only constant in the shifting worlds of the Network made from desires and fears, the yearning for infinity.

Ghost Dogs

IT BEGINS WITH A WHISTLE. It echoes in the cool summer evening air and fades into a high note. Ruby immediately pulls her nose out of the hole we have dug in Mum's dead flower bed to look for pirate treasure. She whips around and runs to the fence, thick Labrador tail wagging like crazy. Princess perks up too, puts her bone aside, yawns and pads after Ruby, dignified.

For a moment I think that it's Dad coming home early, and my heart jumps. But no, it's Dog Boy, crouching behind the fence, lanky teenage frame bent almost double, ruddy face pressed against the boards. I stare at him, still kneeling in the dirt with my pirate sword, but he does not seem to notice I'm there.

And then he starts barking, really loud, deep from his chest, like thunderclaps. Princess and Ruby listen, ears pressed flat against their heads. When he stops, there's just the sound of the two dogs panting. And then he stands up and looks at me, eyes big and white.

"Hey, wee man," Dog Boy says. "You know you've got ghost dogs in your house?"

He stands up and crosses his hairy arms across a Nike-vested chest and glares at me. There are mean-looking dark smudges around his eyes, and he stares at me intently like a dog that wants something. My throat is dry, but Princess and Ruby are still wagging, so I don't run inside. I get up and walk to the fence.

"Ghost dogs?" I say.

"Dead dogs, like. Old ones." He scratches his nose and shows his teeth. I catch a whiff of stale sweat and earth from him, and hold my breath. "You better watch out. They can go inside you, make you do bad things."

Grown-ups have this look they get when they are winding you up, like a grin just under their skin. But Dog Boy looks like Mr. Gunn when he's talking about geography at school, dead serious.

"Okay," I say and take a step back, digging my fingers in Ruby's fur. Dog Boy pushes a hairy hand through the fence and Ruby sniffs it, grinning a dog grin, tail still wagging slowly. "Can't be too careful with ghost dogs," Dog Boy says, eyes still fixed on me.

"Simon!" I hear Mum suddenly. "What are you doing?"

She is standing at the kitchen door, a frightened scowl on her face. Dog Boy gives Princess and Ruby one more growl and a yip and starts backing away.

"Looks like you're in trouble," he says.

"You again!" Mum shouts. "One more time and I'm calling the police!"

Dog Boy looks past her into the house at something and lets out a low growl. Then he turns on his heels and starts running down the street, low, loping steps, dirty Nikes slapping the asphalt.

"Simon. Come here," Mum says. "It's getting cold. And you know you shouldn't talk to that boy."

"I didn't want to be inside. And he wasn't talking to me, he was talking to Ruby. And Princess."

"Well, it's bedtime," Mum says and takes my shoulder. "Dad will be home soon."

"Can Ruby sleep in my room?"

"I suppose." She sighs, looking tired. She hugs me tight for a second. She has changed her perfume, third time this month, and she smells strange, like the tanned ladies at Jenners. "But don't tell Dad, okay?"

"Okay," I say and go inside, back to the quiet.

I lie awake in my room for a long time. Ruby twitches and yips in her dog dreams next to me.

It makes perfect sense. If dogs don't go to heaven, they will just stick around after they die, and there will be more and more of them. Loads. Everywhere. I think about every dog I have ever seen. What if every one of them ends up like a ghost? I wonder what so many ghost dogs would eat, and decide that the only thing that would work would be each other. So some of them would be getting bigger and stronger, like in *Highlander*. Thinking about it makes my skin go clammy, like the time when I found the dead bird in the garden, crawling with white worms.

The gurgling of the pipes in the new house sounds a little like dogs growling, and suddenly I really need to pee. I wonder if there is a ghost dog in the room, just waiting for me to get up. But Ruby's breathing and dog smell make me feel safe, and I decide she would know. So I get up, careful not to wake her up. If you do that at night she'll think it's morning and will want to go outside to play.

I decide to use the loo in the utility room so I don't have to go past the bedroom. I sneak down the narrow stairway. The boards under the thick carpet squeak like Ruby's rubber toys.

The utility room is hot and smells of drying laundry that Mum hangs in the rack in the ceiling. The boiler rumbles in one corner. Mum does not like us using the loo there—getting your germs all over the place, she says—but it is harder to be afraid of ghost dogs with an empty bladder.

I open the tap to wash, and something closes around my right hand.

It feels like a dog's grip, cold teeth pressing into my flesh, and it hurts. A wet thick sewer smell rises up from the sink. I try to pull my hand away. The ghost jaws hold tight. Teeth grate against the bones of my wrist. I scream.

Through the pain, I see a wet black dog looking at me from the mirror with bright green eyes.

Far away, a door slams. Then the lights come on and Mum is there.

"Simon," she says, blinking in the light. There are rollers in her hair, they make her head look like a flower bed. "What are you doing?"

The cold pain in my wrist goes down to the pit of my stomach and comes up as tears. "What's wrong with you?" Mum says, grabbing my wrist exactly where the dog's teeth were. The knuckles of her bony hand are white under the Canary Islands tan. "I don't know what to do with you, I really don't."

I look at her eyes, see a glint of green in them and suddenly know where the ghost dog went. She drags me up the stairs to my room and almost throws me back to bed. "Get that dog out of your room, it's filthy. Ruby. Downstairs. Now."

Ruby gets up and shakes her head, ears flapping. Then she darts down the stairs, tail hanging low. Mum slams the door shut behind her.

I curl up under the blanket, pain still pulsing in my wrist. I try to go to the warm spot that Ruby left but it's cold soon.

Inside the walls, the pipes gurgle and bark.

The next day at school, I feel tired. Mr. Gunn's chalk scrapes against the blackboard like a little white dog yipping.

After school, I take Princess and Ruby for a walk, just to get out of the house. They pull at my arm—or Ruby does, Princess is too dignified for that. I let them lead me, just walk and breathe, not thinking, looking at the white marks around my wrist. They still hurt.

It is too late when I realise where the dogs are taking me.

There's three of them sitting on the bench between the Chinese laundry and Scotmid. Dog Boy stands a little away from them, leaning against a lamppost and smoking. They keep looking at him, with a kind of quiet reverence. Princess and Ruby both pull me now, eager to see them.

"Not there," I try to tell them, yanking at the leash so that Ruby's eyes bulge out, but I'm not strong enough. And it's already too late.

The biggest of the three gets up, tosses away a candy wrapper and walks to me lazily. The white flab of his body is barely contained by his tracksuit, and his thick neck makes him look like a bulldog.

"Who's this then?" He is still chewing something, and his pouchlike cheeks jostle.

For a moment the cold weight is back in my gut and bladder.

"I want to talk to the Dog Boy," I say.

"Dog Boy? Well, he only talks to doggies. Are you a doggie?" He crouches down, and even then he's taller than me. There is an angry pimple on his chin, like a tiny white eye. "Why don't you give us a bark, little doggie." He gives me a chocolate grin.

Suddenly I get angry. He's not a ghost dog, he's just a fat kid. "Ruby," I whisper. "Say a big word."

Ruby explodes into an angry bark—except that she's really happy to do it, she's beating the air with her tail. But of course the bulldog boy can't tell and almost falls down on his backside. Princess joins in too, short ladylike barks, like she's telling someone off.

"Fucking mental," shouts one of the other boys, sloughing on the bench, eyes hidden under his cap. "Go, Itchy." The bulldog boy's face goes red. He clenches his fists but doesn't dare to move or take his eyes off the dogs.

"That's enough," says the Dog Boy and walks over. He hunches down and scratches Ruby between the ears. She gives him a dog grin. "That was a good bark. Good girl." He smells of stale cigarettes but Ruby doesn't seem to care.

Then he looks at me and I realise that his eyes—brown, flecked with gold—aren't really dog eyes. They're wolf eyes.

"That bad, huh?" he says, looking at my wrist.

I nod.

"There's always a leader. A boss dog. You find it, you beat it. You stare it down, you show it you're the top dog. That's how you get rid of them."

"Like vampires?" I ask.

"Like vampires, yeah."

"But how do I find it?"

Princess wags her tail at Dog Boy and he gives it an odd, sad look. "They like water. Like wild animals do."

I don't want to go to the utility room again, and it must show in my face.

"Hey," Dog Boy says. "I know what it's like. No one told me how to get rid of them, so you do it. All right?" He squeezes my arm gently: his fingers are sticky and sweaty, but it's a friendly gesture somehow. "Good man."

Then the wolf is back in his eyes. He turns around and flexes his shoulders. "Lads!" he shouts, a bark in his voice. "Let's wake the fuck up!" He picks up a broken pavement stone and flings it, right through the

Scotmid window. An alarm goes off, and the whole gang takes off as one, laughing and hooting as they go.

When I come home, Dad is sitting on the couch in the living room, the gym bag still at his feet, tennis shirt collar open, hands in his lap.

"Hey," he says. I give him a hug. He pats my back clumsily.

Dad smells like he always does after gym, shower gel, and there is a little bit of shaving foam behind his right ear. But I can tell there is another smell underneath, stronger, and his face is flushed. Ruby does her tail-chasing welcome dance around him and Princess puts her head on his lap, offering him her bone. He smiles, but just a little, like a door opening and closing.

"Have you been smoking?" he asks.

I shake my head.

"You smell like you go through three packs a day."

"Maybe you should be a little more interested in what your son is doing," Mum says. She is barefoot, wearing pyjama bottoms and a T-shirt. I can tell she has been home all day, watching the telly. She looks pale and angry.

Dad swallows, jaw muscles clenched. Dad has black hair on the backs of his hands and when he's like this he looks a little like Dog Boy. Or the Wolf Man.

"It doesn't seem to matter what I'm interested in," he says quietly. There is an edge to his voice that makes my wrist hurt again.

"No. It doesn't," Mum says. "There's some leftovers in the kitchen." She doesn't look him in the eye and goes upstairs.

Dad gets up so suddenly that Ruby and Princess scramble up too, ears perked up. "What are you looking at?" he says. "Don't you have home-work to do?" Then he kicks his sports bag aside and walks out through the front door.

I eat the cold pizza slice by myself in the kitchen and decide that the ghost dogs have to go.

I lie in bed until late, until I'm sure Mom and Dad are asleep. It's not difficult to stay awake. There is a rhythm to the sounds in the pipes now, like they are expecting me.

Finally, I get up and go downstairs, bright purple shapes from my table lamp dancing in my eyes. Princess and Ruby follow, their nails clicking on the floor.

I sneak past Dad: he is sleeping on the couch again, underneath the tartan-patterned rug that he likes, the one whose edge Ruby chewed when she was a puppy. Maybe that's what ghost dogs do to people, chew them around the edges until they wear thin and unravel.

Dad takes a deep, rasping breath and turns in his sleep. Ruby suddenly decides that it's time to go out and is about to go and nudge him, but I manage to grab her collar in time. "Ssssh," I tell her. She looks back at me, confused. Then Princess brushes past her towards the utility room, and we both follow.

The utility room feels hot and stuffy. The washing machine's light is blinking, and its window looks like a huge dark eye.

I close the door behind me. It's almost completely dark, just a sliver of summer night sky from the small window near the ceiling.

I step into a puddle of water on the floor and make a small sound at the sudden cold beneath my bare feet. Just as my eyes get used to the darkness I see two pinpricks of green in the shadows. The ghost dog is standing in front of me.

I imagined it would look like a ghost, transparent like some CGI effect, but it doesn't. It's terribly solid, a real dog, a German shepherd with a brown-black, shaggy coat. It's all wet. The puddle on the floor comes from the thin rivulets running down its back and nose. Ruby and Princess make yipping puppy sounds and retreat behind me, their ears flat against their heads. Fear uncoils in my gut and I flip the light switch. There is a dim orange flicker and then the light dies. The toothmarks on my wrist burn white-hot, suddenly, and I bite my tongue to keep from screaming.

There are other shapes in the dark, other ghost dogs, shapes moving in the walls as if under a blanket, different sizes. There is the muzzle of a terrier, the shape of a dachshund. They are all around us, watching. But the black dog is the only one that matters.

My heart is a fist inside my ribs. My nostrils are full of a wet-dog sewer smell. *Small dog*, the smell says. *Yield*, the eyes say. I dig my fingers in the scruff of Ruby's neck, but she whines and backs away, snarling like an angry puppy. The eyes of the black dog are like two car headlights in the distance, coming straight at me. It's like somebody is trying to force me to swallow. Dirty water, like drinking from a toilet bowl, fills my mouth, and angry ghost dog thoughts come with it, into my head. *What are they doing not thinking about me they don't love me anymore I should just take the matches in the kitchen and make some warmth—*

Princess growls. She lunges at the ghost dog and goes for the throat. The ghost dog barely moves, but Princess is tossed aside like a bag of bones, crashing against the wall. She lets out a short painful howl and then lies still. Behind me, Ruby whines quietly.

I don't have time to feel sad. My head clears, and I stare at the ghost dog like I stared at the bulldog boy. It makes an angry sound that is like engine rumbling. I feel it in the wall and the floor. But there is a snarling reply, and it takes me a moment to realise that it comes from my chest.

The eyes come for me again, but I'm ready now. This time it's me who goes inside the ghost dog.

Cold thirsty wet places hiding a master no pack eating the pack strong strong in the dark but cold warm inside let me in—

For a moment I feel sorry for it. Then I think about Dad and the silence in the kitchen and Princess, and the anger comes back and makes me strong.

I walk over to it and grab it by the scruff of its neck. The coat feels wet and oily, but I hold on like I was its mum, shaking it, staring into its eyes. Its ears are flat now, and its tail goes down. Then it rolls over and bares its throat. All the dogs in the walls around us howl, a wet sad sound.

I whistle quietly and they come out of the walls and surround me, my pack. We walk through the sleeping house and leave a trail of wet foot-prints. Princess's old bone is on the floor, next to the telly, and I pick it up.

I open the garden door and throw the bone, as hard as I can. It arches up into the cold morning sky and all the ghost dogs run after it, an avalanche of dark wet dogs out of the door, crazy wild joy in their run. I feel sad when I close the door behind them.

Then I remember Princess.

The utility room is nothing special now, just a stuffy place with laundry hanging from the ceiling. But Princess lies still next to the puddle. Her coat is still warm, but she does not breathe. Ruby pokes her with her nose and whines.

We bury her in the flower bed that morning.

"Princess was a good dog," Dad says, leaning on the shovel. He wipes his face with a dirt-smeared hand. Then he holds me close. He smells of sun and sweat, and looks me in the eye. "You remember her, Simon. That way she won't go away."

Then it's like I can see a bit of her in Dad's eyes, old and wise. And I know that Dog Boy was wrong about ghost dogs.

Mum cries, although she is trying to hold it in, and Dad pats her back clumsily. She flinches, but doesn't pull away. "We could have some flowers there again, I suppose," she says. "Come on, you lot. Let's have some tea."

We sit around the kitchen table together and the shortbread is dry and crumbles all over the place, but I don't care.

Back in the garden, Ruby is playing.

The Viper Blanket

It was All Hallows' Eve when Markku and I went to the church for the last time.

I had found Markku in the TV room of the nappy home. That's what Markku called it, the nappy home. He'd been wearing a nappy for more than a year now. Against a man's nature, he said. It hadn't improved his temper much.

Markku sat in a swing chair and watched *Wheel of Fortune*. The volume was loud, probably because Granny Ruuskanen was making her sound again in the corner, a low painful bleating. Her mind came and went. At least this time she didn't think I was her son.

I cleared my throat. Markku jumped a little, looked at me and nodded.

"So. Are you coming this year?"

Markku didn't look good. He was unshaven, had mottled skin and a fresh pimple on his cheek.

He looked just like Dad used to.

"Sure. Sure I am," said Markku.

"Well. Let's go then," I said. "Do you need to go to the toilet?"

"Nope. I just went."

"You better be sure," I said. "The churchyard has no toilet."

"Nag nag. I'm sure," said Markku. He took his walking stick and wrenched himself up. "Can't keep the family waiting. Wouldn't be proper."

"Nope," I said.

Markku grinned. It was a lopsided grin: a stroke had taken the life from the right side of his face.

"Do you remember the one time we arrived late?"

"Of course," I said.

"Dad was in a hurry then. Where on earth did he find that gypsy?"

"Dad knew what he was doing," I said. "Come on now, let's get these boots on. We should get going."

Markku looked around, confused, and I knew that he was in that October fifty years ago, when Dad brought the family a gypsy from the Rapa swamp and Markku had to hit him over the head with a crowbar when he tried to run.

"Where are we going?" asked Markku.

"To the church. To the family reunion," I said and grabbed Markku's elbow.

Markku wanted to drive. I didn't let him.

"At least give me some smokes," he said. "So my brother has to be my chauffeur, *saatana*. I can still do it myself."

I had known that Markku would be cranky, so I gave him a pack of Marlboros and lit one of them with my Zippo.

"So. What do you have for this year?" asked Markku, mellowed by the first few drags. "We had trouble even before you put me in the nappy home."

I started the car and motioned towards a large plastic sack in the back of the van.

"Just a little something," I said. The lie tasted bitter. "From Somalia, I think. Found him passed out in a ditch after midsummer. Kept him in the basement and fed. So much trouble. Almost gave him to the dog already."

"You sure he's a pagan?" asked Markku.

"I'm sure."

"That's all right, then," he said. "So you found the strength after all."

"Somebody has to," I said. "The young ones don't care."

The Tango Market at Seinäjoki had started a week ago, so I put the radio on. Reijo Taipale sang about Fairyland.

"They couldn't care less," said Markku, and lit another cigarette.

We drove on in silence. The sun was almost down.

The churchyard was quiet. The wooden walls of the church had started flaking since our last visit. The red ochre coating of the tower was almost gone.

We stopped in front of the gate and I helped Markku out. Then we went to get the sack. It wriggled a little, like it was supposed to.

"There's some life left in it," grinned Markku. Leaving the nursing home had cheered him up a bit. Lifting the sack wasn't easy, though: we both started breathing so heavily that speech became impossible.

"Sure there is," I hissed and went to get the cart that somebody had left leaning against the stone fence surrounding the graveyard. Once we got the sack in the cart, I opened the gate using Dad's old key.

The graveyard air felt cool on my sweaty face, much fresher than the nursing home. We pushed the cart together, Markku holding one handle and me the other. Markku still had a burnt Marlboro in his mouth. When I looked at him, a memory came and bit me with sharp viper teeth.

Markku was twelve and I was ten when Dad took us with him for the first time. The horse's flanks steamed in the cold and I kept looking at the big jute sack we had in the back of the cart. I thought Dad had kittens in it. Our cat popped them out like a little fur factory and we had to drown them in the river—nobody in town would have taken kittens from us.

We stopped at the churchyard. Dad adjusted his misshapen cap, lit his pipe and patted the horse on the neck.

"Boys," he said, looking at us more seriously than ever before. "Do you know where the dead go?"

"Heaven," I said.

Dad laughed coarsely, and spat in the snow, staining the white at his feet with brown.

"And how do you know that?"

"From school," I said, uncertainly.

Dad sucked on his pipe and looked at the graveyard, a slight grin on his face.

"Markku, what do they say about us in town?" he said then.

"That we worship Satan," said Markku quietly. "And they always look at you like they're afraid. Always give way. Never ask for a ride."

I remembered that Niilo Liikainen called me a pagan when he lost to me at a billy goat fight during recess at school, and Markku came and hit him so hard that he lost a front tooth and had a nosebleed for the rest of the day.

"You should know, boys," Dad said slowly, "that the Hurme lineage is long and proud. We've always lived on this land. We've been rich and poor, witches and pious men. But always they've been afraid of us. In the bad years they hunted us down and burned us alive. But they never managed to drive us away. Or if they did, we always came back."

"Why?" I asked, and bit my tongue. But Dad looked at me and nodded. "Why?" I repeated. "Why did we come back if we had it so bad here?"

The fire returned to Dad's eyes.

"Because our mother lives here," he said.

The horse whinnied out its fear. And then we saw our family, coming up from the earth.

I lit up while we waited. It was quiet: fallen tree branches rattled in the wind, the trees swayed like thin fingers. We sat on a gravestone quietly and waited.

They came silently, the family from the earth, and their footsteps didn't disturb the leaves. They walked past us, to the church, men and women and children. The first one to go past was an iron-shirted warrior who had a broken sword and blood on his hands. He looked at us with eyes of dirt and knew us.

Dad was the last, his cap perched atop his head. We waved at him as he passed. And then it was our turn to enter the church.

Markku had to take a nitro when we carried the sack up the stone stairs. His face went beetroot red.

"Ticker's gone bad," he puffed.

"They won't mind," I said and gave him such a mean look that he went up the stairs like a man half his age.

The family waited silently in the church. I remembered to take off my hat as we went inside, closed the doors behind us and took a hymn book from the shelf next to the entrance. Markku and I sat at the bench that was almost at the front, next to Dad. We looked around, seeking familiar faces. There were plenty. Grey-skinned, empty-eyed, dark-born. Our family.

At that same graveyard fifty years ago Dad told us about the daughter of Tuoni.

In the ancient times there was a man who went to Tuonela, the land of the dead.

He sought power and words, from the land beyond the black river, from the house on the dark hill. And the daughter of Tuoni took him across, brought a living man to the house of the dead, for he called her fair and she had never heard such words from a man before. But there were no words in Tuoni for the man and so he went away, turned into a snake, slithering through the iron net in the river.

And the daughter of Tuoni followed.

She came from the dark below, sharp-nail, pale-face, dug her way up to the surface of the earth. But the wise man was already gone, who knows where. Beyond the sea, some say.

There came a warrior, Hurmerinta Bloodbreast, who saw the daughter of Tuoni crying on a battlefield. The sight of her made his blood hot and so he took her there, atop dead men's bones, took her and bled her virgin blood.

And that's how we came to be, the red-haired Hurmes, Tuoni-children, twice born.

She lives beneath the church now, the daughter of Tuoni, black worms in her hair, cold iron in her claws, suckling her children with heathen sap. And the family is with her, sleeps in Tuoni-mother's lap.

Waiting for the Hallows' Eve feast.

We started singing. The family hymns had many words, old and strong. Of the birth of blood we sang, and the birth of iron, and other things besides.

> *Three maidens there were,*
> *Three brides strong and hale,*
> *Giving their milk to the earth,*
> *Feeding ground from their breasts,*
> *One gave black milk,*
> *White spilled the second,*
> *Red blood poured the third.*

When the song ended the family arose as one. A wave of thick earth smell rushed through the church.

The daughter of Tuoni came.

She pushed the floorboards aside and arose. She had grown tall: her hair was a tangle of whips or dead birch branches, black and flowing. I didn't dare to look at her face. Her body was pale and stick-thin, draped in dirt and tree roots. Tall she had grown, and I was afraid.

But then I remembered Marketta and the words I had been given.

I held Marketta's hand when she died. It was a warm hand, even after she stopped breathing and closed her eyes, and her grip did not have enough strength left for me to know the difference between life and death.

"Remember to pray," she said, just before the final sleep. It was good that she went like that, sleeping, even though I couldn't say goodbye. But we had been saying our goodbyes for many months already, so maybe they didn't have to be said aloud.

"It's better for her like this," said the doctor.

How was it better? I thought. Better than what we had? Better than when we were young and Marketta was such a *körtti* girl that it stopped my heart, wore a black scarf and talked about God and Jesus, but never without a hay-barn twinkle in her eyes?

And I knew where she was going. To the house on the black hill. How was it better there? Better than here, under the bright sun?

I told Marketta about the family once. Or tried to, anyway. She just laughed and said that Dad was a mad pagan and had made his sons into mad pagans. And it was God's hand at work that I had been given to her, her own mad pagan to be brought to Jesus.

And that was all we ever said about that.

In the end, her hand started to feel cold. I squeezed harder, willing the cold to take me as well. I wanted it to go into my veins and all the way to my heart so that we could lie under the viper blanket together and laugh at the tickling bites.

I knew then what I had to do.

Markku squeezed my hand. "I have to go now," he said. "Mother is waiting."

I watched Markku go, watched him walk between the benches, the family whispering all around him. Dad looked at me and smiled his grey smile. I wished I could have told him what I was going to do, but he would not have understood me. His thoughts were family thoughts now, thoughts that lived in the place I did not wish to go to, in the cold grave-yard earth, in the place between above and below.

And the daughter of Tuoni came and took Markku to her breast. My brother kneeled at the altar and seemed to drown in her hair, and I remembered how it felt, the cold black breast, the smell of the earth, the bitter dark blood in my throat.

Few were the drops of blood that Markku had left, and he fell asleep there, in the Tuoni-daughter's embrace. Hooked fingers caressed his hair.

Finally he arose, and walked back to his seat, effortlessly, without a walking stick. There was a content note to the whispers around him, and I knew that the next morning Markku would still be sitting there, his face pale and cold, and I'd take him and bury him quietly in the spot in the utmost corner of the graveyard. He sat down next to me and started whispering family words to Dad. I had become a shadow to him, a warm wraith of the waking world.

Then the family was quiet again, waiting. I got up and shouldered the sack. It was heavy, but the strength of the family blood was in me now, and I carried it easily towards the altar.

It was September when I burned Marketta and scattered her ashes. She went away lightly, carried by the north wind.

I cried again, surprising myself: I had thought I had no tears left.

Then I walked into the woods. I walked until it was dark. I walked until a sleep came, or perhaps a waking brighter than waking, I do not know. And the cold of Marketta's hand was in my mind and in my heart and it led me on, took me deeper and deeper into the forest.

I came upon a black river, deep and wide. On the opposite shore was a dark hill upon which stood a crooked house, larger on the inside than on the outside. Quiet moans drifted across the river.

A woman waited for me on the shore. Her hair was darker than the river water, and her dress flowing black velvet. Her face was proud and beautiful, but etched with sorrow. I knew it was the face of a mother.

"What brings you here, grey-haired warrior man?" she asked. "Is it iron that brings you? Or water? Or fire?"

"It is grief that brings me," I said. "Will you carry me across?"

"Grief will not take you across the river; grief will not bring a man to Tuoni," she said. "Only one man has come deathless, and that is enough. I have no more daughters to be stolen away."

She paused, and touched my cheek, and her hand was cold. In her eyes there was iron, and fire, and blood. And something older besides.

"I believe you are my kin, warm man," she said.

"I am your kin," I said. "Although I wish I wasn't."

I faced the daughter of Tuoni in the church. Her eyes were blood red, her lips black, her face bone white. And I was no longer afraid.

I put the sack down and saw the hunger in her eyes.

"Look, my Tuoni-mother, fair daughter of Tuoni, look what I have brought you," I said and opened the sack.

The hissing of vipers filled the church.

I had gathered them with my own hands, and fed them, and now they came, the saw-backs, the worms of Tuoni, sharp-toothed vipers. They came like a black river, and swarmed over the daughter of Tuoni, climbed her limbs and covered her in a hissing, squirming blanket. She screamed: a high, furious keening, and it cut me to the bone. But I bit the pain down and spoke the words I had been given.

> *So says Tuonetar, the good mother:*
> *My old back is tired, my arms are too weary,*
> *To ferry the dead across the river,*
> *To weave their blankets in my house.*
>
> *Come back to me, my daughter*
> *Come back to my dark house,*
> *Come and row across the river,*
> *Be the joy of your mother worm.*

There were more words I said. The birth of iron I said, and the birth of fire and blood. But older than them is one, the birth of worm, the birth of Tuoni, the birth of death. And that I saved for the last.

When the family saw the viper blanket and the pain of the daughter of Tuoni, they let out a terrible cry. They arose and rushed to the altar to sweep the snakes away: but when their grey hands seized the snakes, the snakes bit and the burning poison of Tuoni went into the family blood. I stood and watched. The fire lit up in their eyes and fiery tears poured down their faces, burning, consuming. Markku and Dad looked at me, snakes in their hands.

"I'm sorry," I said. "But it's time to go home. It can't be so bad, not if Marketta is there. And she's all the family I ever wanted."

There was such hate in their eyes that I had to turn away. I ran, and slammed the doors of the church shut behind me.

The fire of Tuoni passed from the family to the wooden walls and ceiling and went wild. It took a long time for the church to burn down. I sat on a gravestone and watched and listened to the screams of the family inside. And I had no more tears to cry, except smoke tears, false tears.

I live in the nappy home now, although I don't have a nappy yet. I checked myself in: I had nowhere else to go. It's not too bad here. Sometimes I have a quick smoke when the nurses can't see.

Sometimes I see the faces of all the unbaptized we gave to the daughter of Tuoni, and grieve. But if they have something to say to me, they can say it when I meet them in the dark house.

And I know that Marketta waits there too. Waits for me, and weaves a viper blanket.

Paris, in Love

It was his mother who sent Antti there, of course. "You need some glamour," she said. "With those rough hands and rubber boot feet, you will never find a woman." He did not believe her, but went anyway. And so he found himself getting off the bus from Beauvais, staring at the most beautiful city in the world. Antti did not know it, but Paris looked back at him: at the dirty straw-blond hair, the rough boots, the plaid shirt and jeans, the forty-year-old ruddy face; and it fell in love.

At first, Paris just flirted with him, coyly, like a court lady showing a hint of an ankle under her skirt. Antti saw richly carved stonework, wrought-iron balconies and crowded riverbanks. There was a playful shower of rain that felt refreshing after the hot bus journey. Everywhere, there was the smell of fresh bread. Pastries and éclairs were sold at every corner. Elegant women rushed past him, tendrils of every hue of perfume after them. And there was not a single dog turd in sight.

The flow of the crowd carried him past the little hostel his mother had booked, and to the Ritz on Place Vendôme. Not knowing any better, he accepted the Suite Impériale for a week from a pencil-moustached concierge—who had, in fact, mistaken him for a Formula One driver.

The next day, the city put on some makeup for the first date. She brought Antti to the Louvre just after sunrise. There was a haze in the air, and light poured through the glass pyramids like fine chardonnay. As if by accident, he passed the queues, going in through the Porte des Lions entrance while looking for a toilet. Blinking, he walked through Galerie d'Apollon. The gold and the art were like a sea of beauty he could feel himself drowning in. He held up his N95 to take a few pictures for his mother, but it was too much.

Paris gave him her best flirtatious smile through that famous one in the Denon gallery, but Antti didn't even notice. Exhausted and perplexed, he made his way out of the endless corridors and sat down at the tables next to the statues on the balcony of the Louvre cafeteria. He saw a man with a serious face whom he instantly recognized as another Finn, trying to read the museum guide.

Sakari was a policeman on holiday: he looked like the weight of the world pressed down on his shoulders, and there was a hint of wildness to his sunken cheeks. But Antti gladly accepted a countryman's company in this strange place. One thing led to another, and they found themselves having a drink or a few, first in Harry's Bar, then at Hemingway's in the Ritz. Amazingly quickly they found themselves in a state of proper Finnish drunkenness, with that special edge that being abroad grants it: throwing a hundred *perkeles* and *saatanas* in the air at anything that looked even remotely strange or foreign.

It was Sakari's idea to see the Crazy Horse girls. Later, Antti had recollections of women clad only in multicolored lights. Futilely, he tried to stop Sakari trying to climb onto the stage to grope at one of the girls clad in strangely revealing military uniforms.

Then it was suddenly hours later, somehow, and they were having an impromptu wrestling match with Sakari in Jardin du Luxembourg, next to the Grand Bassin. The children who sailed the little boats screamed delightedly at them, but they got disapproving looks from the lovers (and through them, from Paris) sitting on the olive metal chairs. After Sakari threw Antti into the basin using an improvised full nelson, a gendarme came and firmly escorted them out.

In the subway back, Antti fell asleep, listening to a guitarist playing a heartfelt Pink Floyd melody. Sakari got annoyed that no one would look him in the eye and got off at the wrong stop. Antti never saw him again.

The next day Paris finally came to Antti as a woman. She asked him for a light on the bank of the Seine. She was beautiful even through his hangover: legs like the arcs of Pont Neuf, nose as straight and perfect as the obelisk on Place de la Concorde. Her smile was not unlike that famous one, the one he had seen in the Louvre. And at last, he smiled back.

They had no common language, but it did not seem to matter. They watched the riverboats from Ponts des Arts and played boules on hot sand in Arènes de Lutèce. His heart jumped when she laughed at a sausage dog diving into the Seine with a splash.

When they made love in the Suite Impériale that night, the Eiffel Tower had all its ten thousand lights on, running up and down its length like a celestial sparkler.

But in the morning, he looked at her sleeping form that fitted perfectly against his body, and a familiar terror rose in Antti: the one that haunts the men of Pohjanmaa, that there might be an end to the drinking and the hard work somewhere. He gathered his things quietly, without waking her, and took the bus to Beauvais. As the plane left the soil of France, he felt a strange mixture of longing and freedom.

When Paris awoke, her anger was a terrible thing to behold. Later, the police argued about how the riots started and how the hundreds of cars were set aflame. But in the end, in Paris, what else could it have been but a woman scorned?

Antti was not able to escape Paris completely. When he slept in the bedchamber of his old house in Pohjanmaa, he dreamed of her. Every morning he kept his eyes closed just a little longer, dreading the cold of the floorboards, knowing that the view outside did not promise a lover's touch: just the cold glare of a grey sky and the sullen yellow of the fields.

One September morning, when the fall had just arrived, he slept even longer than usual, dreaming of feathered boas and a midget juggling chainsaws and female forms clad in light. Suddenly it seemed like the French of his dreams spilled out and into the cold air: there were voices outside, shouting, and somebody was banging on his door.

When he opened the door, the Crazy Horse girls were there, with goosebumps all over that lovely flesh, standing in puddles of mud and fragile ice. They were shivering, hugging the little birds of their identical bare breasts. They spoke urgent French to him through chattering teeth, waving their hands, feathered headdresses like an autumn forest.

And out there, in the fields of his farm, next to the toothpick piles of the hay barns, were buildings, like stone ships emerging from the light morning mist, covered in statues and glinting gold.

He warmed up the sauna for the Crazy Horse girls, and refused politely, blushing, when they invited him in. Then he drove them to town in threes and fours in his battered old Mazda. Antti later heard that they joined up with a group of Lapp rap stars and took a tour bus up north to Rovaniemi, successfully adapting their act for the colder climate by introducing reindeer skins into their skimpy wardrobe.

After the last trip he came back and stared at the pieces of French national heritage on his fields. There was Dôme des Invalides, and Opéra Garnier, and of course Crazy Horse, sitting there like discarded slices of Camembert, all the fragments of Paris he had dreamed about through the cold night.

The next morning it was the bookshop from Montmartre that he had liked, and Pierre's pâtisserie from Rue de Rivoli; and the day after that, the Louvre. They arrived on Antti's fields out of nowhere, like baroque flying saucers, one by one, just stood there like they had always been in a flat land with a grey sky. Soon, Antti's farm was completely swallowed, his house wedged between the Panthéon and Notre Dame.

Paris brought people with it, too. Shivering mimes prowled the streets of Oulainen, trying to make enough money for one cup of bitter Finnish coffee. Young lovers defied hypothermia in the thin snowdrifts of late September. One morning Antti was woken up by a gentle rain of parkouristas, one of whom fell through his roof. He took care of the stray Parisians the best he could, turning his barn into a temporary shelter.

Still, the situation was not without its advantages. He was able to take his mother to visit Louis Vuitton, and they had coffee together in a little cafe that was determined to keep going even though most of the clientele consisted of Antti and his friends who frequented a nearby gas station. Antti's mother looked at the early autumn sunset, red and gold above the rooftops and riverless bridges of Paris. She touched his cheek with quiet pride, tears shimmering in her eyes.

Finally, the authorities took notice: since everybody in France had been on holiday until September, the matter had escaped the Parisians' attention. Once the French caught on, they blamed Al-Qaeda, aliens, or a Nokia mad science experiment, depending on which day of the week it was. Glumly, Antti watched Finnish Army troops moving carefully through the heart of Paris. When the urban planning commission of the EU got involved, he knew it was time to act.

The next morning, Antti went outside before the dawn, stood on his porch and wished Paris had a face for him to look at. He settled for the mosaic window of Notre Dame. The constant plain winds of Pohjanmaa blew between its towers softly, almost sounding like the language of love.

"It's not you, it's me," he said. "I can't fill you on my own. They will take bits of you back, and build you again, and you'll be empty."

"I don't want that. Because—"

Antti struggled to say that thing that a Finnish man only says very quickly, with something caught in his throat, his face a little red perhaps: but meaning it more than anyone else in the world.

"Because I love you."

And Paris held its breath in the stillness of the morning, and waited.

"Tell you what," Antti said. "In the winter, I will come back."

The next night Paris returned, as if it had never left, taking it all with it—the hill of Montmartre, and the boules players and even the mimes and the girls of the Crazy Horse (much to the disappointment of the reindeer herders of Lapland). The only thing that remained was a thick layer of dog turds, all over Antti's fields, meant as a gift of fertilizer.

Now the people of Oulainen smile knowingly when the first snow falls and Antti drives away in his tractor, going south for the winter. But during warm summer nights, just before that moment when the sun dips below the horizon, he walks across his fields with a bouncy gait. And if you listen carefully, you can still hear distant chanson music all around.

Topsight

THE NIGHT before Kuovi was supposed to fly home, the four of them went to bring back Bibi's soul.

She waited for the others on one of the Lily's landing stages. Her mouth tasted of sleep and her eyes stung. In the dark, the floating city of the Estuary—decommissioned oil platforms and moored ships—looked more like what they actually were. The builders had covered the Lily with colourful housing units and green gardens. But underneath, it was still a thing of ugly rusty metal and concrete, made to suck oil from the ground until there was no more left. It had cheated Kuovi when she first came, showing her bright colours and reflections in the water. But now she knew the truth.

It didn't matter anymore. Today, she would go home. But there was one last thing left to do.

The low whine of an engine broke the silence. A small boat approached, a low shape against the lights of the Island. Kuovi waited until it slid to a stop by the landing stage. She held up her phone to cast dim light over the three figures on board.

"Hi," she said quietly.

Branjo sat at the back, hands in his lap, steering with a cheap halo—a clear plastic headband with brain-computer interface circuitry printed into it. He squinted at the light, chunky kickboxer's shoulders hunched, and gave Kuovi a barely perceptible nod. But Aoko got up, almost fell when the boat swayed beneath her, offered Kuovi a soft hand and pulled her in.

"Sorry for being late. Chris couldn't get up. Lazy sod."

The bearded, heavyset man wearing a padded vest waved a hand at Kuovi. Aoko grinned, white teeth flashing in the dark.

"Sorry, buddy, but we need to do it early, before the sorcerers wake up. Did you bring it?"

Kuovi held up the small soul bottle she had run off from Mum's fabber the day before. It was blue glass and had a delicate, arced neck.

Aoko took it between her hands and looked at it critically. "It's a bit small," she said. "It's not going to hold very much."

A thick gob of anger rose into Kuovi's throat. She should have been sleeping. She had one day left with her Mum before going home. She had already said goodbye to Bibi. The whole home-bringing ritual thing had been Aoko's idea. Some African tradition she had no idea Bibi's people even cared about. To make sure her spirit was at rest. To make sure she would look after them all. To keep her ghost from being used for evil ends by sorcerers that were supposedly everywhere, just waiting for people to die.

"I thought Bibi would like it," she said, and reached across the boat and grabbed the bottle.

"I think it's nice," Chris said. He sniffed and started rolling a cigarette with thick fingers. "Like a bird."

Branjo said nothing.

Aoko sniffed. "All right, sweetie. Let's get going. We don't want to keep her waiting."

Branjo frowned and the boat started moving across the dark water, picking up speed.

Aoko used her phone to find the exact spot where they had scattered Bibi's ashes a month before. She stretched it into a big screen so they could all see. Profiles from Threads flickered across it, and the girl whispered to them, tapped them away with her logo-encrusted fingernails.

Kuovi looked away. She hadn't used the app for a month. Whenever she did, she would see Bibi's Thread, her digital ghost, automatically liking things she would like, even after the police had found her in the water, floating, face down. It took such a long time to die properly. It wasn't fair.

When they approached the spot—in the middle of the Estuary, far from the shore—there was the first hint of purple light in the sky. A small swarm of quadrotor drones followed the boat at a respectful distance: the silver discs of their blades caught the first rays of the sun. Bibi's other friends, watching through Threads.

When Kuovi scooped up the water from the river, there was a leaden feeling in her gut. Her father had told her about funerals in old multiplayer games and the griefers who would raid them, diving down from the sky on dragons and flying mounts, raining spells on mourners. But nothing happened. The water was cold. Her sleeve got wet. The bottle filled with a gurgle. Aoko laughed when Kuovi held it up, blue and wet and filled to the brim.

"That's our girl," she said. "Now, let's take her home."

On the way back, Kuovi huddled behind Chris's back against the wind and held the bottle close to her chest.

Bibi's flat had been empty for a month, but Branjo still had the key. Kuovi had only been there a couple of times. It was in one of the decommissioned ships, and getting in required a long climb up rickety metal stairs along the curve of the hull.

Inside, there was a cramped living room, a cupboard that served as the kitchen, and a small bedroom. A roughly fabbed low table. Mixed clothes Bibi brought from her charity shop job. A gutted dragonfly drone sat on a foldable desk. The watercolour painting Kuovi had given Bibi was still there, the one with the godwits in flight. Later during the day, Amazon would come and pack everything up. Kuovi wondered if Branjo would keep the painting.

"Welcome home," Aoko said solemnly and set the bottle in the middle of the table.

Chris clapped Branjo on the back. "Did you hear that? Let's get the party started." He took out his phone and started playing music on it, booming, heavy drum and bass. Branjo put his backpack on the table and took out plastic cups and three screwtop bottles of vodka, poured for four. Chris lit a scented candle that sat on the table next to the soul bottle.

They all drank. Kuovi only tasted a little: it was sour and cheap. She pushed her hands into her armpits and sat as far away from the table as she could, under her painting, her back against the wall. The music made it easy to stay away from the conversation. She kept looking at the soul bottle, the blue hue she got from Bibi's eyes, but Bibi wasn't there.

"It was crazy," Chris was saying. "She just came to the office one day, asked me if I wanted to buy a city in Mongolia. I thought she was crazy, but it turned out there was a whole ghost city there, all wired and ready to go, control systems, ubicomp, you name it. Built for a supply chain war somebody lost. They rented it out for testing city apps. I own it now. I was there last week. You haven't played Pac-Man until you've played it with trams. I'm going to open source the whole thing, give it to city hackers. Tiritror, it's called."

"She was from somewhere called that," Branjo said. His voice sounded rough.

"Well, I don't know where she was *from*," Aoko said, "but I know she was homesick. We worked at the Nero at the airport, see, and whenever we'd have a break, she'd go and look at the planes. I thought she liked them, but you see them all the time there, get used to them, you know? But she would always look. So I asked her. You know what she said? 'I look at the big snakes in the sky, fighting.'"

Branjo tossed back the contents of his cup, looked down, eyes dark. Aoko squeezed his knee. "She's here with us, you know. Don't be sad." Then she turned to Kuovi. "What about you, Finnish girl? Do you have a story about Bibi?"

Kuovi looked at their faces. Her head felt heavy. She stumbled up, hit her knee on the table; the soul bottle wobbled. Her heart jumped.

"I need to go to the loo," she muttered, went to the bedroom and closed the door behind her. She bit down tears and lay down on the bed. The sheets were crumpled where Bibi had slept on her last day. She hugged the pillow to keep the sound of her crying down, wrapped her arms around it. It smelled of Bibi's coconut shampoo, mixed with dust.

There was something under it, a soft, knitted thing, with a hard band inside it.

Bibi's halo.

Bibi had always worn it as long as Kuovi had known her. Plastic and sensors under a knitted hat of white wool that had looked a little dirty against the perfect ivory of her teeth. Bibi had not had it when they found her in the water. That's where the mugging theory had come from. The police had not bothered looking for it, they had the backup image anyway.

The door opened. Music and light poured in.

"You shouldn't be here."

Branjo looked at her, holding a bottle in one limp hand, and closed the door behind him.

"She never liked people looking at her things. I guess you don't understand that," he said.

"I understand," Kuovi said quietly. But not why she was with you, she thought.

Branjo took a step forward, swaying.

"Did you ever run? Really run? So hard that you can't breathe, but if you stop they catch you." He grabbed Kuovi's shoulder with his free hand, suddenly. She let out a little shriek. Then Branjo let go and made a sound that was somewhere between a cough and a laugh. "Of course you didn't."

Kuovi got up, a cold knot in her stomach, fingers around her phone in her pocket. She took a step towards the door, but Branjo made no move to follow. He sat down on the bed. It creaked under his weight.

"It wasn't my fault," he said. "I set her up with some drone jobs, nothing bad. She was really good. Never anything dangerous. Never anything with the Jamaicans. It was just an accident." He dropped the bottle and squeezed his temples with his wrists. "Just a bloody stupid accident."

Kuovi ran. The aluminium of the walkways rang under her feet, long legs, long steps. The air cleared her head. She felt cold and light. The platforms and the ships were putting their morning faces on. The boat buses to the city roared past, white foam in their wake. Everything looked sharp and clear. It's the last morning, that's why, she thought.

She was breathing hard and sweating when she got to the Lily. It was not until she was taking the elevator up to Mum's flat that she noticed she was still clutching the halo. She put it in her coat pocket. Her phone was buzzing as well, apologies from Branjo, a request to come back from Aoko, calls from Mum. She ignored them, walked through the rooftop garden and went inside.

Mörkö greeted her in the flat and rubbed its spiky spine against her legs.

Mum worked for BAE and the other big ones as a consultant. She liked to show pictures of Scooby Doo, the old remote-controlled anti-IED bot that soldiers had sacrificed themselves for, just a piece of metal with camera eyes. People saw themselves in everything, she said. She tried to make things that were purely Other.

Mörkö was one of her failures. It rolled onto its back to show its plastic belly, waved its six legs in the air. The rat brain emulation inside its ugly head was smart enough to know something was wrong.

"Kuovi?"

Mum turned on the lights. She had a cup of tea in her hand and she wore her Marimekko night shirt. Her golden hair was thin and wild. Mörkö ran to her, claws scrabbling on the floor.

"Kuovi, you should have said it was going to go on so late. Early. I was worried."

"I guess the sorcerers woke up," Kuovi said wearily. "I'm sorry. I'm going to go to bed."

"Well, it sounded like a nice ceremony," Mum said. "Did I ever tell you about a friend of mine who got his ashes made into memory diamonds, and then they entangled them at Caltech—"

"Mum." Kuovi closed her eyes.

"All right, all right. Sorry. Too late for stories." Mum took her hand. "Goodness. You're cold. Have a shower, go to bed. But don't sleep too late. I'll make breakfast. I was hoping we could do something together before you go. I should have bought you clothes as well. And we never talked about trying again next year for the schools, I never spoke to Maggie at RCA, we could—"

Kuovi's shoulders shook. Mum's hand was rough and warm. She allowed herself to be hugged, just for a moment.

"Ssh, it's going to be okay," Mum said.

Kuovi took a deep, shuddering breath.

"I'll need different clothes in Finland, Mum," she said weakly. "It'll be winter there." Grey slush and rain and wind.

"It's winter here too," Mum said.

"Good night," Kuovi said gently. She bent down and kissed her mother's forehead. There was a faint 3D printer feedstock smell in her hair that never seemed to wash away.

Before Mum hugged her again, Kuovi pulled away, kicked off her shoes, went to her room and closed the door to stop Mörkö from getting in.

Kuovi undressed, threw her clothes onto the floor and lay down on her bed. She smelled and felt sticky but could not bring herself to care.

It was hard to get to sleep. The room looked empty without her things in it: everything was in clamshell suitcases, and the BeadBrick walls were bare. Maybe she would sleep on the plane. Maybe she would sleep when she was dead, face down in the water. Or snow, if she was lucky. Snow would be better, cold and powdery. She missed snow.

She wished she could talk to Bibi about going home.

It was nice that Mum had waited. When she remembered to, she tried very hard. That's why Kuovi had chosen to spend the gap year with her in the UK, that and the half-hearted attempts she had made to get into art schools. Dad would never say it, but he would be pleased that it hadn't worked out.

One time, Mum had even asked Bibi to join them for dinner. Bibi showed up early and brought a present, an old paper book on the Canvey Island Monster from the charity shop where she worked on Sundays. Mum turned it in her hands, delighted. She clearly wanted to go away and make sketches of the strange gilled, web-footed creature that had supposedly washed ashore eighty years ago. But she made an effort and stayed. It was the perfect gift. Bibi had always known what to do, always what to give and say—

Kuovi sat up. Suddenly, she was completely awake. She picked up her coat from the floor and took out Bibi's halo.

Bibi never did anything without a purpose.

She put the halo on. It was a little tight, and got stuck in her long hair. For a moment, nothing happened. Then there was a brief faint headache, like from being upside down. Was that supposed to happen? She had only tried a halo a couple of times, long ago, to play a silly swordfighting game. Halos were illegal in Finland, after the Kokkola shooting.

The headache faded. It was pointless. There had to be a password, or some specific pattern you had to think about. She grabbed her phone and opened a sherlock app.

"How do I unlock the halo of a . . . dead person?" she asked.

A lot of the answer was geekspeak, in the soft, hesitant voice of the app. It sounded like Kuovi would have to do something like open up Mörkö's head, plug it into the halo and write a program that would search through the space of all possible thoughts. The police could do it. She quizzed the app further, asked about how to guess halo passcodes. Her stomach tightened up when she did, that sort of thing could be picked up by the cops. She shook herself. She would be out of the country in a few hours. She told the app to go on.

Halo passcodes could be anything. Memories. Dirty images. Old-fashioned passwords, typed out on a mental typewriter. Usually something strong you could summon up quickly. But the sherlock said it wasn't necessary to get it perfectly right. The halos were based on machine learning algorithms. They had to be trained by their wearer, but the matching was fuzzy. Getting close might be enough.

Kuovi closed her eyes. It had always been so hard to see what was going on behind Bibi's constant smile. She had no idea what Bibi would consider important. But if Bibi had wanted her or somebody else to have the halo, it had to be something obvious. She thought about the faces of Branjo, Aoko and Chris in succession. Nothing. What did Bibi have in her flat?

A painting, with a flock of godwits, taking to the air.

Kuovi thought about the birds, about the day she had met Bibi.

She had been trying to get a photograph of a godwit, on a sunny Saturday. It had been a long walk along the marshland in her Nokia rubber boots. The birds were in shallow water, pecking it with their long beaks, running around, rust-coloured necks bopping up and down. Kuovi hunched a good fifty metres away, balancing her freshly printed 400mm objective for her phone in the crook of her arm. It had taken several iterations in Mum's fabber to get it right, for quick shots and a good zoom. She wanted a picture of a bird eye, with a landscape reflected in it, some of the Estuary platforms perhaps.

But it was difficult to get close to the birds, and mostly she ended up with blurry shots of wings. She thought about using the phone in full lifelogging mode, and then just finding attractive frames that would work, but that would have been cheating.

People forgot about that now, she thought, the ability to catch just the right moment, the right light and angle, with intuition and instinct. You could get apps trained off the brains of professional photographers to do it for you. But they couldn't *see* for you.

That didn't mean she could do it either. She looked at the latest sequence of shots. "*Paska,*" she swore. Rubbish again, just things, not a pattern. She just saw a bunch of birds running around while marsh water sloshed inside her boots.

Somebody laughed. Kuovi's cheeks burned. She felt like a stork, stepping out of the water onto a small grassy clump of earth. She righted herself with some effort and tried to ignore the sound.

The clump crumpled under her feet and forced her to take several stumbling steps. Her boots took another deep slurp of the marsh water. Kuovi almost collided with the person who had laughed. She was small—although everybody her age was small compared to Kuovi—angular dark face, an old Afghan coat and a white knitted hat. She looked at Kuovi intently, her eyes two blue points that seemed to swallow the world.

"I'm sorry," the girl said. "But you do it wrong."

Kuovi sniffed. "I know," she said. She bit her tongue. Kuovi, master of snappy comebacks. Perhaps she should have a sherlock for that, like some people at school back in Finland. Only, once you all did that, you were left with nothing: a chorus of nonsense. She could do nonsense on her own.

Kuovi pushed past the girl—what point was there in living in the Estuary if you could not get away from annoying people when you wanted to?

"No, no," the girl said. "I will show you."

Kuovi stopped. The girl's smile was warm. Kuovi snuck a peek at her phone. No trust tingle in her palm that would have revealed a Threads connection. It was a bit rude to have such a long googleblink, but the girl had been rude first.

"All right," Kuovi said finally. "Show me."

"You have to look up," the girl said.

Then she ran right at the flock of birds, waving her hands and shouting, *coo-ee, coo-ee*. The birds took off in a cloud of fluttering wings and cries and beaks. Their shadows played on the water. Kuovi looked up. The flock made a beautiful arc above her, and there was a pattern in it, sudden like a smile. She lifted her phone.

The girl grinned at her and waved. "See?" she shouted.

The halo vibrated gently. Ultrasound fingers tickled her brain.

A forest of apps opened in front of her, little icons like faces. She did not recognise any of them, except Threads, of course. The most-used one was called Topsight. The icon was a bright blue eye. She tried to open it, but the halo fumbled, did not recognise the commands her brain was trying to give. There was feedback, too. It felt like the hangover after the night she and Bibi had walked along the Canvey sea wall with a bottle of white rum. The halo was smart enough to open a calibration screen, made her move a ball around with her mind, flashed shapes and colours at her until the feeling subsided.

Then she opened Topsight.

At first, there was just a slight dizziness. The edges of her vision blurred.

She felt strangely light, like in a dream when she could sometimes decide to float up and look at things from above. Everything looked the same—except that there was a faint green outline around her suitcases. She looked at them.

Suddenly, they became serpents of green light, flowing out of the door and beyond, highways of ghost suitcases that extended all the way to the horizon. She followed them with her gaze and was swept up, a bodiless viewpoint looking down a green line drawn across Britain and the North Sea, crisscrossed by a moving, shifting spiderweb of airplane routes. She blinked and was back in her body. Her legs trembled.

She sat back down on the bed and pulled on her trousers—and saw another winding light snake that stretched across the Earth, more complex this time, supply chains and logistics and manufacturing. She shook her head and the vision vanished again. She pulled on dirty socks, staying focused on her room, and nothing moved this time, except for a vague awareness in the back of her head of a city in China that made all the socks in the world.

Light-headed, she opened her door. Mörkö had been sleeping behind it and scrambled up, did its morning dance around her. She could barely look at it: the little drone was an explosion of lines and facts and connections. Was this how Bibi had seen the world? Overlaid with all the invisible things everybody had forgotten about? There had to be more to it than that.

She went outside, past the neat flower rows and trees of the garden: interconnected boxes of metabolism and ecology, entwined with the sea and the sun and the sky.

Then she climbed up to the observation deck of the Lily.

She looked at the hulls of the ships, and saw the shapes of their journeys, overlaid as a spiderweb on Earth, saw the shifting of supply chains that were everywhere like living things, Bibi's snakes dying and being born: saw network links severed and converging to the Estuary like snapped rubber bands leaping back to their origin.

London, a great blaze in the mouth of the river. Emotion maps made from halo data spread over the city. Little stars where people had sex, great blue swathes of sleep, a network of yellow stress and anxiety of the early morning commuters. Financial markets crashing over them like waves. With a thought, she could go back and forth in time, like in Threads, except it wasn't just a timeline of people; it was a timeline of everything. It showed how everything fit together. But Threads were there too, social networks forming and dissolving. She saw how they fit with the locations and the economics and the transportation and the great snakes of economy that swallowed all the little serpents of light that made the world work.

She saw everything, and it all made sense. It had to be more than just the app, there had to be a community out there, people who saw meaning in data and shared it with others. Suddenly, she had a vague awareness of others out there in the app. She wanted to talk to them, ask questions.

And then she saw Bibi.

She was there, in the weave of Topsight, a little thing that moved between big things, making connections, pushing, nudging. The app was not just for seeing, but for changing. The realisation was a tingle across Kuovi's back. There were shifts in the picture in Bibi's wake, like birds taking wing from the marsh, like a sudden smile.

Kuovi smiled back and waved.

"Kuovi?"

Mum, behind her. What would she see if she looked at her with Topsight?

But that wasn't the right question.

Kuovi took off the halo and turned around. The world spun. Mum was there, holding her up. Kuovi blinked at the bright sunlight.

"Sweetie, what's wrong?"

"Nothing," Kuovi said, wiping her eyes. "What would you like to do today?"

The Oldest Game

ORANEN'S KNUCKLES TREMBLED on the BMW's steering wheel. The road to Turtola was a winding snake of dirt, pockmarked with puddles full of piss-coloured rainwater. The sky was the colour of recycled toilet paper.

He had been dry for three days now. It had been an eight-hour drive from Helsinki, and fatigue stung his eyes. The veins at his temples were dark and thick in the rearview mirror, throbbing to the rhythm of his headache. The inane chatter of the local radio station made it worse, but he did not want to drive in silence: the barley fields around him were too big, too empty, their monotony broken only by lopsided hay barns that looked like they were made of toothpicks.

The house was much as he remembered it: a squat, two-story affair, flaking yellow walls, thatched roof. He parked the car in front of the barn and got out, a little unsteady on his feet. The wind felt cold. It smelled of dead leaves.

Oranen was home.

The old man had kept the place clean: his Nokia rubber boots were still sitting next to the stairs in the front room. Oranen's mother had always made such a fuss about coming inside with shoes on.

He lined up the bottles on the kitchen table, a row of Koskenkorva bottles and two crates of brown beer. Then there was the package from Dimitri, cold and heavy. He weighed it in his hand and put it into a drawer.

It was getting dark, and Oranen had to fumble around in the pantry to find the main switch. When he turned it, the kitchen lamp flared and died. He looked in the drawers for bulbs but did not find any. *"Perkele,"* he swore. Drinking himself to death was one thing, but he sure as hell was not going to do it in the dark.

Oranen walked to the village briskly, both to be warm and to shake away a city-dweller's unease on a road with no streetlights. The leafless birch trees cast long shadows across the driveway.

The village store was a squat building close to the church. Oranen went inside, trying not to look at the flaming red-and-yellow headlines of the tabloids: they didn't know the true story. He ignored the now-familiar stab of anger and shame and went looking for light bulbs.

He heard a familiar voice when he made his way to the cashier.

"Saatana, it's Saturday, and a man can't get a goddamn drink. Keijo, you gotta sell me a couple of beers, some Karjala, look, I've got money. Just a few bottles, what's that? Come on, Keijo."

Pengerkoski hadn't changed much. There were more broken veins in his potato-shaped nose, but the mop of blond hair, the stained overalls and the rubber boots were the same. He was two years older than Oranen but there hadn't been that many kids his age in Turtola when he was growing up and so they had hung out a lot. When Oranen started going to high school in Haahkala, taking the bus every morning, Pengerkoski had stayed on the farm, fiddling with engines and drinking. Oranen remembered Dad mentioning Pengerkoski running over somebody while drunk. That hadn't surprised Oranen much.

Pengerkoski's face lit up.

"Oranen *jumalauta*! Fuck, it's really you! I thought I was seeing things. Been known to happen." He laughed, revealing yellow teeth, and offered his hand. It was greasy, but the handshake was solid. "Your mug has been all over the papers. Your old man used to talk about how good you'd done for yourself in the south. *Perkele,* it's good to see you."

"You too." Oranen found himself smiling. He had planned to make sure that he didn't see anyone he knew. What the hell. "I heard Keijo isn't selling you beer."

"Aw, he's just giving me shit. I did a bit of damage here a while back." He showed Oranen his hand: the knuckles had fresh scars. Pengerkoski grinned. "Don't worry, just fell against the window while pissed. Haven't taken to breaking skulls yet, much as I want to. Nothing but cunts here."

"Fuck you, piss artist," hissed the shopkeeper. "I'll have the pigs on you if you don't—"

Oranen cleared his throat. "I'm just here to get some bulbs."

Keijo took his money, scowling at Pengerkoski.

Pengerkoski shook his head. "Damn shame to be dry tonight," he said.

Oranen thought for a second.

"I've got beer. And *kossu*. Was thinking of heating up the sauna as well. How's that sound?"

"Pretty fucking good. *Saatana!* The world hasn't turned Oranen's son into a cunt!" He slapped Oranen's shoulder. "Unlike some." He gave Keijo the finger as they walked out.

"Promised your dad I'd keep an eye on this place," said Pengerkoski, when they arrived. "Haven't done it as often as I should have. You'll get a harvest this year, though. Barley."

"It's okay."

"But, you know, let me know and I'll get this place sorted out. Not enough to do anyway. Had a mad cow. Had to put all the cattle down. Bad times."

"It's the same in the city," said Oranen.

Pengerkoski nodded knowingly.

Inside, Oranen replaced the bulbs and this time the lights came on. Pengerkoski whistled when he saw the array of bottles on the kitchen table.

"That's a big party you're planning, Oranen."

"Not big enough." Oranen opened two beers and passed one to Pengerkoski. He dreaded taking a sip at first, even though it was only beer, but the liquid was soft on his tongue and he quaffed half a bottle without thinking.

"So how about that sauna?" asked Oranen, wiping his mouth with the back of his hand.

The sauna was one of the few things that Oranen and his father had had in common. The old man had been a farmer to the bone, tolerating but at the same time disdaining Oranen's success at school. The argument about him going to the university had resulted in the sullen silence that lasted all the way to the success of Oranen's company and his marriage. But in the sauna there had never been any arguments. It was only there that they talked about the important things. Like death.

He remembered a Saturday night, five years ago. The old man sat hunched on the sauna bench, the ridges of his spine pulling the thin skin tight.

"Your mother was a good woman," his father said, suddenly. "Too good to go into the church ground." His tone was even more measured than usual. Oranen did not know what to say and threw another dipper of water onto the stove-stones: hot steam kneaded their backs with stinging fingers.

"I watched them bury her, the priest saying the words," continued the old man, "and that's when I stopped believing. You've seen how nothing grows there, in the churchyard? Dead earth there, and dead words.

"Whatever God there is should at least make things grow."

Oranen wasn't so sure, but the sanctity of the sauna kept him quiet. His father took the dipper, filled it with beer and threw the contents onto the stove. There was another hiss, and the sauna was filled with a strong barley smell.

"That's God for you." They sat together in silence, breathing in the heady smell. Then Oranen's father sighed.

"Your grandmother was a seer. They always said I had it. Never believed it until I saw the death in your mother. I've seen it in you too." He gripped Oranen's shoulder with bony fingers. "Make me a promise, boy. If there's ever death in you, come here to find it. Here, where things grow. That field there, it's been watered with Oranen sweat. You ever have to do it, gun, rope, drink: go there to do it. Promise."

In spite of the heat, Oranen felt cold. But he nodded.

"I promise," he said, breathing in the barley.

It was five years later, and it was Pengerkoski who sat hunched next to him on the sauna bench now, laughing and throwing another dipper of beer onto the stove. The heat and the beer and the vodka made his head buzz. He leaned back against the wall that was sticky with sap, letting the steam burn his face. The embers were dying in the stove, but the round stones on top of it were still hot and thirsty.

Where had he found his death? He wasn't sure anymore.

"Turtola's boys in the sauna again, *jumalauta!*" roared Pengerkoski. Oranen chuckled. Pengerkoski hadn't changed. "What you laughing at, Mr. Helsinki, eh?" Pengerkoski drained his bottle and climbed down to get another. They had left the beer bottles in a bucket of cold water outside. "*Saatana*, this wind," muttered Pengerkoski when he returned, teeth clenched. He looked at Oranen.

"You're an odd bird, Oranen. Here's me talking and talking and you're not saying a word even though it's your house and your booze.

"Now, even a shit-pants loser like me knows what the papers say. I don't care. You want to keep your peace, that's fine.

"*Perkele*, I'm just here for the booze and the company. Not much of that around these days. I got to be pretty good friends with your old man after you left. He was worried about you. Just so that you know."

Oranen stared at the glowing stove-stones.

"Looks like he had reason, too," said Pengerkoski. "Fuck, I've been on a two-week binge and I swear you look worse than I do."

Oranen sighed.

"It all went to shit," he said. "Marketta wanted to have a baby. But we couldn't. We tried everything. *Perkele*, if they had cloned that sheep back then we'd have tried that. But nothing worked.

"So she had my best friend Antti screw her instead. And we had Tuomas. The rest kind of followed from that. I was jealous. I thought they carried on the affair. Hired PIs. Turned out they did. Then we started tearing each other apart, for the control of the company. Antti framed me for that Sonera thing that the papers talk about. I started drinking, pretty badly. Marketta got a divorce, and—Tuomas." Oranen laughed bitterly. "I was dry for three straight days to see Tuomas once, before I came here. Well, not any more. See, just the same in the city?"

They listened to the hiss of the steam and drank.

"I buried your father," said Pengerkoski.

"What?"

"Buried him. He made me promise. In the barley field," said Pengerkoski hastily. "Didn't like churches much, your dad."

"Why didn't you tell me?"

Oranen shook Pengerkoski, shoving him against the wall of the sauna. Pengerkoski's bottle smashed on the floor.

"How did he die?"

"Shot himself," muttered Pengerkoski. "I'm sorry."

"Jesus," said Oranen and let Pengerkoski go, biting down tears.

After a while the stove died down and the sauna was cold and dark.

"You know what I'm here for, right?" said Oranen finally.

"Yeah," said Pengerkoski. "I'll come down in the morning, see how you're doing."

Then Pengerkoski climbed down, cursing when he stepped on a piece of glass from the broken bottle, and was gone.

Oranen sat alone for a long time. He didn't really even taste the vodka anymore, but kept drinking anyway.

What god did you find in the barley field, Dad?

Oranen got up. The air felt thick and his legs had a will of their own. *Good*, he thought. *On the right track.* He got Dimitri's package from the drawer: a 12-gauge sawed-off shotgun. He put it under one arm, grabbed the half-empty Koskenkorva bottle from the table and went out.

Oranen shivered on the stairs for a second, bare-footed, went back inside and put his father's boots on. They were just a bit too tight, but by now his feet were numb anyway. Then he walked along the trail that led to the fields. There was frost on the ground, crispy and white. He trod on frozen puddles and they made a sound like breaking glass.

It was no longer dark. There was a smear of orange light in the horizon, just above the dark teeth of the pine trees, and Oranen saw that Pengerkoski had kept his word. There was Oranen's barley, dark yellow in the dawn, reaching up to his waist. The soil was black and thick, its surface porous and frozen. The wind moved around in the field like a hand caressing a yellow dog's fur.

Oranen took a long draught of Koskenkorva. *Nothing here but mud and mad cow turds*, he thought. *Dad was a crazy old man in the end.*

Then he saw the naked giant in the barley.

At first he thought it was a large animal—perhaps a bear—rolling on its back. Then the first rays of the sun fell upon it and Oranen saw that it was a man, impossibly large. It lay on its back, hands spread out, moving them in arcs like a child making snow angels. Its hair was the same colour as the barley. It had a long beard and a generous paunch, bare feet stained by the soil. It was both young and old.

When it stood up it was like a tree growing from the red-gold sea. And then it spoke, its voice like the wind.

> *Why have you come,*
> *What do you seek,*
> *Son of Oranen,*
> *Child of barley?*

Oranen took another swig of vodka and laughed. It was all strange enough to be funny, and the booze sang in his veins. "*Perkele*, I don't know! Can't a man fucking kill himself in peace?"

> *There is no death here,*
> *No daughters of Tuoni dancing,*
> *Only harvest ripe,*
> *Only Pekko, the field's blessing.*

The giant strode towards Oranen. Its feet sank deep into the half-frozen soil and its footprints steamed. The barley stalks bent their heads as it passed. Warmth emanated from its body. Its smell reminded Oranen of beer hissing on the stove-stones.

The giant reached out one shovel-sized hand and grabbed the bottle Oranen was holding, sniffed it and cast it away.

Little man's drink this,
Wine of small measure,
Not good enough for barley's water,
Not worthy of Oranen's son.

There was rumbling laughter, like an earthquake inside the giant's chest. Tears of anger started running down Oranen's cheeks. *It's mocking me, the dirt-grown troll. Or maybe I am seeing things. I'm certainly drunk enough.* He found himself still gripping the shotgun. *Only one fucking way to find out.*

He fired both barrels into the giant's chest. The shot was like a thunderclap. Something warm splattered across his face. The giant staggered back a step and started laughing. There was a black bleeding crater in its chest, but it was closing, knitting itself shut.

"Leave me alone, *saatana!*" muttered Oranen. "Leave me alone."

Then a tendril of the giant's blood trickled into his mouth. It tasted like—beer, deep and slightly bitter—no, like mead, sweet and heady. It was like a mixture of every ale, beer or bitter he had ever tasted, and something more besides. It was like liquid soil.

Oranen dropped the shotgun, burying his face in his hands. The giant squatted down beside him, smiled gently and laid one hand on his shoulder.

Drink with me,
Drink deep my draught,
Son of Oranen,
Son of barley;
Play the oldest game with Pekko,
Try your manhood and your mettle,
The one that drinks more is the stronger,
The man who holds his drink the longer.

"I don't want to play games," said Oranen. "I just want to die. I thought that's what Dad wanted, for you to be my death."

If you best me, I will grant your wish;
If Oranen wins, old Pekko will relent,

I will carry you down to Tuoni on my back,
Take you under to the black swan's river.

"And what if I lose?" asked Oranen.

Gentle is old Pekko become,
Kind-hearted Hittavainen,
Only the seed of your loins wants he,
The heart of your first-born to keep.

Whispered Pellonpekko, and now its eyes looked darker, the color of dried blood.

My first-born? Oranen thought. *But I have none—unless Marketta lied, the bitch. Did she? Is this real?* But the giant's challenge burned in his mind. Perkele, *drinking is the only thing I've ever done right.*

Oranen forced a grin.

"Do your worst," he said.

Pellonpekko smiled. Then it dug its right hand into the soil and withdrew its fist from the ground clasping something. It opened its fingers. On its dirty palm rested a human skull with its top missing, crowned by jagged edges of bone. It was filled to the brim with a dark frothy liquid.

Oranen seized it and drank deep.

Oranen lost track of how long they sat there, on the barley field in the light of almost-dawn, passing the skull back and forth. Each draught was an explosion in his mouth. Memories that were not his passed through his mind: hunched stubborn men growing barley on this field, sacrificing to Pellonpekko, drinking the beer that they made from his flesh in harvest-time to warm the long dark days of winter.

At first the mead made him feel lighter. He laughed and mocked Pekko and told dirty jokes. Pekko smiled and asked him riddles whose answers meant nothing to Oranen.

Gone are Vipunen's words,

Dead Antero's wisdom,
From the minds of little people,
In the hearts of the wee folk,

said the giant and shook its head sadly. For some reason that was so funny that it made Oranen laugh aloud.

Soon the drink in Oranen's mouth began to taste sour. Swallowing became difficult, and the mead was like lead in his belly. But he kept drinking. He thought about Antti and Marketta and his stupid, stubborn father who had got him into this, and kept drinking, burning the darkness with the anger he had left. And then he started drinking his death.

Pellonpekko matched him drink for drink, a sad smile on its face.

When his death was gone, Oranen drank for Tuomas. For his son. For Tuomas's blond curls and yellow raincoat and his love for Powerpuff Girls. Little by little he began to slip and then at last when his hands felt like oversized mittens and his head like an iron anvil, he spilled some of the mead to the ground.

The last thing he saw before the world went away was Pellonpekko standing over him, holding his father's skull.

He had lost.

Tuomas. Don't take Tuomas, he thought. *Please.*

And then Oranen slept.

Pellonpekko watched the sun rise over the fallen man.

Well he was crafted, old Oranen,
Cunningly wrought, your old father:
Bested Pekko in the drinking-game,
Bound Hittavainen to his word.

Better than you old Oranen drank,
Deeper mead took your father:
More iron in his blood,
In his belly, more fire.

Seen his son's death had Oranen,
Seen the passing of his seed;
As his boon, his son's life he wanted,
Pekko to best him in the oldest game.

Pellonpekko his word has kept,
Free from boon is Hittavainen,
Your first-born is yours still,
Oranen's grandson a man his own.

Go back to the world, young Oranen,
Back to the winds barley scatter,
Go find your true death, and your seed,
Seek the true evening of your days.

Oranen woke up when somebody poked him in the side with something sharp. He blinked at the sunlight.

"Perkele!" exclaimed Pengerkoski. "I was sure you were dead! I heard the gunshot last night. I even brought a shovel."

Oranen sat up slowly. Somebody hammered nails into the back of his head, and his mouth tasted foul. He got up, staggered a few steps and vomited. Everything hurt.

"So you didn't do it, then? Odd bird, you are, Oranen, odd bird," said Pengerkoski, leaning on his shovel.

Oranen sighed. He didn't remember much about the previous night. But he felt clean and empty. Like a drained cup.

"No. I've got family to look after," he said, smiling weakly. "And family looking after me, I think."

"You know, there's still some Koskenkorva left in your kitchen," said Pengerkoski.

Oranen shook his head.

"I think I had enough last night," he said.

The two men walked to Pengerkoski's tractor. Behind them, the barley sang gently in its sleep:

> *Pekko will lie here waiting,*
> *Pellonpekko here sleeping,*
> *Blessing harvest golden, ripe,*
> *Blessing mead brown and deep.*

Shibuya no Love

THEY WERE EATING TAKOYAKI by the statue of Hachiko the dog when Norie told her to buy a quantum lovegety.

Riina's Japanese was not very good in spite of two years of Oriental Studies and three months in Tokyo, and the translation software on her phone did not immediately recognize the term, so she just stared at the small caramel-skinned girl blankly for a few seconds, mouth full of fried dough and octopus. "A what?" she managed finally, wiping crumbs from her lips.

Norie, who sat on the edge of the fountain and dangled her impossibly tanned legs in the air, giggled.

"You don't have them in Finland? How do you meet boys there? Oh, I forgot, you have the sauna!"

"It's not a—" Riina stopped. The concept of non-erotic unisex nudity in a steamy room was something only her Canadian friends had grasped so far. "Never mind. Tell me about the lovegety."

"It's the most kawaii thing! I keep mine on all the time. Look!" Norie held up her wrist. Her phone was embedded in a Cartier platinum bracelet with a jewel-studded Hello Kitty engraving that her boyfriend Shinichi had given her for her birthday. Riina had admired it several times, but had not paid attention to the little teardrop-shaped plastic thing dangling from it until now. It was hardly bigger than the tip of her index finger, and its pink surface had the characteristic teflon sheen of a nanovat-grown product. There was a silvery heart-shaped logo on one side.

"They had these already when my mother was a schoolgirl—that's how she met my father! Then they went out of fashion for several years, but now there is this crazy otaku in Akihabara making new and better ones. Quantum versions. Everybody has one!"

"So, what does it do?"

"I can't tell you—you have to try it! C'mon, let's go find you one!" Norie leaped up, took Riina's hand in her own and tugged her towards the techno beat of Shibuya and District 109 that was its heart. A forest of orange hairdos, brown legs and spidery eyelashes swallowed the girls. There was a crowd around the statue: it was one of the few clear landmarks in the district, and tourists loved the story of the dog who waited for its master for years after his death.

Riina hesitated. Norie tended to assume that she was equally good at assimilating the new memes that boiled up from the teenage paradise of Shibuya as her Japanese friends, who seemed to be able to turn the latest otaku toy into a subculture or a fashion statement in a matter of minutes. She was starting to become desensitized to future shock, but the labyrinths of the new and the old in this country still confused her. She wondered how her father managed: good protocol/etiquette software, probably. It was simply impossible to figure out the right kind of bow, the correct form of address towards a senior or a superior.

Let alone get a date.

She sighed, and allowed Norie to tow her deeper into the crowd. The Japanese girl's neon-rimmed eyes were bright, and her small white teeth were flashing, her canary-yellow backpack bopping up and down.

"Seriously—lovegetys are sooo kawaii!"

The boy looked like a painted little satyr: silver lips and eyelids, orange ash-streaked hair and a heavy gold chain around his neck. He couldn't have been older than twelve, but then in Shibuya a fifteen-year-old was ancient and venerable. The drone of the bass beat that seemed to permeate everything in 109 obscured the rapid-fire exchange between Norie and the boy, but it wasn't long before he smiled hungrily and held his palm out towards Riina, the little pink thing bright against his dark skin like a tiny flower. She took it, and it was still warm from the boy's hand, a living thing almost. Her MasterCard thumbnail sang an inaudible song to the boy's account, and suddenly she was the proud owner of a quantum lovegety.

Norie gave her a nymphlike smirk as the satyr boy vanished into the seething mass of Japan's young around them.

"Now comes the best part. We go to Starbucks, and you get to try it out!"

Most of Shibuya was like a graffiti: clashing, bright, screaming colors over a drab concrete surface, the clothes shops and holograms and neon signs and rainbow crowds a stark contrast to the utilitarian '90s architecture. Starbucks was an exception—an intricate, cylindrical two-story glass monstrosity, a ten-meter hologram of the white-green all-seeing mermaid hovering above it.

The girls sat at a small table on the second floor sipping cardboard-flavored cappuccinos. Norie helped Riina to calibrate the lovegety: it talked to her old Nokia toothphone eagerly, a little light blinking in the center of the silver heart. Menus with swirling Japanese characters danced on her retina, barely comprehensible. "Get2 setting? What is that?"

"Never mind that, you don't want to set it that high for the first go. We'll go for 'karaoke.' Your VR stuff is a bit old-fashioned, but—there. It's mining the web and creating your profile now—done!" Norie visibly enjoyed her big sister role, affecting a firm motherly tone.

"What do I do now?"

"Now? Silly girl, now you go and find a boy you like, and enjoy the show."

"Just a random guy? But what will I say to him?"

"You don't have to say anything, that's the point! Off you go now—just wander around and pretend that you're looking for the ladies' room. I'll call Shinichi, and we'll go for dinner with him after he gets off work—it'll be fun!"

Riina swallowed the last of her coffee and got up, feeling awkward.

She took her purse, pocketed the lovegety and walked towards the signs pointing to the ladies' room, trying to look innocent and casting passing glances to the men sitting at the tables she passed. There were a couple of businessmen, a glazed look in their eyes as they imbibed caffeine seasoned with the latest stock fluctuations, a couple of rare daylight otaku wearing ill-fitting jeans, anime T-shirts and subterranean mutant complexions, and trendy neo-jinrui oozing illusory wealth, talking loudly and dressed in pin-striped gangster suits. She felt silly and focused her eyes on the white skirt-wearing pictogram ahead, shaking her head.

The lovegety beeped. A female voice chattered something in her ear like an exotic bird. Flashing icons guided her eyes towards a lone figure sitting by one of the large windows. Riina stopped, felt blood rising to her cheeks and tried to think about lying face down in a snowdrift, cold and dead: usually it worked.

Not this time. He had good cheekbones, short-cropped black hair and large brown eyes behind rimless AR glasses; he was scribbling something furiously with a stylus on the screen of an old-fashioned palmtop, forehead furrowed in concentration. Suddenly he stopped and looked up, straight at Riina, a surprised look on his face. His name was Hiroaki, she suddenly knew: twenty-three, studying communications technology at Keio University, single, four previous relationships, likes old Takeshi Kitano films and Japanese jazz, owns a cat.

The lovegety buzzed again. Riina caught a glimpse of a brief animation: clunky cartoonish figures of a boy and a girl holding lovegetys. The devices sent out little arrows that shook hands in the air. "Karaoke Mode Initiated!" chirped the shrill voice of the gadget through her jawbone.

Riina was suddenly overwhelmed by a nauseatingly powerful sense of déjà vu mixed with vertigo. It was like she was falling, only sideways, weightless. She closed her eyes, and the feeling subsided. When she opened them again, she was looking straight into Hiroaki's eyes, and felt his hand touching her cheek gently. A confused tangle of new memories unfolded in her head: a seafood dinner, games at the arcade, strolling through 109's boutiques of the bizarre, joking about the latest fashionable trinkets.

Tension, hands and limbs brushing against another ever so lightly, Hiroaki missing his train to walk Riina home. And then—"The First Kiss!!!" piped the female demon in her ear, and her mouth was suddenly full of Hiroaki's tongue and taste, his lips moving a bit clumsily, uncertainly. But there was no clanging of teeth, no awkwardness.

It was perfect.

And then it was over.

"To Experience Adult Situations, Upgrade To Get2 Mode!!!" sang the lovegety and plunged Riina into a warm sea of afterglow, into soft jazz tunes sung by a Japanese voice. They lay on Hiroaki's futon, Riina listening to his heartbeat, her cheek against his smooth chest, as he leaned on one elbow and toyed with her hair.

"Pillow Talk!!!" crooned lovegety.

"I'm going back home this fall," she said, not knowing where the words came from, head heavy with newly discovered plans and dreams. And the butterflies in her stomach, the fear of losing all this perfection—where did that come from? She looked up at Hiroaki, touching his cheek.

"Would you like to come with me?"

"Yes," he said, and smiled, and the lovegety carried them away again.

Finland. Snow. Perfect weekends by the lake, in her family's summer house. Hiroaki learning to ski, nose peeling from mild frostbite. Hiroaki making her tea. A big warm water balloon swelling in her chest as she thought about him. Staccato images punctuated by the voice of the lovegety. Arguments. Hiroaki's inferiority complex. Her endless need to overanalyze her problems, the desire for a safe male figure to replace her father. The usual things, the pitfalls of pillow psychology. And finally, Hiroaki's back receding into the distance on one of the moving walkways of Helsinki Airport, Riina holding back her tears and squeezing the little ivory cat he had given her in her pocket.

"Karaoke Mode Ends!!!"

The voice was like a guillotine, sharp-edged and unstoppable, cutting through the illusion. She fell back to the mutter of Starbucks, felt her knees buckling under her. Strong warm hands grabbed her by the shoulders and supported her. She took a deep breath and opened her eyes. It took only seconds for her head to clear a bit, and she found herself looking into Hiroaki's eyes again. She almost cried from relief and covered his face with kisses, but the lovegety world was already fading away, the memories attaining a dreamlike quality.

"Are you all right?" asked Hiroaki, a concerned look on his face.

"Yes, fine," she stammered. "I was just—"

"Oh dear. That was your first time, wasn't it? Come, sit down and we'll get you some coffee."

"No . . . no, I'm all right now."

"No, really, it's no bother. I owe you that much at least." He winked. "Although I did hope that you'd have set it all the way up to Get2." He saw Riina's expression and laughed. "Only joking. C'mon. It's safe, I promise."

Riina felt a bit better after a steaming cup of mocha. Hiroaki watched her intently as she sipped the frothy liquid. She heard a short buzz from somewhere far away, and jumped in her seat: but nothing happened.

"Look, I'm sorry you got so shaken up," Hiroaki said finally. "Your friend should have explained to you how it works. Are you sure you're okay?"

He touched Riina's arm gently, his fingertips little points of electricity on her skin.

"Yeah . . . yeah, I'm fine. Thanks for the coffee, by the way."

"Any time."

Norie waved at them from the other side of the room and walked over, her pink Hello Kitty handbag swinging in the air. Riina glared at her angrily, but her irritation turned to astonishment as her friend bent over Hiroaki and kissed him on the lips, full and hard. He smiled sheepishly. "Sorry. While you were drinking your mocha, we went to Get2. Kind of accidentally."

Norie pursed her lips. "Well, it didn't seem to work out between you two, and he is cute! You don't mind, right?"

"What about Shinichi?"

"What about him? He's not really a boyfriend anyway, it's more of an enjo-kosai thing, you know. We do stuff, and he buys me things. Very practical. He doesn't mind, really—and we're still meeting him for dinner! Hiroaki can come along."

Riina stood up.

"No, you guys go ahead. I . . . I think I need some fresh air."

"Really? Are you sure? Look, I'm sorry, these things happen quickly. Try some other setting sometime, it's really fun!" Norie gave her a tight little hug. "I'll see you soon, OK? Call me."

As Riina started walking away, Hiroaki called after her. "Riina! You are invited to our wedding, of course! Next week! Try to make it!"

She ran then, tears in her eyes, towards the endless heavy beat of Shibuya, trying to find an ivory cat in her pocket, and her heart jumped when her fingers closed around something small and warm: but it was only the lovegety.

She threw it into the fountain by the statue of Hachiko the dog, and watched it sink. The statue seemed to be looking at her sadly with its bronze dog eyes, and she knew that it too was still waiting, waiting for love in Shibuya.

Satan's Typist

TAP TAP *TAP TAP TAP*, said the typewriter. "Excuse me?" *Tap*. The determined sound of the last period punched in was like a needle piercing an eyeball, final and a little moist. "Yes?"

She looked at me from behind horn-rimmed glasses with eyes like iron nails. You could have balanced an apple between her shoulderblades. Her skin had a wrinkled, worn-out look, like paper that has been folded and opened too many times. Her lips were blue and her gums were as pale as her skin, barely hugging the coffee-yellowed teeth when she opened her mouth in a rictus that was not a smile. Her mahogany desk was an orderly kingdom of documents and stationery. Her sticklike fingers rested lightly on the keys of the typewriter, a black, polished Underwood. Somehow it reminded me of a throne, the seat of some invisible king.

"They sent me from upstairs," I said. The air down here was humid and hot and I could feel a droplet of sweat running down my spine, like the teasing finger of a dirty old man.

"Ah," she said. "One of those."

"The, uh, manager said that you'd type up the contract." I waited for her steely gaze to soften a fraction. It didn't.

"That's my job," she said.

"So . . ." *Tap-tap-ta—* ". . . do you need any extra information or do you have it all there?"

The carriage of her typewriter had started moving again even though her eyes were still fixed on me. A slightly pained look appeared on her face.

"It's perfectly fine," she said. *Tap-tap-tap.* "Take a seat, please. This will only take a minute."

As I waited, she attacked the typewriter with an intensity that approached fury. The sound of typing rose to a machine-gun crescendo, punctuated by the little songs that the carriage return sang. Droplets of sweat appeared on her forehead. An errant curl escaped from her tight bun but she did not stop to brush it away.

When she was finished, she leaned back in her chair and sighed. Then she stood up, pulled the document from the typewriter's maw and handed it to me. As she leaned over the table, we were very close for a moment. I could smell moisturiser, a tang of bitter sweat and something more putrid beneath. Then her lips brushed my ear, dry as paper.

"Please," she whispered. "Kill me." She pressed something cold in my hand. It was a paper knife, terribly sharp. Her eyes pleaded.

I looked at her. Her hands rested on the table. The fingertips were red and raw, mottled with dried blood and thousands upon thousands of scars, the marks of tiny sharp teeth.

Only when I looked at the document I was about to sign and saw the wet crimson words slowly seeping into the bone-white paper, I understood.

Tap-tap-tap, said the typewriter.

Skywalker of Earth

CHAPTER ONE. THE HOUSE OF DR. DUPRES

Twelve hours before the rain of ships.

I am four years old and wearing my best dress. The last man on the Moon is on TV. He moves in slow, deliberate bounds and leaps, next to a long-legged spidery craft wrapped in tin foil.

Grandmother sits on the edge of the couch, laughter in her eyes. The dim light of the TV screen brings out the hollows in her cheeks. She catches me looking at her, and winks, as if we're sharing a secret, like she's been there already—

I wake up with a start.

"Kate? You all right?"

"Hmmh?"

The car window is cold and hard against my temple. I open my eyes slowly. The night of lost sleep stings. Gomez is looking at me, an awkward smile on his round face.

"We're there in five minutes. I thought you might want to get ready."

"Thanks. I needed my beauty sleep," I say. "For my date."

I look at the sleepy Washington suburb that the hard-faced agent is driving us through. It is calm and serene at five on a Saturday morning. The road is lined by cherry trees in full blossom, and under other circumstances, I'd enjoy the view. But the two black field team vans driving ahead spoil it, and I know that there are helicopters above us, too, insect eyes in the sky.

"He's ninety-seven," Gomez says.

I dig out a small mirror from my pocket and look at the ruins that used to be my face. Tired wheat-coloured curls, glasses that keep sliding down my nose, dark pouches under my eyes.

"And I *look* like ninety-seven. Perfect match." I get my laptop out and bite my thumbnail while it boots up. "I shouldn't be here," I tell him. "We have more and more data coming in from the Object. ETINT has more important things to do than talking to a geriatric. *I* have more important things to do."

"You've read the file, right?"

"Dr. Marc C. Dupres," I say. "A PhD in applied chemistry from Cornell in 1926, when dinosaurs roamed the earth. Work in Rare Metals Laboratory in D.C. Consulting for a big machinery company that went down in the crash of 1928. Not much between 1930 and 1938. A lot of work for General Atomic in the fifties, including ORION. Maverick scientific papers ranging from general relativity to quantum mechanics and obscure mathematics. A loner. No wife. No living relatives. A few old patents in chemical industry that still make money. Apparently hasn't done much for the past twenty years."

"Show-off," Gomez says.

The laptop throws up a blank screen full of static and its hard disk makes a painful grinding noise. "Shit!" I push the power button again angrily, rebooting, but the machine refuses to come to life. Sighing, I put it away. "Doesn't matter, I've got hardcopies. A budget of three point six billion, why do we get these pieces of crap?" I look at Gomez. "And for that matter, *why* are we sending two armed units to cover a friendly talk with a retired physicist?"

Gomez blinks, and I know that the next thing he says is going to be a lie. Filing such things away in a relationship is an occupational hazard.

"It's not what you think, Kate. He's a dangerous man. We don't even want you to try to extract information from him. Strictly non-confrontational. Just show him the pictures and see how he responds."

We lock eyes for a moment. The classic mistake of having mixed work and pleasure is really starting to backfire, big time. I swallow the need to shake him by the shoulders and make him tell me the truth. I close my eyes. I can imagine how the argument would go, like an ETINT scenario: angry words falling like rain. I want to be back in my office at the Palace, sit at my computer and analyse the images from Spaceguard, pixel by pixel. I don't want Gomez looking at me with apologetic puppy eyes like he did when we ended our little fling.

So I simply sigh instead. "Fine. Whatever."

Wordlessly, he hands me a little earpiece, a lapel mike and a handgun in a belt holster. I fumble with them for a moment: I haven't worn this kind of gear for a while. He almost tries to help me, but stops himself in time.

"Oh, Gomez?" I tell him as the car stops. "I'm not helping him to go to the toilet. That's your job."

For most of my adult life I've been trying to think of ways for the world to end.

Reagan started it. Maybe it was just his Alzheimer's kicking in or maybe he'd wandered into a '50s B-film set while shooting one of his horse operas: I don't know. In any case, he told the NSA that there had better be a unit that would be ready the day the aliens came. Ergo: ETINT. A loose group of weirdos in the Puzzle Palace, science geeks like me. I started out as a cryptanalyst, but drifted through the corridors of Black City to its darkest corners where black-book budgets pay for the obsessions of senile presidents. We ground Seti@Home packets to little number crumbs on the spare cycles of Maryland supercomputers, concocted paranoid scenarios and response strategies ranging from alien viruses to the spontaneous emergence of artificial intelligence and churned out recommendation memos. We all knew they got lost somewhere in the system or got fed to the Elephant, NSA's house-sized, furnace-mouthed devourer of secret documents, but it was great fun anyway.

Until two days ago, when it became real.

The house is a beautiful two-story stone building. Its walls burn red in the morning sun. The two vans are parked farther down the street. I'm the velvet glove, they're the iron fist. There will be lasers trained at the windows, picking up every sound.

"We're here," says Gomez in my ear. "Any sign of trouble, we come and get you."

"I bet," I mutter.

I walk up the sandy footpath, grasp the brass knocker above the plaque that says MARC C. DUPRES, PhD, and tap it a bit too hard against the door. After two minutes or so, it opens.

Dupres is not what I expected. A hook of a nose, skin like tanned hide, wavy iron-grey hair; piercing dark eyes beneath bushy snow-white eyebrows that grow together in one quizzical chalk line. He is stooped, but has the broadest shoulders I have ever seen in a man approaching his first centennial. He is wearing a bathrobe.

He looks at me and makes a little ticking sound at the back of his throat.

"Is it death or taxes, young lady?" he asks. "Because I won't concern myself with anything else at this hour."

"Dr. Dupres," I say, clearing my throat. "Sir. My name is Kathryn Leroy. I work for the National Security Agency."

"Not taxes, then." Dupres's eyes widen slightly. "Leroy? Curious. I knew a Leroy once—" There is a ghost of a sad smile on his lips. "I see they still know how to play the game, sending me Baby Face Leroy's daughter."

"Granddaughter, actually." *They never told me he knew my grandfather.* Black sheep of the family, that's what my mother always said. He even had a gangster nickname. What on Earth was he doing with Dupres?

Suddenly, there is a lost look in Dupres's eyes. He blinks several times rapidly. But then the steel is back. "Yes, yes, of course. Well, they are wasting their time. I have no emotional handles to twist. But I am an old man and I don't enjoy feminine company as often as I used to. Old men do not sleep either, so you might as well come inside."

The house smells of pipe tobacco and coffee. Furniture is sparse and new, almost Spartan. The walls are bare. The photographs and mementoes that I associate with the homes of old people are conspicuously absent, except for one: a large framed black-and-white photograph on the hallway wall. It shows a group of men, all young, some in lab coats, some in their shirtsleeves. I recognize Dupres immediately, dark-eyed and serious, remarkably handsome, standing slightly apart from the rest of the group. A small copper plaque attached to the frame says RARE METALS LAB-ORATORY, WASHINGTON, D.C., 1928.

He leads me to a spacious living room where a laptop is humming on a low coffee table. A cable attaches it to a complex-looking contraption that looks like the guts of an old vacuum-tube radio. Dupres motions me to sit. I steal a look at the computer screen. Symbols that mean nothing to me float across it like aliens from an '80s video game.

"Coffee?" Dupres asks. "That's the one drug they still let me have."

I smile. "Yes, please."

While Dupres goes to the kitchen, I open my briefcase, sorting the pictures on the table. I still can't believe the pictures are real, even though I've been poring over every pixel of the TIFF files for two days. It was a Spaceguard team in New Mexico that saw it first, moving through the Kuiper belt. They would have mistaken it for an unusually large dwarf planet, except for the fact that its trajectory showed blatant disregard for the Newtonian traffic rules of the solar system. They shot the data to us and all hell broke loose. We shouted at NASA until they turned Hubble away from the latest nebula that looked like Jesus and trained it on the Object. Even now, my mouth goes dry when I look at it.

It's a gigantic angry eyeball, perfectly smooth and round, outline slightly blurred, exactly one thousand kilometres in diameter. The NASA boys figure it's a thin shell surrounding a larger central mass. The images have been corrected for blueshift. The Object is moving at roughly 0.3c. And as far as we can tell, it is on its way to Earth.

That's what I should be thinking about, not the mind-game bullshit they like so much at No Such Agency.

"What is this about my grandfather?" I mutter in the lapel mike. "That's why I'm here, isn't it?"

"Casey found the connection," admits Gomez's voice in my ear. "Your grandfather used to work for him. Hired muscle, as far as we can tell. You know Casey: she never ignores serendipity. But never mind that. Just show him the pictures."

Dupres emerges from the kitchen carrying two mugs of coffee. He sees the pictures and his hands start shaking violently, spilling hot liquid to the floor.

"Doctor—" I help him set the coffee on the table.

"I'm fine," he snaps and collapses on the couch. He closes his eyes and takes a deep breath.

"Please bring me my pipe," he says. "In the drawer. There."

I do as I'm told. He fills it with foul-smelling tobacco from a little pouch from his pocket, lights up and leans back, smoking furiously. Then he goes through the pictures, one by one, pausing occasionally to tap the keys of his laptop.

Suddenly, Gomez is in my earpiece again. "Kate," he says. "We can't hear anything. There's something wrong with the laser setup. The thermal imaging is not working either. Get out of there—we'll—"

The white noise that cuts the sentence is so sudden and violent that I bite my tongue, tasting iron. I take the earpiece out, hands trembling, tears in my eyes, and pocket it, a sudden knot of fear in my stomach.

Dupres looks at me, the faintest hint of amusement on his face. His eyes are like two pieces of flint.

"Dr. Dupres?" I say, slowly getting up. "What is going on here?"

He blows out a thick cloud of smoke and coughs.

"I told those idiots that he would come back. He always did. Always," he says. "There was the time those accursed von Neumann probes tried to eat the ship. He put us in the escape module and rotated us across the fifth dimension onto the Planck brane. I should have known that he would survive the black hole. What a fool I was."

"Who are you talking about? Who always came back?"

"Richard Soane."

Suddenly his voice is hollow and distant, and strands of darkness bleed into my field of vision. I drop the coffee mug and watch it fall to the floor in slow motion. The stain spreading on the carpet is like a Rorschach pattern.

"I am more sorry than I can say, but this is necessary," says Dupres. "I fought my battles with him long ago. It's time to retire. Somewhere with three suns, I think." I hear staccato keystrokes.

I struggle to reach for my gun, but it is so much easier to yield to the warmth rising in my belly. I collapse on the couch. The soft surface swallows me.

As the world gives up and decides to go away there is a groaning, rumbling sound. Like a stone tree being uprooted—

Chapter Two. Dr. Soane, I Presume

I feel like I've been spinning around in a schoolyard game. Slowly I recognise the sensations. The free fall exercise in Florida, three years ago: the thirty-second headlong dive in the belly of the vomit comet.

A leathery hand touches my face gently and presses something on my lips: a straw. "Here," says Dupres's voice, and then I have a cardboard carton in my hand. The orange juice goes down the wrong way, and I cough and sputter. The choking sensation suddenly switches on the lights in the dim rooms of my head. I open my eyes, blinking at the bright light, and see perfectly spherical droplets of juice floating in the air. Dupres's face looms behind them like a scarred planet.

"You're handling this better than your grandfather, if that's any consolation," he says.

"What the hell is going on?" I manage.

"Well, we are approximately fifteen astronomical units from Earth, moving at 0.1c. I'd go faster, but we are not out of the Sun's gravity well yet. There is an Earthlike planet in the M75 globular cluster, outside the Milky Way. I'm hoping that it will be far enough."

He's insane. I reach for my gun. It is gone, of course, tucked under Dupres's belt.

"It was not my intention to kidnap you, Miss Leroy. You should be grateful. I've given you the opportunity to escape what is to come."

I struggle to clear the cobwebs from my head. *It's your job to think about impossible things, Leroy. You can handle this.*

I take a look around. Dupres's living room is unchanged, except that we're floating close to the ceiling. The bareness of the house makes sense now, and for the first time I notice that the furniture is bolted to the floor.

The window shutters are closed, but there is a strange glow around their edges, like the shimmer of oil on water.

This has to be a training exercise. Maybe they shipped me to the ISS. Or we are in a vomit comet, and this will be over in 30 seconds. Maybe—But no. ETINT is a low-budget outfit who survives on crumbs from NSA's table. *They wouldn't do this. This has to be a hallucination. Or virtual reality. Or*—

Damn you, Occam's razor.

I glare at Dupres, who is floating cross-legged in the air in front of me like a wrinkled Buddha. "Show me," I tell him.

He smiles indulgently, taps a laptop key and the shutters open. A cold sea of stars stares at me, unblinking. They are strangely distorted, though, amber-tinted and bloated. But they are there. The Object was just pixels on a computer screen. This is . . . real. Somehow it makes me both terrified and angry at the same time.

"You turned your *house* into a spaceship?" I ask, ashamed of the hysterical edge in my voice.

Dupres laughs, a thin, scraping sound. "My house and about a hundred thousand cubic metres of soil and bedrock. You never read Jules Verne as a child? A gentleman doesn't go anywhere without his library and smoking room. Besides, your people were watching me constantly. It was the simplest thing to do, and I had the technology. From 1928, in fact." He taps the vacuum tube contraption attached to the laptop gently, eyes distant. "Soane called it a bias drive. Simple, really. Wiggle the M-theoretic compactification moduli locally and the value of Newton's constant is altered. Creates a tidal propulsion gradient." He motions towards the distortion effect beyond the window. "There is a useful side effect: a potential energy wall that only light can pass through, and even that gets red-shifted. Keeps the air in: I have life support systems in the basement."

I try to take it in, but the words keep slipping from my grasp. *Somebody had this in 1928?* But it doesn't matter, not now.

"That's not what I meant," I say. "*Why*, not *how*."

"I'm leaving a sinking ship," he says slowly. "Soane is coming. I suppose that it's the wisdom that comes with age that tells me that even then he was my better. God alone knows what he is now." His mouth is a thin line. "He is going to tilt the world from its axis and there's nothing your bosses can do about it. And that's why they sent you to me, isn't it?"

"Jesus. You *really* are afraid of this Soane character. How do you even know it's him?"

"Because of the way he thinks. The pictures you brought show a craft that's like a giant's version of the very first ship Soane and his partner Cranston built. He always had to make things bigger, and he never throws anything away. And yes. I *am* afraid of him. Because of what he is. A moral man."

"I don't understand."

"I don't expect you to. But it doesn't matter now. We're going away from all that. Far away."

There is a sudden bell-like sound from Dupres's machine. A pulsating blue spark appears inside one of the vacuum tubes. He frowns and stares at the screen intently.

I look at the gun in his belt. I start playing the scenario out in my head but my mouth goes dry before I can even start. So I just do it without thinking, let the movement come out in a sudden burst.

I throw the juice carton away from me and Newton's third law gives me enough momentum to cross the distance between us. I grab the gun and give Dupres a good shove: we drift apart, and I can't help but relish his surprised gasp.

"All right," Dupres says, breath wheezing. "Baby Face's granddaughter, all right. I wasn't really expecting to use that. You can keep it if you want." He is holding his shoulder, just the spot where I pushed him, and I feel a stab of guilt.

"Thanks. I will," I tell him, clicking the safety off. "And you are going to turn this . . . *ship* around. We are going home."

In the background, the M-theory machine sings again. Dupres gives it a resigned look.

"I'm afraid we're not, Miss Leroy," he says, grimacing. "Soane is here."

The air in the room turns hot. My skin tingles. And then a ghost is floating in the centre of the room, a half-transparent, colorless image. I recognise him as one of the men in Dupres's photograph. The one with the set jaw and broad shoulders—but there is something different about his eyes. A coldness.

The figure moves its mouth and a static crackle explodes in my ears. Then the noise resolves itself into a deep male voice that has a boyish ring to it.

"Dupres, you son-of-a-gun! Still alive? Made of rawhide and whale-bone, eh?"

The ghost-thing flashes past me and then Dupres is pinned against the wall, struggling to breathe, unyielding fingers squeezing his throat, his face turning blue.

"Let him go," I say. The gun shakes in my grip.

"Do not interfere, dear lady. Me and this swarthy-skinned rascal here have had some unfinished business for the past century or so—"

I fire. The gun kicks. The bullet zings through the apparition and ricochets from the opposite wall.

"Better put the boomstick away before someone gets hurt."

An irresistible force yanks the gun from my hand. It floats away and flames into incandescence, radiating heat. After a second it is only a floating, gleaming sphere of molten metal.

The ghost grins. "That's more like it, doll. A pretty thing like you shouldn't be hanging around the likes of him. You'll go rotten before you know it."

He lets go of Dupres. The old man gasps for breath. There are blue fingerprints imprinted on his wrinkled neck.

"How did you . . . find me?"

"Oldest trick in the book, old bean. Quantum entanglement. Cranston and I thought it was a good idea to make sure you didn't get away from us again. We've got a polarised photon that has your number back on the *Skywalker*."

Dupres closes his eyes.

"Richard Soane?" I ask.

He smiles, old-Hollywood-movie teeth flashing.

"At your service." Then he glares at Dupres. "We need to talk, Darkie," he says. "But not here. Better hold on to your knickers!"

Chapter Three. The *Skywalker*

For an eye-blink, everything is soundless and dark. Then my stomach lurches as gravity returns like a bad hangover. The fall is only a metre or so, but I hit the ground painfully, landing on my side. Dupres grunts, slides down the wall and lies on the floor in a heap, helpless anger in his eyes. After a second, I regain my sense of *downward* and manage to stand up again.

"Please help me up, Miss Leroy," Dupres says in a hoarse voice. "I'm not meeting *him* on my knees."

Together, we get him on his feet. He sways a little, grasping my shoulder with one spiderlike hand.

"Thank you," he says, breathing heavily. "Now let us see what the stage for this passion play is."

We walk to the window—both of us unsteady on our feet—and stare, blinking at the sunlight.

Outside is a *Little Prince* world whose horizon curves too sharply for comfort. In spite of the warm yellow glow, there is no sun—the sky is uniformly blue. Two houses sit in the middle of a green field in the distance, side by side: a well-kept colonial-era mansion and a smaller, more modern two-story building with French windows. The air is humid and smells of summer. I give Dupres a wide-eyed look.

Dupres grunts. "Toys," he says. "He's been playing with his new erector set."

"Jesus," I whisper. "It looks like a Magritte painting."

"Never cared much for splashing paint on a perfectly good canvas," says a voice. I smell strong tobacco, and the door opens. It is Soane, impossibly perfect and tanned in the fake sunlight. He is wearing a white shirt, sleeves rolled, and old-fashioned grey trousers held up by suspenders. He is barefoot, biting the amber stem of a large pipe. The muscles of his forearms and chest ripple as he moves.

"That's one of the reasons why we never really saw eye to eye," says Dupres calmly. He lets go of my shoulder, steps out to the porch and crosses his arms. The two men lock gazes for a moment. Then Soane blinks.

"You know," he says, emptying his pipe onto the grass, "I've known that you've needed killing for seventy years now and I've never finished the job. What's it going to be this time, Darkie?"

"You have no reason to kill me," says Dupres.

"You have always made sure I have reasons not to. But you've finally gone too far."

"What do you mean?"

Soane shakes a finger at Dupres.

"Come on, Darkie, don't take me for a fool. I took a sweep of the electromagnetic spectrum in a sphere of a couple of light-decades in diameter, watched some of the televisor transmissions. *You took over.* In secret, not showing your hand, but by God you took over. The biggest war in history. Atomic explosions. Mindless entertainment for the masses. All those fancy new gadgets that could only be based on the bacon we brought home a few decades back—"

"None of it my doing," interrupts Dupres.

For a moment, I listen to Soane, and the little girl inside me who thinks about possible worlds whispers in my ear. What if there was supposed to be a different twentieth century, with shiny spaceships and abundant energy and flying houses? What if it *was* Dupres who took all that away from us, ruling the world in secret? What if—

No, I tell it firmly. *This is madness.* I step forward and clear my throat. "Dr. Soane, he's actually telling the—"

"And still an eye for pretty ladies, I see," says Soane. He looks at me for the first time, lips curling in a boyish grin. But his eyes are empty and lifeless, like painted eggshells. "Now, doll, I don't know if he's hypnotised you or what, but I can tell you for a fact that Marc C. Dupres, PhD, is the slimiest, slipperiest rattlesnake you'll find this side of Andromeda, no matter what honey he's poisoned your pretty pink ears with."

"Listen—"

"So you think I'm the master of Earth?" interrupts Dupres, an incredulous tone in his voice.

Soane scratches his head. "This is getting a bit tiresome, Darkie. But I can make it easy for you. What say you if I just use the educator to have a peek in that wonderful twisted brain of yours? Find out exactly what you have been up to?"

"You know that I'd die before you'd get anything out, even now," says Dupres haughtily. "I've had sixty years to work on my meditation techniques. I was always better at it than you."

Soane chews the stem of his pipe.

"Well, how about this: you let me poke around or I find an infinite time-like geodesic, dematerialise you and launch you along it in a suitable container. You know I can do it, too: I know both the words and the music. Long, long time to think about your sins. What's it going to be?"

"You can't threaten me with that," says Dupres. "In case you haven't noticed, I've aged a little since we last met." He smiles sardonically. "Immortality is becoming a concern when you are almost a hundred. And I'm sure I could think of something to occupy myself for an eternity."

Their eyes lock again, and this time it looks like they are prepared to stare each other to death. I want to scream at them, make them stop this idiotic dick-measuring contest. But I bite my tongue and force my voice to remain calm.

"Dr. Soane, please listen. We mistook you for an alien ship and—"

Soane laughs. "An alien ship? Why, there isn't a space-faring civilisation in this spiral arm of the galaxy! Not any more."

I stare at him and clench my fists.

"Dr. Soane," I say as slowly as I can. "I *order* you to contact my government immediately via whatever means you have at your disposal, enter Earth orbit and subject your craft to an inspection by the Ministry of Homeland Security."

A puzzled look appears on his face. "Excuse me?"

"Dr. Soane, if there's anyone here who represents the authorities on Earth, it's *me*. I work for ETINT, a branch of the National Security Agency that deals with potential extraterrestrial threats. You are an American citizen; I am a government agent conducting an investigation and would appreciate your co-operation in this matter. I need to contact my agency and let them know what is going on. I'm sure they can have you on the phone with the President of the United States within ten minutes, and with the Secretary-General of the United Nations soon after that." I narrow my eyes. "But first I need to know precisely what your intentions are, and where exactly you acquired—" I make an arching motion with my hand, trying to encompass the technological vastness all around us and take a deep breath—"all this."

Dupres pinches the bridge of his nose.

Soane lets out a long, high-pitched whistle. "That was a pretty deafening report, sweetheart. I don't know where you find these minxes, Darkie. She really isn't a very good actress. I've seen gangster's molls before: she handled that gun pretty neatly back there, for a gal. And besides, I know who's really in charge here—"

"Wait. He can read minds?" I ask Dupres, taking some satisfaction in the fact that the absurdity of the sentence doesn't even register on my weirdness scale any more.

The old man nods. I cross my arms. "Fine," I say. "Read mine. I'm telling the truth."

Dupres shakes his head slowly, horrified.

Soane arches his eyebrows. "That's an interesting idea, toots. Just stand still. This won't hurt one bit."

Suddenly, a swarm of silvery insects hovers around Soane's head like an unholy halo. A cold metal band squeezes my temples, and there are a million tiny pinpricks across my scalp. A scream builds up in my throat. But it is too late. Memories come in a rush that drowns me, a Niagara of nostalgia—*moon and Grandmother and the snowman I built when I was five and the secret I never told anyone*—and I know *he* sees it all and takes it away from me.

I try to fight it. I think about hash functions and finite fields and elliptic curves. The hungry alien mind inside my own sweeps them aside, demanding more. And then I'm empty, all dry, no longer aware that the aching feeling in my head is pain—

"Stop," says a voice.

I collapse on the grass, my mind a blank sheet of white paper.

Memory returns, sudden and painful. *Flying houses and mad scientists and strangers in my mind and crazy old men and the smell of freshly mowed grass somewhere in space please let me go home please.* I sob, but there are no tears. My breath seizes up.

"Breathe," Dupres says, gently. He touches my cheek and looks at me. I swallow nothingness.

"A long time ago," he says, "before you were born, I travelled in the Orient. I studied with a lama who taught me how to breathe."

I blink, helplessly,

"It is easy. You do *not* breathe. You open yourself to it, let it fill you. It is a hard thing, and an easy thing. Do it right, and you will never be afraid again."

I listen to his voice, gasping for air, a heavy black animal sitting on my chest.

"Slowly," Dupres says chidingly. "Repeat after me."

"Lead me from Ignorance to Truth. From non-being to being lead me, from darkness to light lead me, from death to immortality lead me."

He whispers it to me several times, and I repeat it, the act of saying the words slowing my heartbeat, calming like water.

"Have you gone soft, Darkie?" asks Soane. "Time was, you wouldn't have batted an eyelid if I had put a bullet between her eyes. You give me your word that you'll co-operate, then? That, at least, was always good."

"You fucking bastard!" I get up, push Dupres aside and punch Soane in the face as hard as I can.

I actually take him by surprise. Pain explodes in my hand as bone impacts on bone. Soane does not fall, but for a brief moment there is surprise and anger on his face. The halo around his head goes dark red and I feel a wave of searing heat around me. The sun goes dim, and there is a distant sound of charging machinery, a giant humming. Behind me, I hear Dupres's sharp intake of breath.

Then the cold thing returns to Soane's eyes.

"Dang," he says with a mirthless grin, rubbing his jaw. "That was more than a thistledown falling on Gibraltar. And I felt it." Then he frowns. "But you only get one shot for free. Why don't you run along to the house and see my wife, Barbara. She'll fix you supper, and make you see sense. I'll finish dealing with this serpent-tongued double-dealing bastard here."

I want to hit him again, but Dupres lays a spiderlike hand on my arm.

"Miss Leroy, please do what our host says. I'll try to sort this out." He smiles wanly.

"But—"

"This is the best way, believe me. Please?"

"Fine," I mutter and start walking towards the house with French windows, tears of anger on my face.

I find Barbara playing the violin in the garden behind the house, sitting on a wrought-iron bench.

Even though I'm still seething with rage her music takes my breath away. She is wearing an old-fashioned dress, a solid, high-collared blue affair made from some preternaturally light, flowing fabric. There is a gigantic jewel in a bracelet on her upper arm, shooting out dazzling beams in the artificial sunlight. Her hair is deep auburn red, and like Soane, she glows with health, to the extent that makes me instantly aware of all the Pilates classes I've missed.

"Hello," I say. She stops playing and gives me an irritable look. But then her face lights up.

"Ah. Dick mentioned we'd be getting visitors," she says in a warm voice. "You must be Kate. I'm Barbara. Do sit down, dearie-dove." Then she frowns. "Oh my," she says. "Are those *trousers* you are wearing?"

I sit down on the bench next to her and bury my face in my hands. *They are all mad.* But I am too numb and exhausted to say anything.

"There, there," Barbara says. "We'll get you something nicer to wear in no time, don't you worry about a thing." She pats my arm in a firm, friendly way. "Peg! Peg, we have a guest!"

A slight, short woman with dark chestnut hair emerges from the shadow of a rosebush, a book in her hand, wearing a dress that resembles Barbara's, except for its lavender hue.

"Oh, Babs," she says. "That awful man, Dupres, is back." A look of confusion passes over her face. "And he looks so *old*."

"Never mind that," says Barbara in a determined voice. "We'll let the boys worry about him. I won't let that scoundrel make Kate here think any less of our hospitality." She gives me an utterly trusting smile. "Blinding flashes and deafening reports, both of them. They've handled him before, and I'll happily leave them to it. *We* are going to get some supper!"

They take me into the house. Peg slips a tiny arm through mine as we walk, chattering away.

"You really must tell me *everything*. We have been away for so long—it feels like years! What do people wear these days?"

"Trousers," I say, forcing a smile.

The house is a perfect replica of a New England mansion. The walls are decorated with paintings and sports trophies and pictures of a man that I guess to be Martin Cranston, posing next to old aircraft.

The kitchen is not exactly what I expect. The shelves and racks are empty, although there is a large oak table. A floating metal headset that looks like a cross between a dentist's headgear and a Buck Rogers jet-pack descends slowly from the ceiling. Barbara dons it. "Now, sweetheart," she says. "What would you like?"

"What is that?" I ask.

"Oh, this? Just something my Dickie whipped up one day to save time on cooking. I just think at it and it creates food out of molecules or some such nonsense. He's got one too in the control room, of course, a really big one, but that's for the whole ship—or its Brain, that's what he tells me. He has to be really, really careful with it. One errant thought and he could blow up the whole ship, he says. Good thing this one can only make stuff." She closes her eyes. A steaming plate with thick slabs of steak buried under a pile of caramelised onions and gravy appears on the table. I expect some sort of shimmering effect like in *Star Trek*, but there isn't any: it just pops into being without a sound.

"There. Tuck in!"

A small bell goes off in my tired brain. There is something I can use here, if I just ask the right questions.

We eat, making idle conversation, and even though I'm still shaken, it feels amazingly good to have warm food in my stomach. I tell them about Jean-Paul Gaultier, and they ooh and aah appreciatively.

"Where did you get that wonderful bracelet?" I ask Barbara.

"I'm not even sure I remember anymore!" she says, an odd, blank look in her eyes. "We have been *all over the place*. I'm so glad Dick built this new, better ship. You couldn't even have a proper *bath* in the original. It was horrid."

"How did he build it?"

"Oh, it's completely beyond me. I don't really worry about these things. There was this green place, like a goldfish bowl around this star. Dickie got along very well with the machines there. They did most of the work. Although of course Dick and Marty designed it all. They are frightfully clever, you know." She smiles. "Do you remember, Peg? That was the place where we died. It's a good thing Dick brought us back."

Peg nods.

"Of course I do." She shivers. "I really don't like to think about being dead." Then she smiles brightly. "But we're both better now."

I stare at them, a suspicion dawning in my mind. I remember Dupres's words. *He never throws anything away.* I think of the way Soane took the memories from my mind, and look at their perfect complexions, like Photoshopped magazine pictures brought to life in the flesh.

"Let me ask you something," I say. "What year do you think it is?"

Confusion flickers on their perfect faces.

"Why, what a thing to ask!" says Barbara. "It's 1932, of course!"

Afterwards, I lean back in my chair. "That was wonderful, Barbara. Really, extraordinary. Dickie is a lucky fellow."

Peg giggles.

"You know what would go really well with this?" I lower my voice. "Although I really shouldn't. Have to think about my figure."

"Do tell!" says Barbara. "We'll keep your secret." She winks.

"My mother's raspberry pudding," I say wistfully. "I wish I could have some. And some coffee."

"I'll make some coffee!" says Peg eagerly and dons her headset. Three beautiful china cups materialise in front of us. "I'm afraid I can't help you with the pudding, though."

"Maybe I could try?" I say innocently.

"I don't know," says Peg. "Marty said that only we were supposed to use these."

"Don't be a silly goose, Peggy!" says Barbara. "Of course Marty would say that—there is no one else here! Let Katie try." She gets up and hands me the headset. "There. Just put it on and think hard about raspberry pudding. But be careful, we don't want to drown in it." She lets out a little high-pitched giggle that makes me think about an out-of-tune violin.

I summon an image of the ex-Marine boyfriend who took me to the shooting range and taught me how to disassemble a M16A2 assault rifle. *No. It didn't work before.* I need something more subtle.

And then the idea comes. It is callous. I am in a callous frame of mind. I put the headset on.

The pudding starts eating Barbara's face. And the table. And the house. It is a grey, expanding, seething mass that radiates heat, growing, growing like a stain in a fast-forwarded film, flowing and growing hungry tendrils.

"My, Katie, this is really lovely," says Barbara, a tumorous grey growth blooming on her cheek. "You must give me the recipe." More of the goo drips to the table from her mouth. A classic Turing test trick: introduce something outside a chatbot's reference frame, and it just keeps going, like it wasn't there. The Peg-thing is already gone, consumed by the seething mass.

I have eidetic memory. ETINT did an evaluation of existential threats once. We reviewed hypothetical designs of self-replicating nanobots, tried to evaluate what their destructive potential was. We concluded that starting from scratch they could destroy the entire biosphere of Earth in less than an hour.

If the schematics I thought into the headset—a molecular assembler of some kind, I'm pretty sure—work as they should, I have something in the region of five minutes.

I take one last look at them. What happened to the real women? Did they really die—or go mad? Is there a little graveyard on this ship some-where? Is even *Soane himself* the original anymore?

I decide that I don't really care, turn around and run.

I make it out just in time. The house groans and collapses, its support structures gone, and there is a hot wind at my back from the waste heat the grey goo is radiating as it grows.

Then I do something I've never done before: I scream. I let all the anger and fear and frustration out in a high-pitched sound that comes right out from the bottom of my belly like my Tae-Bo instructor always told me a proper *kiai* should be. I'm pretty sure that it sounds more like a battle cry than a damsel in distress. But it works. Suddenly, Soane and Cranston are there, catching me as I fall.

"Oh, Dr. Soane, it was terrible," I say. "I don't know what happened. I thought into the machine and it went mad—" I let my eyes roll back.

Cranston freezes. From the terrible confusion on his face I can see that he is really no more than a puppet either, another extension of the little world Soane has built himself.

Behind us, the grey goo swirls upwards in a boiling mushroom cloud.

"I have to go to the control room to contain it," says Soane. He smiles brightly. "Don't worry, doll. It'll all be all right in no time." Then he vanishes without a sound.

I notice Dupres standing thirty feet away, looking at the spreading destruction curiously. The heat is searing now, and the cloud is moving towards us at a growing speed.

"Come on! We don't have much time!" I shout. Dupres looks at me, eyes wide.

"You did this?" His lips curl into a sardonic smile. "Bet *he* didn't expect that."

"Can you get us out of here? Does that contraption of yours still work?"

Dupres nods. We run towards his lopsided house, and he manages to keep up, sounding like a high-pitched steam engine.

Then we are inside. I slam the door shut, and hear a rasping, painful sound.

Dupres is laughing.

Chapter Four. Capital D

Dupres steers the house up from the little planetoid, fingers dancing on the keyboard of the M-theory machine. The glow of the bias field surrounds us and the gravity is gone, but this time I almost welcome the nausea and vertigo.

"That stunt you pulled down there was impressive, but omitted a crucial detail: we can't get out of the *Skywalker*," Dupres says. "I don't even know if the outer shell is matter. It might be some sort of flaw in space, or picotech pseudomatter."

"I didn't see *you* doing anything back there," I say tartly.

Dupres gives me a little smile. "No. You didn't."

"What's that supposed to mean?"

Suddenly, Dupres's machine tinkles again. *Is he already after us?* Fear grabs a hold of my guts and gives them a cruel twist.

"Hah," breathes Dupres. "I can't believe it. It's still here. That's Soane for you: he never throws anything away if he can help it."

"What?"

"My ship. The *Capital D*." He gives me a devilish grin that makes him look like a much, much younger man.

"We'll need spacesuits. I'll have to cut the drive once we get to the stable region Soane has set up for his toys. Icosahedral symmetry orbits: trust him to show off with an N-body solution like that. Anyway, that means we'll more or less fall apart: nothing to hold the house together when the bias field is gone. That locker over there, open it."

As I open the door Dupres is pointing at, junk spills out. Helmets and thick, padded overalls with a silvery sheen, emblazoned with the Soviet flag.

"Russian surplus," Dupres says. "I love eBay."

We float through Dupres's door together and into a giant's junkyard. My breath wheezes in my ears and I am painfully aware of the vacuum just beyond the thin fabric of the spacesuit.

Immediately next to Dupres's house—which has now lost its shape almost completely, with loose bricks drifting off from the roof in all directions—hangs a riveted copper-coloured sphere, perhaps thirty feet in diameter, dotted with gun-ports and round high-pressure windows. Below us is a larger sphere, this one made of something transparent and faintly green-tinted. Beyond that there is a shape that I cannot define, something that seems to pulse and move as I watch it. It reminds me of a 3D projection of a hypercube I once saw. Above and around us there are stranger things, revolving silver seashells and some sort of medieval armour that I judge to be the size of the Empire State Building.

There are living creatures too, in suspended animation. A many-eyed monstrosity with six pairs of wings and tentacles, something out of Lovecraft's nightmares. A black tree whose branches form a Mandelbrot set and whose trunk is dotted with eyes. A humanoid with a ridiculously oversized head, a thin, withered body: its skull is transparent, and the contours of its brain throb as I watch.

And all around us there is a cloudless blue sky that curves up and left and right and down and fades into an opaque haze in all directions—the outer shell of the *Skywalker*.

"We'll see if the old girl remembers me," says Dupres through the rattling radio link. "Dupres alpha gamma three four one," he whispers.

It rises from the machine sea below us, a matte-black cylinder at least a mile long. I feel vertigo again as the impossibly smooth surface fills our field of vision, a soap bubble of sheer black bigger than the sky.

"They made it for me in the green worlds," Dupres says, his voice far away. "So trusting. So old. Ancient machines made to bring desires into being. And this was what I thought I wanted. A toy."

"D responding," says a rasping feminine voice in my earphones. *"Welcome back, Dr. Dupres."*

"Come on," says Dupres. "Let's get out of here."

A giant mouth opens in the skin of the ship and swallows us.

Inside the ship, there is gravity again, and a moving walkway—a metal strip that flows like water beneath our feet—that takes us through seemingly endless blue-lit tunnels, through chambers with gigantic humming machines, vast coils and electric arcs. As we pass them, they wake up, as if welcoming Dupres.

Dupres shakes his head. "Most of this stuff is for show: they wanted to give me something that I could visualise at the time, something I could understand. All the real stuff is in an artificial singularity: it's not much bigger than a pinhead. But back then, we had to have proper trappings."

And then we stand on a floating platform in a cavernous pilot's chamber. Dupres sits on a velvet-cushioned chair at a control keyboard that looks like the bastard offspring of three pipe organs and a typewriter—it even has pedals. He works furiously with a cable connection for a moment, then taps at the keys of his laptop. Whole groups of keys and levers move by themselves all at once, as if played by an invisible pianist. A soft golden light fills the cockpit and the entire ship around us comes alive. Buck Rogers machines are everywhere, glowing and humming and singing. There is a round viewscreen twenty metres in diameter, showing an awe-inspiring view of Soane's junkyard and the *Skywalker*'s sky.

"You went out there," I say quietly. "You found all this. And you didn't share it."

Dupres closes his eyes.

"Of course I didn't. I really did want to be the Master of Earth. And I could have been—if not for Soane, who thought he could do a much better job. But things change. We were not ready for this, any of us."

Soane. The fear is there again, suddenly.

"So, are you going to get us out of here, old man?"

"No. You are."

I stare at Dupres mutely.

"I can't do this anymore," he says quietly. "I'm old. I'm too slow. You are much faster, and your brain is not nearly as crowded."

"I can't. How on Earth am I supposed to fly this thing?"

Quietly, he holds up a device, a brass-and-vacuum-tubes headset that looks terribly familiar. "I'll help you," he says. "If you'll let me."

"What the hell is that?" I ask.

"Soane calls it an educator."

It starts slowly. Dupres sits on the metallic floor, eyes closed. It is not at all like Soane's violent, relentless attack. Instead, new knowledge blossoms in my mind like a field of beautiful, exotic flowers, an orchard of science big enough to lose myself in. *How on Earth can this possibly work*—I think and then the answer is immediately there, in front of my eyes like something I have always known: microscopic wormholes created out of quantum vacuum by an amazingly simple circuit, extending into my brain and gently potentiating new neural connections.

It is an exhilarating feeling. I think about the ship around us, the adolescently named *Capital D*, and I see the angry, hungry knot of the singularity in its heart, the shell of exotic matter around it, ready to bend the space around us into Alcubierre warps and more: the unimaginable weapons that fire fragments of twisting, seething spacetime. I look at Dupres's immensely complex keyboard and it resolves itself into a shorthand for complex mental commands, there only to serve as a crutch for his mind so used to levers and plungers and typewriter keys. Hungry for more, I ask the headset how to reach out—and do so. There is a brief flash of amazement from Dupres as his mind mingles with mine. *Lead me from ignorance to truth—*

The images hit me in a relentless stream. *Burning worlds, cities beneath emerald seas. A green Dyson sphere filled with machines bigger than planets. A terrible war, things that look like ectoplasmic brains riding great machines of destruction; black insects eating rock and shitting copies of themselves. A planet splitting, unbearable brightness. Guilt, endless guilt, years and years and years of solitude and self-loathing and hate—*

And there, at the core, a moment: Dupres looking at two sleeping forms, an astonishingly beautiful woman and a little girl with wheat-hued hair, curled up together under a blanket. He touches the woman's hair, brushes the little girl's cheek.

And then he walks away, knowing that he is never coming back.

I yank the headset off and throw it away, tears streaming down my face. Dupres is clutching his chest, his face almost purple.

"Too much," he gasps. "You took too much. But it's what I would have done, too. It's what I did, many times." He grimaces, the tendons of his neck standing out. "They died screaming, so that I could have what they had in their brains, the poor bastards. But even there, Soane went further, like he always did. . . ." His face twists in pain.

"Jesus," I say, still reeling from the new vast thing boiling inside my mind. "You're hurt." I reach out to touch his arm. He brushes my hand away and wipes the foam from his lips. "I'm fine," he says. "Just fine."

"That was my grandmother. Maryann Leroy." I whisper. "And my mother."

"I had to leave them," Dupres says. "They would have been used. Soane, or . . . others. Like your bosses. They found out, that's why they sent you to me. I couldn't have them." He coughs. "But it doesn't matter anymore. Baby Face looked after them. And you turned out fine, all of you. Better off without me."

He closes his eyes and leans back. "Get us out of here, Kate. Take us home."

Millennia of knowledge whisper in my brain. I don the headset again, and the ship is there, a mind without consciousness, just a calm pool of obedience.

The bias drive of *Capital D* wakes up for the first time in seven decades, and we break off the icosahedral symmetry orbit, thundering towards the illusory sky. An alarm rings in the ship's brain, and I see silvery spheres— not unlike the ones that accompanied Soane on his planetoid, but vastly larger—hover around us.

"He must be getting your plague under control," mutters Dupres. "Still can't give us his full attention, but this is not going to be easy."

Around us the dead spaceships—the old *Skywalkers*—are coming to life. Through my ship-enhanced unreal vision I watch as the gun-ports of the copper sphere open and the mouths of machine guns start flashing. There are dazzling explosions in the vacuum. *Jesus. Antimatter bullets.* But that is just the start. The transparent sphere darts around the dark bulk of *Capital D* like an angry hornet, stinging us with a blazing energy beam, making our quantum dot skin boil. I pull power from the Penrose generator and increase the binding energies until *Capital D* glows across all frequencies, holding together under the assault.

A thought, and the *D*'s array of weapons comes to bear. The little *Skywalkers* explode into incandescence as I hit them with nuggets of super-symmetric matter.

"We have to get out of here before he activates *Skywalker Three*," mutters Dupres. "Hurry!"

"I'm trying!"

I start accelerating. Time slows down to a crawl. The ship's brain mirrors the functions of my own grey matter and makes my clock spin faster.

I see it coming after us: not dark like *Capital D* but easily twice the size, a tapering, vast cylinder whose insides glow in a tracery of green veins. The ship around us shudders as *Skywalker Three* reaches out a hand made of gravity waves and claws at our skin.

I fire the ship's weapons at the artificial sky ahead. The viewscreen goes black, but the *D* is projecting a representation of what is happening directly into my brain. Supersymmetric projectiles strike the bluescreen surface ahead and scatter in a halo of indescribable light. I curse, shifting through the vast storehouse of information now lodged in my brain. Quantum dot casters, plain old antimatter warheads—there is nothing in the ship's arsenal that will go through that impregnable shell, a picotech construct in the spacetime foam itself.

And *Skywalker Three* is just behind us, keeping pace, preparing to put us out of our misery.

Spacetime. Kate, you idiot.

I kick in the Alcubierre drive. Even the ship's view of the boiling space around us goes black as the warp bubble causally disconnects us from the rest of the Universe, shearing and stretching and molding vacuum. The ship shows me the discontinuity cutting right through *Skywalker Three*, gutting it like a fish, and for a brief moment I exult in triumph.

Then we go through the sky and I scream together with *Capital D*.

CHAPTER FIVE. MASTERS OF EARTH

I expect there to be a bone-jarring impact, a collision. But we just keep going, safely inside our warp bubble, moving faster than the speed of light.

Capital D complains. Its drive has been pushed past all endurance. The black hole in its heart is eating the exotic matter hungrily, threatening to break free of its shackles. If the carefully crafted hyperdense cocoon in which it lives collapses, we will be crushed in a microsecond—or stretched into spaghetti by the thousand-g tidal forces. I have a vision of our crushed bodies trapped inside the warp bubble, careening ever faster towards infinity. I delve deeper into the knowledge I've received from Dupres, trying to stabilise the engine's heartburn before it eats us.

"Help me here," I grunt at Dupres. "How do I turn this thing off?"

"You can eject the drive," he says. "There is a wormhole anchored to the galactic centre, see?" There is a pained smile on his face and I feel his presence join mine in the ship-mind. "Like this."

And we do it together with a thought, like it's the easiest thing in the world: shunt the exotic matter shell across thousands of light-years into the galactic core.

The bubble collapses. The blackness wavers and becomes a field of stars. The viewscreen shows a pale blue dot in the distance.

We are on our way home.

I look at Earth, letting my mind roam the corridors of the ship. There is still power circulating in the superconducting coils that run the full length of the ship, and the bias drive still works. Talking to the ship has an abstract beauty to it, a calmness that keeps my mind away from everything that has happened.

Quietly, I wonder if there is something that Dupres did to my mind, something that allows me to take all this in stride: I have a feeling that if I was really the same Kate as I was mere hours ago, I would be a gibbering wreck by now. Or maybe my system is saving the shock, and once we are back on Earth, I will collapse for good and be carted to wherever NSA hides the agents who have suffered mental injury in the line of duty.

Instead, I feel strangely content and serene. If it were not for the painful awareness of the possibility that Soane will inflict terrible retribution upon Earth in a very short time unless we do something, I would be having the time of my life.

I don't even notice Dupres leaving and returning. I look at him in astonishment as he hands me a metal bulb with a plastic nozzle. It smells of coffee. His hands shake, and laboriously he takes a small bottle of pills from his chest pocket. He opens it and swallows two bright green capsules. Then he leans back and lets out a long sigh.

"When we get back, we need to get you to a hospital," I tell him.

"Nonsense," he scoffs. "We can worry about that if we are alive tomorrow. I'll live long enough."

"I can't believe you have coffee here."

"I told you," he says. "A gentleman always travels in comfort."

The coffee smells like coffee should, strong and faintly bitter, and I let it and the stars and Earth and the humming giant spaceship take me to a Zen-like state of sensory bliss. Then I realise that I'm ravenous.

"I don't suppose there is any food in this oversized tub of yours?"

Dupres gives me a microsecond flicker of a smile, eyes still closed.

"How do you want your steak?"

"Dr. Dupres," I tell him. "If you think I'll let my grandfather cook me dinner, you've got another thing coming. Where is the kitchen?"

We leave *Capital D* hovering above Cheyenne Mountain.

NORAD is ready for us. Steel doors open, and close behind us as we enter the best-protected spot on Earth. ETINT is now running things from here: the fact that one of their agents has a mile-long spaceship may have something to do with it. There is rock and steel and Marines: the whole complex sits on hundreds of gigantic steel springs that weigh seven tons each. It can withstand the direct impact of a multi-megaton warhead: but even with the untold masses of bedrock above my head there is a fearful tickle at the back of my neck.

Gomez and Casey are waiting for us at SCC, and it looks so delightfully utilitarian and prosaic—green-uniformed young men with shaved heads sitting in cubicles and staring at computer screens, wall displays showing news reports—that I almost burst into tears.

Gomez gives me a tight bear hug and I don't even care that his breath smells of onions.

"Hey," he says. "I shat myself when I saw that house go up. It's good to have you back."

I glare at Casey. The head of ETINT is proper and unfazed as ever, her tiny frame showing no signs of fatigue, looking at me over her rimless glasses.

"You," I tell her. "I have a bone to pick with you. But that can wait. Now we have to—"

Before I can finish the sentence, an all-too-familiar titan in slacks and a Hawaiian shirt shimmers into being in the centre of the room.

"Hiya, Darkie," says Soane. "Long time, no see."

"Hey, toots," says the projection, looking at me. "I should have known that you were a wildcat, following that no-good, back-stabbing louse around, but I really didn't expect that last love-tap—more the fool me!" He frowns. "Me and Marty had to pretty much rebuild the whole core of ol' '*Walker* to get rid of your bugs—and that, as the poet feelingly remarked, is going some! Barbara didn't really appreciate your cooking either, and I'm afraid we can't have you over for dinner again anytime soon. My Red-Top would claw your eyes out."

"The feeling is mutual," I say coldly.

"What do you want?" snaps Dupres.

"I told you before. There's a lot of cleaning up to do here, Darkie boy," says Soane. "I tried to analyse the stuff coming through the televisor network and the interbrain, and boy, I don't know what you are trying to do here, devolve them or what. You told me about your empire plans, remember? A sedated working class and the super-rich. I always preferred the green-world way: get rid of the unfit, make people struggle to become better. And there's plenty out there we can struggle against. Those machines in M4, we'll have to take care of those as well before they take care of *us*. And there's all the races who disappeared up their own backsides, got rid of their bodies. They built big stuff out there that no one is using. We can go there and make it ours."

Dupres grimaces. "As you say. So, what do you want from me?"

"I don't want my son to be born into *your* world, Darkie," Soane says.

"Your son?" says Dupres.

"Yes, a son," says Soane. "Some of us have family to care about. And you've had your way with this place for a long time. Time to hand it over. Make a clean Earth. Shut down this interbrain poison, restore *some* sort of social order together. I figure you've got enough dope to sort it out in twenty-four hours. If our home nest is not spick and span by then, we up here on *Skywalker* will start doing some cleaning up of our own. And I don't think you'll like that, not one whit or piffle."

Dupres does not reply. Casey is covering her mouth with her hand.

Soane's gaze becomes like stone. "And just to show you I'm not just talking to make noise, I'm going to remove your naval forces from the various corners of Earth right now. I don't want you equipping them with bias drives and sending them against me. Cheerio now, bucko—see you again in twenty-four hours!"

The projection disappears. The clock strikes five. And the SCC news screens go mad.

In New York, it is raining ships.

They fall in unison, in a perfect, evenly spaced grid: giant metal hailstones raining down from the stratosphere. I see an aircraft carrier go down and flatten the Statue of Liberty. Fighter planes spilled from its deck drift down after it. The ballistic nuclear subs dive through concrete like giant dolphins and keep going, and I imagine their reactors getting China Syndrome and burrowing all the way down to Earth's core. The battleships are giant sledgehammers, crushing skyscrapers like sandcastles.

It lasts less than a minute. Twenty-seven battleships, ten aircraft carriers. Two hundred destroyers. Fifty-six cruisers. Innumerable support craft. The frozen bodies of four thousand sailors. It is like a shotgun blast, straight into the face. God chewing our steel and explosives and atomic furnaces and spitting them back down on us.

Finally, the smoke and dust over the island make us blind and we just listen. After a while I no longer hear the disjointed reports, screams and sirens. I want to cry but the tears will not come. Next to me, Gomez starts screaming obscenities.

Dupres sits in his chair, a mug of coffee in one liver-spotted hand, stroking his grey stubble with the other. I want to scream at him, punch him in the face. *You knew. You knew he would do this.*

Somebody shuts down the satellite feeds and the news channels and the room goes dark. We breathe the deadly silence for a few seconds. Then Dupres speaks.

"It's not over yet," he says, his voice calm. "It's going to be a local gravitational lens next, I'll wager. Just to show us that he can."

Three minutes later, the sun goes out.

"Yes, I knew," Dupres tells us all. "Not that, precisely. But something like it. I knew." He squeezes the bridge of his nose. "I am sorry for all those people. I am sorry. Seventy years ago, I could have put a bullet in the brain that did this, but I did not. I . . . regret that now."

"Then again, if I had—it would be me up there now. And things would be more efficient. But no more pleasant."

"Let me get this straight," the President says from the videoconference screen on the wall. "This madman—this *terrorist*—still thinks *you* are the most powerful man on Earth?"

Dupres leans back in his chair, smiling his dark smile, and I can read the question *How big is your spaceship, Mr. President?* in his eyes.

"All those civilians, sir," whispers Gomez. "And putting out the Sun—"

Dupres grimaces. "Soane was always a social Darwinist. To him, this is a weeding. The strong will survive this night, for his perfect world." He shakes his head. "I would like to say that it's not really him, that it's some amalgam creature made of the minds he assimilated, just wearing his skin, but it is not. Beneath that there is still that stiff-necked man I knew in Rare Metals Laboratory, all his anxieties and worries and bigotry projected to an alien mind and magnified thousandfold. Believe me, I know how it works."

"I'm not interested in his psychology," says the President. "How do we take him out? The National Guard is on the streets. We're trying to saturate the media with stories about a meteor shower and an eclipse, but it's not going to fly. And every amateur astronomer on the planet can now *see* that fucking thing in the sky. Give me some options, people."

"We have a scenario for the nuclear option in case of invasion—" starts Casey.

"It's not an option," interrupts Dupres. "You people cannot possibly comprehend the scale here. Soane can take out *this solar system* with that ship if he wants to." He frowns. "He wants a fight. He is still playing the old game. Our only chance is to play it. For a while. And then change the game. I've had a long time to think about this: I know Soane. There is something I can do—there is something I can make him do. But I need time."

"We'd appreciate it if you'd share your plan with the rest of us, Dr. Dupres," says the President irritably.

"Don't be a fool," snarls Dupres. "Which part of the *he can read minds* section of Kate Leroy's report did you not understand?"

"Doctor, do *you* understand who you are talking to?"

"He gave us twenty-four hours, Mr. President," I say quietly. "Two of those are now gone."

The President looks down. "Fine," he says finally. "Continue. But any operational decisions rest with me." The screen goes blank.

Dupres slumps in his chair and actually looks like an old man. And just as I'm about to go over and cover him with a blanket, he opens his eyes and glares at me, his eyes like flint.

"All right," he says. "It is time for you kids to learn what it means to *think*."

The brainstorm rages for two hours. Packing *Capital D* with nuclear explosives and using it as a projectile against the *Skywalker*. Giving Dupres to him, infected with a weaponised form of Ebola. Enough crazy ideas to kill Soane a hundred times, except that none of them will work in the time we have left or at all. Gomez keeps the news screens dark, and we are blissfully ignorant of the destruction and chaos that is undoubtedly sweeping across the globe. Somehow, it doesn't make it any easier.

Eventually, the fatigue starts to catch up with me in spite of all the coffee and I start nodding off in my chair, the torrent of arguing voices around me like so many ocean waves.

I beat him once before, the thought comes, in that twilight haze just before proper sleep. *The kitchen. I hacked the kitchen. He didn't know about proper crypto. What else does he not know about? New things. New ways of thinking. Combine them with old things, the things Dupres gave me—*

"Even with *Capital D*, we would not have had much of a chance: we had to dump the black-hole core, and its reserve power is almost out," Dupres is saying, his voice reed-thin. "We need a ship."

"We have Earth," I say quietly, opening my eyes.

Dupres looks at me curiously, red-eyed with fatigue but face alive again. "Earth?"

"The educators," I say. "They are not that hard to build, at the end of the day, at least not the old models that work via magnetic induction."

The smartest man on Earth blinks at me, uncomprehending. I grin at him.

"Granddad, are you implying that you have never heard of the open source movement?"

Chapter Six. *Skywalker* of Earth

We release the educator designs on all the open-source hardware sites. It takes us six hours to convert the design to run on off-the-shelf FPGAs and write a protocol that allows them to run over the Internet. Three hours later, there are hundreds of headsets in existence, worn by geeks and scientists all over the world. By four in the afternoon, there are thousands.

Then we start talking to them through the master headsets from *Capital D.*

At first it is clumsy, painful even. A babble of thoughts and sounds fill my head, and I cringe as I let them explore the storehouse of alien physics I received from Dupres, the memory of Soane opening my mind like a gutted fish still too raw.

But after a while, as they absorb the new information like sponges, something strange happens. Our thoughts start self-organising, synchronising. It is Srinivati—fourteen-year-old prodigy from Mumbai—who comes up with the decision-routing algorithm. I immediately relay it to Dupres, who passes it on. After that, work becomes effortless: any idea I come up with is immediately taken up, pursued to its logical completion. And at the same time, I get flashes of ideas and insights that seemingly come from nowhere, passed on from other minds. The flow of information is such that it becomes addictive, like a crack cocaine version of Internet surfing combined with the most engaging computer game. Hesse's Glass Bead Game on speed.

I would want nothing more but to lose myself in Earth's thoughts were it not for the terrible flashes of violence and terror that come through the educator network as well. A teenage girl is gang-raped and killed in

Rwanda while connected, and the fact that the global brain immediately hacks three Air Force attack drones and blows the perpetrators to kingdom come does not make me feel any better. There is looting and blood on the streets in Paris, fire and horror in Beijing. An idea about installing pain filters into the network floats around for a minute or two but is overruled by the emerging entity where Dupres and I are now merely key coordinator nodes: pain and horror make us more determined. Millions have already died. Billions more may die if we don't succeed.

I am not entirely sure what we do with the Large Hadron Collider. It takes hours of crazy programming, Dupres walking around SCC, dictating and typing furiously at the same time, the master headset he is wearing streaming his thoughts to the world.

We work through the evening and night and dream the Apocalypse into being. When it gets too much, I remove the headset, sit still, close my eyes and breathe. And I'm no longer afraid.

Then it is six in the morning again and the *Skywalker* arrives.

It is in high geostationary orbit, visible from everywhere in the world, a giant eye in the sky. Dupres stares at the viewscreen darkly, hands shaking.

"Come on, you bastard," he mutters. "Show yourself."

Precisely on time, Soane's avatar is there, larger-than-life and seemingly fully solid this time, towering over Dupres.

"I told you it's time to stop being the Poo-Bah," Soane says, Titan-like voice making the bedrock shake. "You've toed over the mark this time, Darkie, and I'm going to—"

"Now," whispers Dupres, and together we send the thought out to a cave in Switzerland.

Beams of protons and antiprotons—each microscopic particle the kinetic energy of a flying mosquito—collide deep underground. Through the educator link and the minds viewing the instruments, I can see the characteristic radiation of microscopic black holes, being born and dying in little bursts of Hawking radiation. I can see the ripple in the Higgs field in my mind's eye, expanding outwards like vacuum flames.

Phase two. The hundred educated minds in CERN gather the black holes the accelerator is churning out in a magnetic bottle before they have time to die, and hurl them at the Sun. And what happens there is the hardest part: it took supercomputers and thousands of brains and mathematics that is beyond me even now.

Soane's projection flickers and disappears. Outside, the pale morning sky changes colour. The whole sky is now shimmering and iridescent, too bright to look at, a phosphorescent sheet with colours impossible to describe.

"Sweet Jesus," mutters Gomez.

"It's a stable domain wall around Earth," says Dupres. "Flaw in ice. Except that the medium we froze is the vacuum." There is just a hint of awe in his voice. "He can't get through it. Nothing can, except a couple of weakly interacting specimens we found."

"Are you saying we are safe, Doctor?" asks Casey, face pale and drawn.

"For about eight minutes," says Dupres. He brings a grainy image on the main screen: the feed comes from *Capital D*—our observation post in orbit—on a modulated WIMP channel, received by a million-litre neutrino detector in the Antarctic. The *Skywalker* is there, so very close, a terrible new moon. In spite of the low resolution, we can see its surface shifting, alive like skin with pulsing veins.

"What happens in eight minutes?"

"The Sun undergoes a quantum phase transition and crystallises into a dark star," says Dupres. "Then it explodes as a gamma-ray burst. A hypernova."

"What?" says the President.

"It was the only weapon I could think of that would even rattle him a little," says Dupres.

"We blew up the Sun?" I say incredulously, the pieces of the plan I helped to formulate finally making sense.

"We are perfectly safe here," Dupres says. "You may see some twinkles in your optic nerve in four minutes. Those will be WIMPs hitting the cells in your eye, lots of them."

The President starts praying, and for a moment I want to as well.

"Oh, don't be such a bunch of old women," says Dupres. "I know where to take the Earth if we win. There is a perfectly fine yellow star in

Andromeda. The Sun is just a ball of hot gas, nothing more. This way, he doesn't get *us*."

After that, no one says anything, we just stare at the screens. A background murmur of anxiety passes through the educator net, growing until I have to remove the headset.

It is over so quickly that I almost miss it. The Sun blinks. The pale disc of the Moon glows white and is gone. And then everything in all the screens is engulfed by a wave of light, until only static remains. There is a rain of stars in my optic nerve, purple and blue and green, the only echoes of the most energetic phenomenon in the Universe that come down this far. I blink them away.

"Did we do it?" I ask Dupres. "Did we get him?"

His face is ashen in the light of the monitors. Slowly, he shakes his head, pain in his eyes, clutches at his chest and collapses to the ground.

"Should've known—the bloody neutrinos would mess up—my pacemaker. I was always—a better physicist," he gasps. "It was Maryann who was the doctor."

His face twists. Every muscle in his body twitches. "We need medical attention here!" I shout, tears in my eyes.

"Ssh, girl," Dupres says. "When he comes—" He shakes his head and some of the steel returns to his eyes. "When he comes, remember Br'er Rabbit. Thornbush. The educator. Promise."

Mutely, I nod. When the medics finally arrive, he is gone.

I know that Soane is coming when my headset—and the Internet—goes dead.

He is not very subtle, this time. The mountain shakes all the way to its foundations. There is a terrible, groaning sound as layers and layers of rock are peeled away by unseen forces, a giant hand made of thunder punching through stone and steel. And before I realise what is happening, we all see the glowing sky through a colossal gash on the side of the mountain. The wind tears at my hair and makes my eyes water.

He descends from the sky slowly, naked and frail. The real Soane is an ancient, wizened man floating next to a corrugated sphere of metal the size of a man's head—the housing for the Brain that was the core of the *Skywalker*. Tendrils of light from his mouth and limbs and head connect him to it like bright umbilicals.

The Marines are there, firing at him, before I have the chance to tell them to stop. The bullets flame into droplets of molten metal in mid-air and the soldiers collapse to the ground, unconscious.

"That actually *hurt*," Soane says, looking at Dupres's still form. His real voice is weak and quavering, but the tone is familiar. "I actually had to leave poor old '*Walker* behind, rotate us off the brane to survive. I have to give you some credit, bucko. You haven't lost your touch. But the game is over now. And I will have to make a new Sun as well. What a chore!" He grins. "But then you've always known that making things bigger and better is the fondest thing I am of."

"He's dead," I say quietly.

Soane blinks.

"What?" he says. "No, no. It's a dummy. A robot. Or a heart-stopping drug, he did that once before. He escaped from that M4 drone as it fell into the dark star. He is not dead, toots. He is somewhere laughing at me, scheming. He can't die."

"He—is—dead. Just like your wife. Your friend. And that poor girl Peg. They are all dead. You should leave them alone. You should leave us all alone."

"I don't believe you," he says quietly. The ground begins to shake around me, and the air is hot. "It is a trick. He always had one up his sleeve."

"I thought you could read dead brains," I say. "Why don't you find out what he really thought about you?"

An invisible hand brushes me violently aside. The educator machinery ghosts into being and seizes Dupres's still form, lifts it up. Soane closes his eyes. And when he opens them, it's like he really sees me for the first time. Briefly, his eyes are young, almost childlike. "He had you. He always had you. He watched you. You're his daughter, aren't you?"

"Granddaughter," I say. "But I'm not going to play the game with you. There is no one to fight you anymore."

There are tears on Soane's cheeks. "I never imagined—" he says. "I never thought—"

His skin starts boiling. The Brain glows like a captive star. *One errant thought,* the ghost of Barbara Soane said.

"I never knew he always won," says Soane.

They rise to the sky together, dead Dupres and dying Soane and the alien brain, faster than the eye can follow. There is a blast of heat, and a burst of light brighter than the exploding Sun.

What they leave behind is mountain wind and an impossible, shining sky.

EPILOGUE

It took a while to work out how to collapse the domain wall, but we did it in time. Building a planetary Alcubierre drive was even easier, and we've got a new Sun now—or three, just as bright and yellow as Dupres always said.

Things are becoming very strange on Earth, almost too strange for me. Gomez feels the same way. We had a second first date on one of the moons of our new system's gas giant, and things are working out better than I could have imagined. But I feel restless: I keep thinking of the dreaming green minds that Dupres and Soane found and wonder what they could tell us. And I wonder if we are still too young to talk to them: but there is only one way to find out.

That's why we built the ship. It's not as big or as powerful as some of the *Skywalker*s the educator kids are making—just to show that they can—but it's big enough for the two of us, big enough for a long, long journey.

Gomez let me name it. I call it *Capital D Two.*

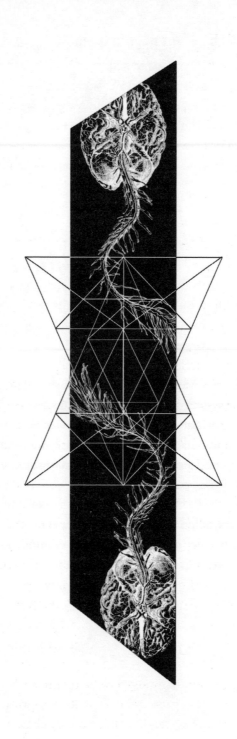

Neurofiction: Introduction to "Snow White Is Dead"

You should really be reading this story on a computer screen wearing an electroencephalography headset.

"Snow White Is Dead" is the most ambitious literary/technology experiment I have attempted so far. It started with me and my friend Sam Halliday—a mathematician and a data scientist—with some time on our hands, deciding we wanted to do *something* with brain-computer interfaces. We were fortunate enough to win a small grant from New Media Scotland to explore the connections between this emerging technology and fiction.

Initially, we just wanted to look at what happens in a reader's brain when they read science fiction in particular. For example, it turns out that the experience of insight has a very distinct brain wave signal, and I was curious to see if we could deliberately evoke it in a reader. But Sam and I quickly realised that the possibility of getting the text itself to change in response to your brain activity was even more exciting. We decided to write a story that reads you, a Choose Your Own Adventure without conscious choice.

For me, finding a story that wanted to be told in such a format was a challenge just as difficult as getting the technology to work. In the end, I decided to go back to archetypes, fairy tales, binary choices. Life or death, red or green, black or white, and there are few stories that embody those more than "Snow White."

We demonstrated the resulting interactive experience at the Edinburgh Science Festival in 2013. You sit down in front of a screen wearing an Emotiv EPOC headset (itself an artefact from a cyberpunk tale, a 14-electrode system for measuring brain waves that connects to a computer via Bluetooth). The story starts by throwing verbal images of life and death at the reader. A machine-learning algorithm tries to determine if the reader's response to each subsequent scene is closer to one or the other. It steers them through one of dozens of possible paths through the story, to an ending that—like the apple—is either red or green.

The project subsequently attracted a lot of media interest and was featured in various UK media, including *New Scientist*. I also gave a talk at Google about it. To my and Sam's delight, people have even taken our code (which we open-sourced) and started creating their own Neurofiction stories beyond "Snow White."

I chose the scene ordering reproduced here based on the most common paths that readers' brains took through the story, but if you want to make your own way, you can download all the code from https://github.com/fommil/neurofiction and see where your thoughts take you.

Snow White Is Dead

The PRINCESS SLEEPS in the hospital bed, and the young doctor watches her dreams.

She is the faded image of a beautiful girl: pale sunken cheeks, tangled black hair, lips with the faintest hint of red. The electroencephalography cap makes her head into a forest of wires and electrodes. She looks gaunt and old. Her skin is paper-thin, full of wounds and bedsores. Her teeth are marred by caries.

She is the most beautiful thing he has ever seen.

She breathes out, and the laptop screen becomes a snowstorm.

They did it with cats first: decoded the visual centre of the brain, stitched fragments of feline dreams together with electricity and algorithms. At first, the images are hazy. The main window shows an amber flame, dancing and wavering. The software tries to match it to a grid of YouTube video clips, a mosaic assembled from fragments of collective subconscious.

A row of skulls, grinning visages of death. Medical images: brains inside fragile carapaces, the dark scribble of a hematoma marring one.

A nuclear explosion. First, a burning golden sun too bright to look at, a perfect disc. White rings smooth like eggshells appear around it. The disc folds into itself, becomes uneven and two-lobed, like a burning fusion brain. An inverted avalanche of dirt rises from the ground to envelop it, breaks the bright colours with grey and brown, until only a faded dark pillar remains. And then the sound comes, shaking the laptop's speakers.

And finally, an apple. It turns slowly from green to bright red.

On the screen, flower grows, in speeded-up time: green tendrils push themselves up, slowly at first, swaying to the tempo of the flickering sky and the shadows of clouds flashing past, then bifurcating into a labyrinth of emerald forking paths and leaves like tongues, finally ending in a fiery explosion of petals and yellow stamen.

A bare heart beats in surgery, red and fleshy and soft, the hue of dirty life against the clinical blue of the patient's hospital gown. It jerks and leaps and shudders like an animal struggling to get free from the trap of ribs in an open chest, a hole held open by square metal pincers.

A fetus moves slowly in a blue-tinted sonogram image, huge dome of a head curled against its chest, tiny hands in fists, dreaming unborn dreams, pulsing to the rhythm of its mother's heartbeat.

Today, she is going to kill her husband.

As she wakes up, the thought brings warm joy that spreads through her limbs like a massage. She stretches luxuriously in the empty bed: he is in an early morning meeting. The girl is gone, too. She feels her absence in the hushed silence of the house, and smiles.

She walks through the house naked, glorying in the morning light on her flawless skin. In a few hours, it will all belong to her: the clean lines of the designer furniture, the calm of the frozen pier and the beach sauna, all the little symbols of power.

She makes herself a coffee, sits on the couch, cradles the hot cup against her bare belly, and turns on the TV.

She does not really watch it, though. She can already see what it will show tomorrow. The shattered glass, the black ice, the blood. The dark sedan that came out of nowhere, crushing the minister's car on the driver's side.

What they won't show is her hand, unbuckling her husband's seat belt, or her last smile in the rearview mirror. Those are just for him.

Afterwards, the TV will show her. She will be stricken with grief but strong, ready to take up her husband's burdens for the party. She will have a single white bandage on her pale forehead, perhaps, dabbed with blood. It will make her seem fragile and beautiful.

Except that something is wrong. The ghosts of tomorrow are whispering. And they are not talking about her, they are talking about *her*. The little princess who died, with the raven hair and rosy cheeks. They can't get enough of her. After today, the little bitch will live forever.

She can't let that happen.

She turns the TV off. An old naked woman stares back at her from the black slab of the screen, hunched and pale.

She has to make them forget her. Make them hate her.

She remembers the dress the girl was making, from the cartoon, yellow and blue with a red bow tie.

Best of all would be to make them laugh at the little bitch.

The smile returns to her lips, and she feels beautiful again. She picks up her phone and makes a call.

The photographer hunts for the princess in the forest of the geeks.

It is late afternoon. Golden light hits the old factory's red brick walls. It would make a good shot, if not for the kids wearing makeup and carrying padded giant swords.

He could be in a helicopter now, stalking the F1 Driver, to catch a candid shot of his mistress who likes to roll in the snow after going to the sauna. But no, he has to be at a science fiction convention, to make a little girl look bad, because of a phone call.

Bring me a picture of her. The kind you do best. You know what I mean.

And he has no choice but to obey the Voice. The Voice knows too much, and has chilly fingers around his balls.

The metal of the camera is cold in his hands. He takes a few shots, just to warm up. Boys with paper bags over their heads, in blood-spattered coveralls. Manga-costumed jailbait chicks in pink leggings and schoolgirl uniforms, pillow lips blue from the cold. Stormtroopers and batmen. No sign of the princess yet. A part of him wonders what she has done to deserve this.

A flash of yellow and blue. *There*. He snaps a photo, and almost drops the camera when a zombie princess growls at him, thrusting a pair of blood-spattered boobs at his face. Her teeth glint yellow against pale white makeup.

There are many princesses here, all in the same colours. Superhero versions, vampire versions, even a cross-dressing one. He swears. It is getting dark already, and there is not going to be enough light for a good shot if he doesn't find her soon. His gut tightens. The shots get better, though. Muscular young guys with spiky hairdos and impossibly large swords, sitting in a circle with a cardboard robot, playing Dungeons and Dragons. Six-year-olds dressed up as Hattivatti from the Moomin books. He realises he is actually enjoying it. There used to be a time he tried to *see* things through the camera, didn't think about the headlines in black, red and yellow. After a while, he just lets the colours and images flow in through the lens, without thinking.

Then he sees her. She sits on the sidewalk, oblivious to the cold. There is a bruise on her cheek that is either very well made up or real. She is smoking a joint, eyes closed. There is his shot: the minister's daughter, passed out in a Snow White costume, getting high. He raises the camera.

But he can't help seeing things as they are, through the lens.

The bruise is real. There are dark rings around her eyes. She watches the crowd with a strange hunger, looking for something. Suddenly, he knows she doesn't want to go home.

His finger freezes on the trigger. For a moment, he just watches her. He waits until the last light dies and all the creatures around him look grey. She disappears among them.

He fumbles with the memory card and his iPad, a cigarette in his mouth. He flicks through the pictures. He picks the one with the zombie princess with the big tits and sends it to the Voice.

It makes a whooshing sound as it goes, like a helicopter blade.

Little by little, we gather all her pieces together, in the glass coffin. Her emails, her Facebook updates, her health records. The duck-face pictures, the cosplay posing. The video from the convention, the one where she smiles.

It takes hours of coding in the dark. Our faces are cratered alien planets in the monitor glow, greasy from lack of sleep. The flat is hot with the breath of our machines.

She came to us on the last day of the convention. We returned home as heroes that evening. We had flirted with cosplayer girls, argued *Star Trek* and *LOTR* trivia with our rivals, hunted for *Babylon 5* star autographs. For once, we belonged. Afterwards, we all felt something had changed.

It was Simo who saw her first and described her to the rest of us. He was good at that. When we played Dungeons and Dragons, he was always the Game Master. With just words, he could paint caverns and orcs and shimmering magic swords and make them real. And so we listened to him and saw.

She slept in Simo's bed, curled up under a blanket, wearing his Red Lantern T-shirt. We had seen her before, from afar, in blue and yellow and red, with the other Snows. She didn't have the cleavage of the superhero Snow or the madcap energy of the zombie one. But out of all of them, she was the most beautiful.

We looked at her and did not know what to do. Then she opened her eyes.

"Do you guys mind if I stay a while?" she asked.

And that was how Lumi came to live with us.

She was always there in the evening. She never said what she did during the day, and we did not ask. But she always had a kind, sarcastic word for each of us. And like manic pixie dream girls do, she would get us to do crazy things. Go to the roof and look at the stars. Compliment random people on the street. Dye our hair and beards in different colours.

We all wanted her, but there was an unspoken agreement.

No one tried to touch her, or to claim her. To do anything would have shattered the illusion that she belonged to us.

So of course Jyri had to screw it up.

It was a small thing, he told us later. She was in the kitchen, one night, sitting at the table. She had done the dishes, lit scented candles. Her old bruise had faded but a shadow was still there. She had been crying. She kept looking at her iPhone. The logo flashed when she turned it in her hand, a silver eyeblink.

Is everything all right? Jyri asked.

It's nothing, she said. Just my mom.

Jyri could see that something had bitten into her mind and she was no longer ours. He felt desperate. He laid his hand on hers, hairy and thick-fingered.

You can tell me, he said. I'm a good listener, not like the others, they just want to make you into what they want you to be. But I'm here for you.

She pulled her hand away and clicked the display of the phone shut.

But I'm not really here, she said. I'm in the mirror.

She kissed Jyri's cheek.

Tell the others goodbye for me.

Her breath smelled sweet. Jyri closed his eyes. When he opened them, he saw her lying on the floor, green eyes wide open. It was only then that he saw the jar of pills, in her hand.

That was how Lumi left us.

When the morning comes, she is there, complete, beneath the glass of our screens. We stare at her, wanting, missing, afraid to touch. Jyri bites down tears. Ismo swears. Mikko tugs at his beard. She is beautiful and bright, and for a moment she is ours again.

Then Ismo makes the site public, and we set her free.

The doctor found her online. It was one of those links you click on when you are bored. A kind of digital shrine to a girl in a coma. There were pictures of her, and a shaky mobile video. In it, she sat on stairs, wearing a yellow skirt.

Suddenly, she looked up at him and smiled. There was a blue bruise on her cheek, but the smile was red and joyous, trusting and innocent.

He watched it three times and knew he loved her.

He requested a transfer to her hospital. The usual weight of names and money made it happen.

He found her in a bare room with yellow walls. She smelled of a brain trauma patient's heavy body cream, and something sweet beneath.

He wanted to see behind her eyes. He wanted to fight the black blood dragon in her brain.

He takes out a glass bottle with an obscure label and fills a syringe. With sure fingers, he finds a blue vein in her arm. The clear fluid goes in, smoothly: another impossible thing that only a prince could buy. When the needle comes out, it leaves behind a tiny drop of blood on her skin, a ruby sphere, perfectly formed. He kisses it away.

He disconnects her from the machines, gently removes the drips, untangles her raven hair from the electrodes. The green lines on the screens go flat.

He holds her hand and waits for her to wake.

Outside, there is birdsong.

I am not who you think I am.

I am death, and you should stay away from me.

It's not personal. You did wake me up. And you are beautiful, sitting there in your white coat, with your slicked-back hair and Biarritz tan and expensive watch and a faint smell of pine in your aftershave.

No, I don't want a glass of water. But I need you to listen.

I was my mother's death. She wanted a perfect daughter, one made from snow and blood and a raven's wing, and there is only one place where such a wish leads.

My stepmother saw it: a reflection of her own end, the death of youth and beauty. She knew what I was, even when I was a child: her death in the mirror.

I read comics about Bamse the World's Strongest Bear and pretended to be his friend Kilpinen the turtle. When I pulled my head inside my shirt, to hide from the world as if inside a shell, she pulled me back out by my hair and warned me about suffocating. But she always sounded wistful.

I could see the slow death I brought to my father, as I grew older. I was a hole in him, shaped like my mother, and through me, his life leaked away. And so I tried to run away.

I will be the death of the man with the camera my stepmother sent after me: he saw something else in my face, did not do as he was told, and in time, she will make him pay.

My friends thought they saved me, but in time, I would have been the death of their friendship. They shared everything: but I was the thing one of them would have claimed all to himself.

In a way, it was a blessing when she sent the message. I knew it was her, the instant my phone vibrated in my pocket. I could feel it in its warm rounded curves and sleek glass.

The letters spelled poison, a chemical formula made of words. IT'S YOUR FAULT HE DIED. There was a link to the car crash.

I stared at it until my eyes hurt.

I found the drugs in Jyri's room. I swallowed them without water: they were dry and tasted like nothing. It was better to be nothing than death, better to be a silence than an echo.

It hurt a bit at first, in my belly and between my temples. Then the dreams came like rain.

I was a vampire princess, cold and hard, who made a pact with the old forces of the earth, ancient gods who took the shape of little men, and fought with a dark queen who wanted an immortal's blood.

I was an android girl, a pleasure machine without a heart, sold off and sent to the scrapyard by a jealous wife; taken in by mining bots on distant Mars and deactivated by a secret code, only to wake again in the distant future where the sun burned red, by a posthuman god looking to understand humanity.

I was a hundred other princesses who existed only to die and come back again and to reflect others' hopes and dreams.

I can see it in your eyes, too. Looking for something you desperately want to see. You think you have won me, rescued me.

You don't believe me. You think we will fall in love and marry. My stepmother will come to our wedding and stare at our happiness, face red with rage, spiky heels tapping impotently on the dance floor. But she won't let me have you. She will ask you to dance, and as the music swells, there will be a syringe in her hand.

That's how it always goes in dreams. But I also dreamt a way out of the mirror.

You said I died, for a little bit, when you brought me back. That's the way it has to be. Lumi never woke up and died in her sleep. If you love me, you can do that for me, change the records and find some nameless body who can be Lumi instead of me.

I will kiss you now, for goodbye.

My body is broken. My teeth hurt, my hair is in tatters.

My limbs are withered and full of sores. It does not matter.

You want me. You untangle the electrodes from my hair while kissing my neck. On the screen of your laptop, the apple is red. And then you are my little death, and I am yours.

You are still asleep when I wrap the hospital gown around me and send a message to my friends from your phone. They will have a passport and a ticket waiting for me, and a new name, forged from the silver of bits.

I whisper a goodbye to you and leave.

It has snowed during the night. The birdsong in the trees is made soft by the blanket on the ground. And all the world is white and empty, like the first page of a book.

I am everything you could ever want. I am everything that you can't buy, you who sit there in your white coat, with your slicked-back hair and Biarritz tan and expensive watch and a faint smell of pine in your aftershave.

I am life. I am innocence. I am fragile. I am sweet. I am the thing you made, from chemicals and electric dreams.

So just for you, I make myself look weaker than I am, after my waking, so you can rush to my side and adjust the pillows and offer me a glass of water. I let your hand touch mine as I take it and drink, slowly. Your fingers are warm, your breath eager and quick. My lips are dry and ragged, my hair a tangled mess. It doesn't matter. The magic is still there.

This is the game of the mirror. I make you see what you want to see.

It was my father the king who showed me how to play. He told me I was special, that I was not like the other little girls. My mother brought me from the fairy kingdom with a wish, made me from snow and blood and a raven's wing.

If I showed him my mother's face, he would do anything I wanted. If I smiled just so, he would smile and buy me a Princess Barbie. If I chewed on my hair just right, his face would darken, and he would go to his office to sit still, covering his eyes with his hands.

All that was his would have been mine. Until she came, to fill the hole my mother had left, to stop my father's life from leaking out. And she knew me for what I was, a thing just like her. The mirror game between us was an infinite corridor of reflections, a labyrinth of glass and smiles.

She was older and stronger, the bitch. And so I had to run.

She chased me, of course. The photographer was easy: his kind exist to see things in a square frame, through a lens.

All it took to send him away was a self-inflicted bruise, a mournful look, to show him what he had lost.

The boys in black would have built me a castle as long as I showed them a sexy little mother. It would have been a safe haven to build myself again, to grow strong. But she sent me a message, summoning me home, masked in grief and love and other lies.

I knew it was a trap. I could never escape her. Unless she thought she had won.

So I took my medicine. I would sleep until the time was right to wake. I slept and dreamed my revenge.

I was a vampire princess, cold and hard, who made a pact with the old forces of the earth, ancient gods who took the shape of little men, and fought with a dark queen who wanted an immortal's blood. In the end, the queen drank too deep of undeath and burned in the sun.

I was an android girl, a pleasure machine without a heart, sold off and sent to the scrapyard by a jealous AI; taken in by mining bots on distant Mars and deactivated by a secret code, only to wake again in the distant future where the sun burned red, by an alien god looking to understand humanity long gone. As a punishment, the AI was trapped in a singularity and turned on itself, devouring its own code as entropy burned it away.

You woke me. I am not ungrateful. Before I take all that you have, I will make your dreams come true, as a true love should.

You will nurse me back to health. We will be on the pages of all the papers, a miracle couple, the princess and her saviour. I will be shy at first, and broken; you will put me together piece by piece, kiss by kiss.

We will get married in your family's country house, in midsummer, beneath the white flowers of bird cherry trees. My stepmother will come. We will smile mirrored smiles at each other, and then you will offer her a dance.

And as the music rises and you swing her around, there will be a syringe in your hand. She will feel a little sting, like the peck of a bird. And then she will dance, dance in her high-heeled shoes until her feet burn, dance her life away.

Now, help me up. I want to see the sunrise outside. I want to see the face of the world again.

Oh yes. A blue sky, golden light, a red horizon. Black branches of trees against the white of snow, like writing. Birds, faintly singing, and then, silence.

Introduction to "Unused Tomorrows and Other Stories"

One of my favourite short stories of all time is Augusto Monterroso's "The Dinosaur": "When he woke up, the dinosaur was still there." I love the fact that most of the story happens outside the frame of those nine words, in the reader's head.

Writing microfiction is the ultimate challenge to a writer's craft. It requires cutting away everything unnecessary, leaving only a sharp, singular image that the reader can grow into a story on their own. Several members of my writers' group in Edinburgh (Andrew Ferguson, Gavin Inglis, Andrew Wilson, to name but a few) are microfiction masters, from science fiction haiku to postcard-sized stories, so I was also inspired to try my hand at it early on.

With its wonderfully arbitrary 140-character limitation, Twitter struck me as a great platform for microfiction from the start. I joined Twitter in January 2007—early enough to capture my first name as a username—but never got around to doing much with it, until New Media Scotland, an arts/technology organisation in Scotland, asked me to be their Twitterer-in-Residence in August 2008.

For a month, I published one Twitter story per day in New Media Scotland's Twitter feed. Squeezing out the daily 140 characters was surprisingly challenging, and effectively meant churning out a lot more material from which to choose the published stories. Some of the characters and ideas that crystallised under the pressure stayed with me. One of them was Imhotep Austin, a half-human, half-mummy, hard-boiled detective, who was later featured in another Twitter serial I published under my own account—"Imhotep Austin in the Time Trap"—which has since become one of my most popular spoken-word pieces.

There are several authors actively producing Twitter fiction—one of my favourites is Jeff Noon (@jeffnoon)—but even big names like David Mitchell are now experimenting. The best Twitter fiction combines the ephemeral, immediate nature of social media with the haiku-like precision of microfiction. As technology changes, perhaps it will go the way of dinosaurs—or maybe one morning we will wake and see a newborn form of narrative there, staring at us, blinking in the bright light of day.

Unused Tomorrows
and Other Stories

OPENING

At night, I stare at the zipper in her spine. Reptile skin peeks out between metal teeth. What if I pulled it down, just a little—

SNOWMEN

Military experiment creates intelligent snow. Icy fists smash the armies of the world. The White Emperor wears a carrot crown.

NO WONDERFUL LIFE

Parallel world: *It's a Wonderful Life* never gets made. Christmas becomes the suicide season. It rains wingless angels.

BALLOON MAN

His girlfriend had been right. Floating over the Tharsis plain, nanoengineered skin stretched tight, the balloon man was full of hot air.

BLITZ CITY

We roll forward on giant treads, spitting out concrete and brick. Tokyo's skyscrapers rise again. Tonight, the monsters will return.

BITE CITY

Bugsy broke its fangs with brass knuckles. We sent it down wearing concrete boots. I smiled. The trench-coat hid the itching holes in my neck.

IMHOTEP AUSTIN IN THE ATOMIC DEATHTRAP!

Next: Imhotep Austin in the Atomic Deathtrap! She was his nemesis from the future. But would she burn him with nuclear flame—or passion?

Chained under the atomic rocket, he grinned. "Imhotep Austin," said the Futurewoman, one blonde lock a second smile. "Defiant to the last."

A Brooklyn private eye gets an edge from a bodyswitch with a 3000-year-old mummy. And the chain had a weak link, melted by the heat—

"You knew about the monkey," he said, buying time. "Of course," she said, body lithe in a silver jumpsuit. "I hired you." A snap: the link broke—

The chain came off. Egyptian rage rose. The robot's eyebeam missed. He seized her, pulled her close. She laughed. Her raygun pressed in his gut.

"I can blast you," she said. "I can drink your soul," he said. "My robot can fire the rocket." "Bitch." "Bastard." Best date ever, Austin thought.

IMHOTEP AUSTIN AND THE TIME TRAP

1. The jetpack kicks. The world blurs. Chronodome glows ahead. In two minutes, they sacrifice his girlfriend to escape the city lost in time.

2. Sentry robot swarm. Eyebeam spiderweb. Skyscraper canyon chase. Twin Smith & Wessons blaze. The mother drone falls, burning.

3. Kidnappings, impossibly aged bodies, green chronal energy dome

in Brooklyn. Routine case—for a half-mummy detective. But now it's personal.

4. He crashes through the Chronodome. Hail of emerald sparks. Jetpack explodes. The blast blows off his fedora. His pet scarab Rosie scutters out.

5. Dr. Dystopia's Crime City. A prison of the future. Gulag time machine, conveying criminals to the Big Bang. They need her life force to escape.

6. He fights through crime mobs to the lab. Strapped under a brass projector, the Futurewoman: 23rd Century villain, reformed by love.

7. The doctor sneers: an equality sign in a formula of death. "Imhotep Austin. Welcome." "No!" she cries. "It's you they want! It's a trap!"

8. "Your life force will take us to ancient Egypt. An eternal empire—of crime!" Neanderthal cyborgs hold him tight. "Now, Rosie!" he shouts.

9. Scarab self-sacrifice: brave insect's bite cuts wire. Projector coil overloads. Chronal beam hums. The beam fist takes out Neanderthal.

10. He shields her with his body. Beam hits them both. Chronal energies collide. Past and future split Crime City's atoms. Dystopia screams. A flash

11. They wake in a jungle. "Austin." "It can wait." They kiss. "I'm pregnant." A feverish hiss. The tyrannosaur charges.